The Supergods

The Supergods

They came on a mission to save mankind

MAURICE M COTTERELL

Thorsons
An Imprint of HarperCollins*Publishers*

Thorsons
An Imprint of HarperCollins*Publishers*
77–85 Fulham Palace Road,
Hammersmith, London W6 8JB

Published by Thorsons 1997
This edition 1998
10 9 8 7 6 5 4 3 2 1

Maurice M Cotterell asserts the moral right to
be identified as the author of this work

A catalogue record for this book
is available from the British Library

ISBN 0 7225 3463 9

Text illustrations by Peter Cox, Jennie Dooge,
John Gilkes and Maurice Cotterell

Printed and bound in Great Britain by
Caledonian International Book Manufacturing Ltd, Glasgow

Contents

APPENDICES

Credits

We would like to thank the following for allowing us to reproduce illustrations:

Figures and Text Illustrations

Maurice Cotterell: 1a, 1b, 1c, 3, 4, 5, 6, 7, 9, 10, 11, 12, 14, 15, 16, 17, 18, 19, 23, 24, 25, 27, 28, 29, 32a, 32b, 33, 34, 35, 36, 37, 38, 40, 44, 45, 49, 53, 54, 57, 58, 59, 60, 61, 62, 65, 66, 68, 69, 71, 72, 74, 75, 76, 79, 80, 82, 85

Fig 2 Novosti, Agency, (London); Fig 8 after Gerald Eveno, (Readers Digest, France) *The World's Last Mysteries;* Figs 13, 55, 56: Bettany G. T., *The World's Religions* (Ward Lock & Co, London 1890); Fig 26 after Augustin Villagra (1952); Fig 30, *Mythology: An Illustrated Encyclopaedia* (W. H. Smith); Fig 31 Werner Forman Archive (London); Figs 36, 37, 39 after Heraclio Ramirez (*Maya Designs of Mexico*, Panorama Editorial S.A.); Figs 43, 46, 47, 48 James Churchward (1931); Figs 63, 64, 67, 73, (81) Mitchell Beazley, *The Atlas of the Solar System;* Figs 77, 78 R. E. Hope Simpson (*Nature Magazine* 275.86, 1978); Figs 83, 84, 86, 87, 88, 89, 90, 91 Kurt Roland, *The Shapes we Need*, GINN & Co (permission Paul & Julian Roland).

Quotations

Doomsday by Warshofsky, Readers Digest (New York)

  Popol Vuh, (1949) English version by Delia Goetz and Sylvanus G. Morley. Translated by Adrian Recinos, University of Oaklahoma Press

Colour Plates

Maurice Cotterell: Plates 1, 2, 4, 5, 8, 9, 10, (10 window head) 11 (11 window head), 12 (12 window mask [see 25], window shell), 13, 14, 15, 16, 17, 18, 19, 20, 21, 22, 23, 24, 25, (after Vautier de Nanxe, Marshall Editions, *The Atlas of Mysterious Places*) 26, 27, 28, 29, 30, 31, 32, 33, 34, 35, 36, 37, 38, 39, 40, 41, 42, 43, 44, 45, 46, 47, 48.

  Plate 6, British Museum; Plates 7, 49 Werner Forman Archive London.

While every effort has been made to secure permissions, if there are any omissions or oversights regarding copyright material we apologise and will make suitable acknowledgement in any future editions of this book.

Acknowledgements

Sincere thanks to Lord Rothermere, Sir David English, Jonathan Holborow and Paul Dacre and all the staff of Associated Newspapers without whose interest and encouragement the work of the Maya might never have seen the light of day; to my wife Ann for her continuing support and encouragement; to Carolyn Cox for typing the original manuscript; to Kevin Burns for help with graphics and art work and finally to Sarah Hannigan for the editing.

They were endowed with intelligence, they saw and instantly they could see far, they succeeded in seeing, they succeeded in knowing all that there is in the world. When they looked, instantly they saw all around them, and they contemplated in turn the arch of the heavens and the round face of earth.

Great was their wisdom, their sight reached to the forests, the rocks, the lakes, the mountains and the valleys. In truth they were admirable men.

And they were able to know all, and they examined the four corners, the four points of the arch of the sky and the round face of the earth ...

THE ANCIENT BOOK OF THE MAYA, THE *POPOL VUH*, PP.168,169

Prologue

This is a true story which began in a field in Northern England in 1960 and ended beneath a pyramid in the jungles of Mexico, 35 years later.

The birds danced in their basket awaiting release. Then they were soaring skywards, clapping their wings as though in applause, before rising beneath the cloud, circling twice, and setting a course for home.

My eight-year-old heart stirred with the birds as they zig-zagged from view, leaving me alone in the field looking heavenwards: how did they find their way home?

Nobody knew how the pigeon found its way home. Nobody knew how a spider acquired the knowledge to build its web. Nobody knew why things fell to the ground when they were dropped. It seemed then that whenever nobody knew anything about something, they gave it a name and somehow everything then became all right: 'because it's a homing pigeon'; 'instinct'; 'gravity'...

As I grew older my questions became increasingly troublesome: who am I? Why do I live? Why will I die? What is life all about?

Nobody had the answers.

It was onboard ship, some 12 years later in the grey wake of a storm, as I watched the steering gear track the compass, making the ship zig-zag either side of its set course, that it occurred to me the pigeon was, after all, sensing the magnetic field of the Earth. The zig-zagging allowed for the sensing of magnetic deviation, the flight path compensated for variance, which together provided a mechanism of course control.

On the long voyages east and west, the restless crew were forever one step behind the day before, as their bio-rhythms chased the ever changing sunrise, and I began to wonder if a 'biological clock' was ticking away inside us. At the same time the crew seemed happier sailing from north to south, rather than from east to west, which somehow made their 'homesickness' worse, and yet the only real difference between those directions was the magnetic field of the Earth.

I had joined my first ship in February 1969 as a radio officer, on a cold and miserable day on the Manchester ship canal, and, in the weeks that followed, headed south around the Cape bound for China. Soon my radio signals began to fade as radiation from the sun disturbed the upper atmosphere, not entirely unexpectedly, as the sun reached a peak in its 11.5-year cycle.

In China it was the Year of the Rooster and it was the ancient Chinese who first recognized this cycle by counting black spots on the sun's surface some 2,000 years earlier. The Year of the Rooster was one of 12 used by the Chinese for astrological forecasts and so, not surprisingly, it was around this time that I began to consider whether the sun's 11.5-yearly cycle might be connected to the 12-year calendar.

In 1957, James Van Allen, an engineer working at NASA, had discovered the existence of belts of radiation encircling the Earth, which caught and trapped particles lost from the sun.

In 1962, the spacecraft *Mariner II* relayed data to Earth showing that the sun gave off considerable amounts of particles collectively described as the 'solar wind'.

In 1969, Jeff Mayo, a British astrologer working with Professor Hans Eysenk at the London Institute of Psychiatry, compiled a psychological profile from respondents of a questionnaire, which supported personality assertions of sun-sign astrology.

In 1979, Professor Iain Nicolson discovered that when solar particles became trapped in the Van Allen belts, the Earth's magnetic field varied.

In 1984, Professor A. Lieboff of Oakland University was experimenting with test tube babies when he realized that magnetic fields, from lights in the laboratory, were affecting the cells of developing foetuses.

The part I was to play in all this became clear in 1986, when I pulled together these threads and showed for the first time that when radiation leaves the sun and becomes trapped in the Van Allen Belts, the magnetic field of the Earth varies. My contribution to the debate showed that the sun gives off 12 types of radiation each year and that this causes 12 types of magnetic field. These 12 types of radiation give rise to 12 types of genetic mutation to developing chromosomes in early impregnated ova on Earth, resulting in 12 types of personality. It was known, since research carried out on twins in the 1920s, that personality was genetically determined. This was what I had been looking for: the scientific basis for astrology.

It was not a popular notion, nor what the astrologers wanted to hear – after all they believed that the moment of birth, not conception, was the crucial moment in astrological understanding – so they abandoned it. It was not what the biologists wanted to hear either, so they ignored it, as did the astronomers.

Around this time, in 1987, Dr Ross Aidey, the White House Medical Advisor for President Reagan, discovered that the bio-rhythm hormone, melatonin, was greatly affected by magnetic fields. The bio-rhythm cycle had already been determined by others as lasting 28 days, which corresponded exactly with the sun's period of rotation. It was a simple step to make a connection between the 28-day bio-rhythm rotational period of the sun. However, measuring the effect the sun might have upon the manufacture of the hormone melatonin and bio-rhythms is more difficult because behaviour is difficult to quantify. It is much easier to measure the female menstrual cycle which is similarly hormone-driven and better understood.

My research turned towards the effects of the sun on the female menstrual cycle and I very quickly confirmed that the sun causes variations in the female fertility hormones on average every 28 days.

Seeking support for these results, I decided to examine the long-term fertility picture on Earth: after all, if the sun's radiation goes up and down, then populations should rise and fall throughout history, as levels vary accordingly.

The problem here was first finding a way to determine the length of the sun's cycle. Eventually it became clear that the sun had a long-term cycle of 1,366,040 days (3,740 years), and that fertility on Earth varied throughout this period.

Remarkably, I learned quite by chance that a number very close to this, 1,366,560, was worshipped as the mythological 'birth of Venus' by the Maya, who built the pyramids in Mexico more than a thousand years ago. They believed that the world had been destroyed on four previous occasions and that we are now living in the fifth age of the sun. They worshipped the sun as the god of Fertility and named their children after a 260-day astrological calendar.

In my last book, *The Mayan Prophecies*, I showed how the sun's twisting magnetic field brings destruction to earth five times every 18,139 years, how the sun actually affects human fertility, causing the rise and fall of civilizations, and how it causes differences in individual personality, reconciling for the first time astrology with science.

Now, in *The Supergods*, I move on to show the causes of the twisting magnetic field and how, in 3,113 BC, one twist caused the planet Venus to topple upside down. Her brilliant light blazed across the cosmos as the Maya gazed skyward at the awesome 'birth of Venus', and their calendar began. Although this weak magnetic turn-about failed to shift the distant earth, quick-frozen mammoths from the wastelands of Alaska, fossilized palm trees from Spitzbergen and coal from Antarctica all go to show that the Earth has suffered the same fate as Venus in the past.

How did the Maya understand these things more than a thousand years ago, in the jungles of Central America? How could they have known that there really are five ages of the sun, that the sun does affect fertility and that astrology really is a science?

To find out, I journeyed to the jungles of Central America, to the ceremonial home of the mighty Maya, the city of Palenque. I explored the temple of Lord Pacal in the Pyramid of Inscriptions and re-examined the evidence as it stood on 15 June 1952, the day the tomb of their beloved priest-king was revealed for the first time in 1,250 years.

I took a closer look at the mosaic jade mask which covered the crumbling face of the man in the tomb. My decoding reveals incredible, breathtaking scenes from a story hidden for more than a thousand years, which show for the first time that the man with the mask was different from all other men.

Gradually it becomes clear that this man beneath the pyramid was capable of incredible super-human accomplishments. He encoded the secrets of his life into the architecture, jewellery, carvings and paintings of the Maya. He introduced the Maya people to a pantheon of gods, knowing that these could be used, like actors in a play, to release his secret knowledge to mankind when the time was right and the code was broken. Now, at last, that time has arrived as 20th-century technology has enabled the breaking of the code and the release of the secret messages destined for our own age.

We are also shown that Lord Pacal, the man in the tomb, shares remarkable similarities with others who have brought the same knowledge to mankind throughout the ages. These miracle makers were the Supergods.

PART ONE

CHAPTER ONE

Frozen Tropics,
Boiling Seas

The river Tanana flows through the Yukon in Alaska. In 1940, while dredging the bed and the gold rich silt, faint cries of discovery pierced the hum and roar and the digging stopped. Through the damp silence the river heaved and swelled with the bones of the dead – at first hundreds and then thousands, of extinct mammoths, mastodon, horses and bison.

And the questions began:

How did these animals meet their sudden and violent death, at the time of the last ice age more than 10,000 years ago?
What brought so many of them to one place at one time?
How did these plain-grazing animals survive in this frozen wasteland, where no grass grows?
What forces tore them limb from limb and mingled them with the roots of upturned trees?

Not surprisingly, enigmas like these have risen in the wake of such upheavals to fire the imagination of a whole school of 'catastrophists' eager to explain the unexplained. One of the most famous was the writer, historian, doctor and scientist Immanuel Velikovsky.

Born in Russia, Velikovsky graduated from Moscow University at the age of 26 and from there, in 1923, set up his first medical practice in Israel, to become a follower of the rising star Sigmund Freud, the psychoanalyst whose theories probed the depths of the human mind. These theories were of interest to Velikovsky in connection with his own work on 'collective amnesia', a term he coined to explain the mysterious loss of historical accounts, by whole races throughout the ages. By 1939 he was suggesting that many ancient stories, whilst perhaps allegorical, might indeed be fact, believing, for example, that Mount Sinai had erupted during the Israelites' Exodus from Egypt, which coincided with tales of great plagues which had swept the land. Further research supported his beliefs, with the study of other ancient documents which confirmed not only the actual occurrence of biblical events, but also that of accompanying catastrophes, the similarities of which could not be explained away by science.

Earth in Upheaval was not Velikovsky's first book but, published in 1955, it followed on from *Worlds in Collision* (1950) and *Ages in Chaos* Volume 1 (1952), each of which had taken the scientific world by storm and stirred up a hornet's nest of controversy. Up to this time geologists had assumed that evolution had progressed only gradually. There was no room for catastrophes as far as they were concerned. The geological status quo that we see around us could be accounted for, they said, by the gentle forces of nature, erosion and sedimentation together with infinitely long periods of time.

But things were already changing and by the 1960s the ideas of explorer and meteorologist Alfred Wegener, who believed that at one time the continents of the Earth had all been joined together, began to gain general support. It had not always been that way. For half a century these radical, unorthodox, and of course 'original' ideas, had been ignored by geologists who claimed he was completely mad. But for Wegener, the fact that, long ago, one single land mass existed on the face of the Earth was the only sensible theory because it explained why the shapes of the continents fitted together like pieces of a jigsaw puzzle;

why mountains occurred in ranges rather than in isolation; how and why sea fossils could be found on mountain peaks; how the small lemur monkey could be found in widely separated geological areas (Madagascar and the east coast of Africa and south east Asia); why fossilised palm trees could be found in Spitzbergen and coal deposits in Antarctica.

The giant continental land mass called Pangaea

Fig 1a Meteorologist Alfred Wegener was ridiculed in 1915 when he suggested that the earth's land was once joined together as Pangaea-land. He was building upon an earlier hypothesis by Antonio Snider, the founder of the Continental Drift theory. Wegener published geological, climatalogical and biological evidence that supported Snider's views.

Modern researchers confirmed Wegener's work when investigating magnetism found in rock samples separated by thousands of miles of ocean. These were found to be identical, persuading modern researchers that the rocks were indeed once joined together. 180 million years ago the original single land mass broke into two sections, Laurasia to the North and Gondwanaland to the South. These then began to break into sections.

Fig 1b By 65 million years ago South America had separated from Africa and started to drift northwest and Madagascar split from Africa. The Mediterranean began to form while Antarctica and Australia were still joined together.

Fig 1c The world today is seen as five continents: Americas, Africa, Asia, Australia and Europe. The Arctic pole is frozen water and the Antarctic a sub-continent.

But it was geologists who in the 1960s and 70s were to confirm from their own researches into palaeomagnetism that Wegener was right, as rocks of identically magnetized structures could be found either side of the great oceans suggesting that they were indeed joined together in the distant past.

Velikovsky questioned how continents could have drifted apart so quickly. Could massive external forces have perhaps helped the process, and if so what might they have been? In pursuit of an explanation for the Tanana phenomena he cites the work of F.C. Hibben of the University of Mexico:

> Although the formation of deposits of silt, muck and bones is not clear, there is ample evidence that at least portions of this material were deposited under catastrophic conditions. Mammalian remains are for the most part dismembered and disarticulated even though some fragments yet remain in their frozen state, portions of ligaments, skin, hair and flesh. Twisted and torn trees are piled into splintered masses...and at least four considerable layers of volcanic ash may be traced in these deposits, although they are extremely warped and distorted...

Thus begins Velikovsky's journey of discovery, argument, counter-argument and unique investigations into catastrophism, which lead to the same conclusion that man is blind not to see everywhere the clues of periodic cataclysmic destruction. Returning to the Tanana extinctions, he asks, 'Could it be that a volcanic eruption killed the animal population of Alaska; the streams carrying down into the valleys the slaughtered animals?' But he dismisses this by noting, 'A volcanic eruption would have charred the trees – but would not have splintered and uprooted them. If it had killed the animals it would not have dismembered them. It becomes obvious that the trees could only have been uprooted and splintered by a hurricane, or a flood or both'. He continues, 'The animals could only have been killed by a stupendous wave that lifted and carried and smashed and tore and buried the millions of bodies and trees.' This is confirmed by the fact that the area affected is much greater than might be the case had a volcanic eruption caused the catastrophe and because such deposits are known to exist throughout the Arctic peninsula.

On the other side of the globe lies Siberia, a vast frozen wilderness too cold for the hardiest of trees. In 1799 an ivory trader named Boltunov found a mammoth, now extinct, beneath the frozen ice at the mouth of the River Lena. This in itself is not too surprising as mammoths are believed to have inhabited the region in warmer times, together with rhinoceros, elk, stags, musk and sabre-toothed cats. A more curious mammoth specimen, though, was found at Berezovka in 1900 buried deep under the Arctic permafrost. It was in an upright position with buttercups clenched between its teeth and undigested food in its stomach. Its meat, witnesses said, was still fresh enough to be eaten by sleigh dogs.

Fig 2 Six-month-old mammoth bulldozed to the surface of the permafrost in the Yakutsk Republic of the USSR in the summer of 1977.

These woolly-haired elephant-like mammoths have been found at regular intervals in Siberia. More than 50 perfectly preserved specimens have been well documented and chronicled along with tens of thousands of bones and tusks which have for the past century supplied the west with ivory.

Orthodox science suggests that for some unknown reason this part of Siberia escaped the most recent ice age which lasted from around 100,000 BC up to around 10,000 BC and at that time the warm climate in Siberia sustained a population of some 50,000 mammoths and other plain-grazing animals, together with the grasses and buttercups which constituted their diet. If we are to believe this then we must also believe that one fine spring day the weather turned suddenly cold and that all of these animals froze on the spot and were buried beneath layers of earth.

But here Velikovsky points out that some of the vegetation found in the stomachs of the mammoths is known to originate far away from the area in which they were found en-masse and also that microscopic examination of the mammoth skin showed red blood corpuscles, which was proof not only of sudden death, but that the death was due to suffocation either by gasses or drowning. Suggesting that once again, like at Tanana, the beasts had been carried a great distance by a tidal wave.

This raised a question about what mechanism might cause a tidal wave to sweep over continents which would, at the same time, account for the instant freezing of certain parts of the globe. Velikovsky's answer to the riddle was that at some time in the distant past some external force caused the Earth to topple on its axis and the accompanying earthquakes and volcanic eruptions triggered tidal waves. Geographical areas once in warmer climates near the equatorial regions shifted to polar regions, accounting for the instant freezing which had been observed in the case of the mammoths.

In a desperate attempt to substantiate his theory, Velikovsky sought a causal mechanism that might support his assertions. Could, he argued, a giant chunk be torn from a planet, the most likely of which would be Jupiter, and perhaps topple the Earth off its axis as it hurtled across the solar system? He later researched the possibilities in ancient annals and came up with much historical data in support of his theory which became more refined as it developed. But this was to prove the last straw for his critics who were all for burning him at the stake by this time. On the face of it their scorn seemed well founded, as such

9

a notion flew in the face of known celestial mechanics accepted since the days of Isaac Newton. After all, gravitational forces exert influences of attraction that pull planets together, not forces which push them apart causing menacing fragments to hurtle through space. Indeed, Dr Harlow Shapley an American astronomer commented, 'If Dr Velikovsky is right then the rest of us are crazy'.

So incensed were Shapley and his colleagues that one of the most bizarre and pitiful conspiracies in the history of science began, to discredit the entire work of Velikovsky. This became known as 'the Velikovsky affair', although history now shows that it was Shapley and his comrades, and not Velikovsky, who were crazy.

Velikovsky's account was summarized in the *Readers Digest* in December 1975 by a writer called Warshofsky in his article entitled 'Doomsday':

At some time more than 4,000 years ago, according to Velikovsky's interpretation of ancient texts, the giant planet Jupiter – about 320 times more massive than Earth, underwent a shattering convulsion and hurled a planet-sized chunk of itself into space. The blazing new member of the solar system – the protoplanet Venus – hurtled down a long orbit toward the sun, on a course that would eventually menace the Earth…

To Velikovsky, it was clear that this fiery birth of Venus had been recorded by peoples the world over. 'In Greece' he wrote in *Worlds in Collision*, 'the goddess who suddenly appeared in the sky was Pallas Athene. She sprang from the head of Zeus-Jupiter.' To the Chinese, Venus spanned the heavens, rivalling the sun in brightness. 'The brilliant light of Venus,' noted one ancient rabbinical record, 'blazes from one end of the cosmos to the other.'

In the middle of the 15th century BC, Velikovsky theorized, Earth in its orbit around the sun entered the outer edges of the protoplanet's trailing dust and gases. A fine red dust filled the air, staining the continents and seas with a bloody hue. Frantically, men clawed at the earth seeking underground springs uncontaminated by the red dust.

'All the waters that were in the river were turned to blood...And all the Egyptians digged round about the river for water to drink,' says Exodus 7:20–24. 'The river is blood ... Men shrink from tasting – human beings thirst after water,' confirms the Egyptian sage Ipuwer.

As Earth continued to move through the cometary tail, Velikovsky claims, the particles grew coarser and larger, until our planet was bombarded by showers of meteorites that were recorded all around the world. Exodus: 'There was hail and fire mingled with hail...there was none like it in all the land of Egypt since it became a nation...and the hail smote every herb of the field, and broke every tree of the field.' Ipuwer concludes: 'Trees were destroyed. No fruits or herbs are found. That has perished which yesterday was seen.' These things happened, say the Mexican Annals of Cuauhtitlan, when the sky 'rained not water but fire and hot-stones'.

Then an even more terrifying event took place. The *Popul Vuh*, the sacred book of the Mayas, tells the story: 'It was ruin and destruction...a great inundation...people were drowned in a sticky substance raining from the sky.' What happened says Velikovsky, is that gases in the protoplanet's tail combined to form petroleum. Some of this rained down unignited, but some mixed with oxygen in Earth's atmosphere and caught fire. The sky seemed to burst into flames, and a terrible rain of fire fell from Siberia to South America.

Earth now penetrated deeper into the comet's tail, on a near collision course with its massive head. Great hurricanes pummelled Egypt and other lands. A violent convulsion ripped the Earth, tilting it on its axis. In the grip of the protoplanet's gravitational pull, the terrestrial crust folded and shifted. Cities were levelled, islands shattered, mountains swelled with lava, oceans crashed over continents. Most of the Earth's animal and human populations were destroyed.

'The heavens burst and fragments fell down and killed everything and everybody. Heaven and Earth changed places,' states the tradition of the Sashinaua of Western Brazil. Plagues of vermin descended on China and the land burned. Then the waters of the oceans fell on the continent and, according to an ancient text, 'overtopped the great heights, threatening the heavens with their floods'.

11

Earth turned part-way over. Part was now in extended darkness, part in protracted day. The Persians watched in awe as a single day became three before turning into a night that lasted three times longer than usual. The Chinese wrote of an incredible time when the sun did not set for several days while the entire land burned.

The catastrophe was also responsible, according to Velikovsky, for the memorable drama in the Old Testament in the Exodus of the Israelites from Egypt. The awful catastrophe toppled the Egyptian Middle Kingdom, and Moses led the people of Israel, erstwhile slaves, out of the ruined land. They fled across the border, before them moved the huge pillar of fire and smoke.

For the fleeing Israelites it marked the way to Pi-ha-Khiroth, near the Sea of Passage. Behind them raced the angry and vengeful pharaoh and his army. Ahead lay the seabed, uncovered, its waters piled high on either side by the shifting movement of the Earth's crust and the gravitational and electromagnetic effects of the protoplanet. The Israelites hesitated, then rushed across the seabed, which, according to rabbinical sources, was hot. As the pharaoh's armies followed an incredibly powerful electrical bolt passed between Earth and protoplanet. The walls of water collapsed.

Through the world, populations were all but annihilated. The survivors were threatened with starvation. And then yet another phenomenon, recorded from Iceland to India, as well as in the Old Testament took place. The hydrocarbons in the comet's tail that had drenched the Earth in petroleum were now being slowly changed within the Earth's atmosphere, possibly by bacterial action, possibly by incessant electrical discharges, into an edible substance – the manna of the Israelites, the ambrosia of the Greeks, the honey-like madhu of the Hindus.

The close approach of the protoplanet Venus produced gravitational dislocations that reversed the direction of the Earth's axis. To the shocked and dazed people of Earth, the sun was rising in the western sky and setting in the eastern sky. Seasons were exchanged. 'The winter is come as summer, the months are reversed, and the hours are disordered,' states an Egyptian papyrus. In China, the emperor sent scholars to the four corners of the darkened land to relocate north, east, west and south, and to draw up a new calendar. For a generation Earth was enshrouded in an envelope of clouds – the Shadow of Death of the Scriptures, the *Götterdämmerung* of the Nordic races. It endured for 25 years, according to Mayan sources.

Slowly Earth and its people began to recover. But only 50 years later, around 1,400 BC, according to Velikovsky's interpretation of ancient sources, Venus made a second pass at Earth. The terrestrial axis again tilted, and Earth heaved and buckled. The few rebuilt towns flamed and collapsed in heaps of rubble. The book of Joshua records that 'The Lord cast down great stones from heaven upon them' (the Canaanites). On the other side of the world, Mexican records speak of a lengthened night. Once again Earth was wracked by earthquakes, global hurricanes, continental shifts, and by universal destruction.

The peoples of the world who survived the second holocaust bowed down before the dreaded Venus, goddess of Fire and Destruction, and each in a manner dictated by cultural heritage placated her with human sacrifices and bloody rituals, with prayers and incantations. Cuneiform tablets found in the ruins of the library palace in Nineveh, the Assyrian capital, record the erratic behaviour of Venus. The fearful Babylonians pleaded with the errant queen of the heavens to leave Earth in peace: 'How long wilt thou tarry, O lady of heaven and earth?'

This summary of Velikovsky's Earth-tilting mechanism is given here not because it provides the answers to the enigma because it cannot, as Shapley correctly pointed out. If it were the case then as Shapley also said, 'Aeroplanes would fall from the sky' and 'the tides would cease to shift'. So why is it included? Because Velikovsky is right, but for all the wrong reasons. Later we will see why. For the moment we agree that pole tilting answers the questions of catastrophes and so we look at the ideas of others who wondered how such a tilting might occur.

How the Mammoths Froze

The most authoritative collection of theories ever put forward by 'pole shifters' is entitled *Pole Shift* by American author John White. It is beyond the scope of this book to attempt to compete with White's excellent research and all I can do here is thank him for his enormous contribution to the subject. In his chapter on Hugh Auchincloss Brown, 'Cataclysms of the Earth', White begins:

On the 11th November 1975 his obituary appeared in the *New York Times*:

'Hugh Auchincloss Brown, Sr, an electrical engineer who devoted more than 60 years of his life to the promulgation of his theory that a vast polar ice cap would tip the Earth over in this century and wipe out civilization, died Sunday night in his home at 115 Prospect Avenue, Douglaston, Queens. He was 96 years old.

Mr Brown graduated from Columbia University in 1900 [with an engineering degree]...

As early as 1911, Mr Brown became intrigued by reports that mammoths had been found frozen in the Arctic "with buttercups still clenched between their teeth". This led him to believe that an accumulation of ice at one or both poles periodically, perhaps every 8,000 years, upsets Earth's equilibrium and causes it to tumble over "like an overloaded canoe".

A Polar Doomsday

Mr Brown continued to push his theories of an impending Doomsday, which he believed was overdue, until his death. For years he bombarded members of Congress, editors of newspapers and magazines, government leaders and scientists with written "proof" of his theories.

Concerning his theories, Mr Brown told a *New York Times* reporter, in 1948, that as an engineer he knew that the bulge of the

Earth around the equator stabilizes its spin. But, he said, an abnormal amount of Antarctic ice, at that time said to be two or three miles thick, could be enough to topple the spin.

This would cause floods of enormous proportions, earthquakes, and other phenomena, Mr Brown said, wiping out civilization. He said such a cataclysm was imminent, and noted that "tales of sudden floods and the mysterious appearance and disappearance of large land masses are found in folklore and legends of all races and men".

Mr Brown recommended establishment of a worldwide Global Stabilization Organization, and recommended that it devote $10 million to a study of how to effectively set off atomic blasts in the Antarctic to break up the ice mass there and thus save the world from certain disaster.

Mr Brown's book, *Cataclysms of the Earth*, expanded on his theories. Published in 1967, it titillated many general readers but failed to raise a great deal of scientific concern, although it contained Mr Brown's statement that a particularly ominous omen for the Earth's future was the wobble in the planet's spin. Such a [wobble] is a scientific fact and continues to challenge scientists seeking an explanation for it.

Mr Brown predicted that in a forthcoming cataclysm caused by the Earth tipping over, New York would probably wind up 13 miles under water, and so would the rest of the world. Among the few survivors, he theorised, would be the Eskimos, because the polar areas would be least subject to catastrophic water action…'

A pole shift, according to Brown, would hence be caused as the ice-cap grew in weight and size and the planet toppled. At such time the tropics may become repositioned at the poles and the poles at the tropics and hence the riddle of the frozen mammoths would be explained.

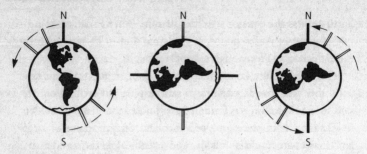

Fig 3 Pole shift according to Brown.

This was all very well, except for two or three loose ends. Firstly, for years geologists had noted that the Earth's magnetic field had reversed from time to time and also that the position of the magnetic poles had 'wandered'. Brown's explanation did not reconcile this, which in all fairness he never set out to do. Secondly, growth of the polar caps is not very well understood at all by modern scientists, nor is the cause of ice ages, as we shall see later. Thirdly, another researcher, Charles Hapgood, pointed out that Brown's theory was untenable for one basic reason: calculations showed the impossibility of the mass of the Antarctic ice-cap developing sufficient momentum to capsize the Earth. As White says, 'A radical modification was needed if the notion of shifting poles was to be retained.'

Hapgood teamed up with Scottish mathematician and engineer James Hunter Campbell, who was able to demonstrate that (when movements did take place) it was only the crust of the Earth that moved and in 1958 Hapgood published his book *Earth's Shifting Crust*, which detailed his years of research. In the foreword Albert Einstein commented, shortly before he died:

The very first communication I received from Mr Hapgood electrified me. His idea is original, of great simplicity and if it continues to prove itself, of great importance to everything that is related to the history of the Earth's surface…this rather astonishing, even fascinating idea deserves the attention of anyone who concerns himself with the theory of the Earth's development.

In essence, Hapgood was suggesting that Wegener's continental drift owed its existence to crustal shifting. It should be pointed out here that Hapgood never suggested a rapid tilting due to crustal shift but only, perhaps to satisfy orthodox geologists, a mechanism that accommodated a slowly shifting crust. This notion, though, as I have pointed out, accommodated magnetic reversals: for if the mantle of the Earth were to remain geostationary and the crust above moved, then the magnetic field contained in the crustal rocks would change, providing a causal mechanism for magnetic reversals.

The Science of the Ancients

Bringing this information together it becomes clear that if a pole tilting mechanism could be found which could tilt the Earth off its axis, a mechanism for catastrophes would be established. Secondly, if a mechanism could be found that tilts the Earth off its axis and shifts the crust, then not only would a mechanism for catastrophes be found but a mechanism that explained magnetic reversals would also be found. Finally, if a mechanism could be found that tilted the Earth off its axis, accommodated crustal shift and explained away ice ages, then we might reasonably agree that such a notion must be given serious consideration.

In *The Mayan Prophecies* I published my own research which put forward such an explanation and I showed that these new ideas were already well understood by the Maya of Central America more than a thousand years ago. These discoveries involved a lengthy and systematic search of often complex and seemingly unconnected information. It began in the late 1970s, with a search for a causal mechanism that could explain just how sun-sign astrology might work (*see the Appendices, particularly Appendix three*) and was to culminate in the publication of my book *Astrogenetics* in the spring of 1988. This showed that astrology, the science of the ancients, could in fact be reconciled with the most recent of scientific knowledge, most of which has only become available as space age exploration has developed over the past two decades.

Later, this proved to be only the beginning, as I continued to work, fascinated by the possibility that the sun's radiation might not only affect personality determination but might also be the cause of biological rhythms, and from this line of enquiry I discovered that the sun's radiation also controls fertility on Earth (*Appendix four*).

Already bells were beginning to ring: the ancient Egyptians, Maya and Inca were all known to worship the sun god as the god of fertility, and all were keen followers of astrology. For this reason the Maya named their children after the date of their birth in a recurring 260 day astronomical/astrological cycle.

So it was a natural progression to look at the long-term behaviour of the sun to see if any links could be found between patterns of radiation and long-term fertility trends on Earth. It was these that led me, in 1989, to the successful calculation of the long-term sun-spot cycle which showed that civilizations could indeed be seen to rise and fall with the sun's radiations and that the sun's magnetic field reversed every 3,740 years (1,366,040 days).

It was this discovery, finally, that inspired me to study the classic Maya of Central America. For they had a sacred number which had been spoken of in ancient times and carved in their sculptures. It was 1,366,560. Could it be simply coincidence that the Maya understood astrology and astronomy better than any race that had ever lived before, without understanding the science that lay beneath? Could it be coincidence that they worshipped the sun as the god of Fertility without understanding that the sun does actually affect fertility? And could it be coincidence that their magic 'super number' of 1,366,560 days, which they worshipped as 'the birth of Venus' was almost exactly the same as the sun-spot number that I had calculated on a modern computer?

This is not all. Was it completely coincidental that the Mayans mysteriously 'disappeared' from the face of the Earth 1,366,560 days after their calendar began, in 3,113 BC? or did they know that the sun would fail their reproductive needs around 750 AD as the sun's magnetic field reversed. We know they believed that the Earth had been created and destroyed on four previous occasions and that we are now living in the 'fifth age of the sun'. Was this another complete coincidence or did they understand that the sun's magnetic field actually does reverse five times every 18,139 years, resulting in fertility cycles and possible pole tilting?

Is it a complete coincidence that modern science acknowledges that magnetic reversals have accompanied mass extinctions of species throughout the history of the planet? or does this simply confirm the link between magnetism and fertility in the animal kingdom?

These are not the only intriguing echoes of the past: one of the things I learned whilst investigating sun-spot cycles was that as the cycle diminishes, the Earth enters periods of mini ice ages. This was significant because it was around the same time that I became interested in Hugh Auchincloss Brown's pole-tilting theory. Apart from Campbell's calculations, which disproved the notion mathematically, Brown's theory seemed an unlikely answer to the question from a commonsense point of view because although the size of the polar ice cap and the advance and retreat of glaciers are often compared with cold periods on Earth, it gives rise to a paradox: glaciers are comprised of fresh water and fresh water is derived from precipitation (rain, sleet, hail and snow), which is in turn formed by evaporation of water from the oceans. In order for glaciers to grow, <u>more</u> evaporation must take place, to fall as more precipitation. For <u>more</u> evaporation to take place temperatures must <u>increase</u> not decrease. And if temperatures <u>increase</u>, glaciers should melt – not grow. Evidence to support this comes from 19th-century British physicist John Tyndall, who once calculated that it takes as much energy to melt a block of iron weighing 5 pounds, as it does to completely evaporate just one pint of water.

So Brown's cap, on the face of it, did not fit. And yet we know that from sediment samples the caps have increased and decreased in size from time to time. So what is the answer? What causes ice ages on Earth?

Velikovsky pointed out that in order to increase evaporation from the oceans sufficient to increase glaciation, the oceans must boil not from above but from below. In other words some phenomenon must subsist to cause the Earth's crust to become super-hot. Addressing this problem, he explained that all it would need for this set of events to take place was that the Earth should pass through the tail of a passing comet. Electrical currents (eddy currents) would be generated in the Earth's surface as the two magnetic fields interacted causing the earth's surface to become hotter, perhaps causing the oceans to boil. Under such conditions increased evaporation would take place and this would fall as increased precipitation, thus increasing the size of the poles.

Velikovsky, as we have seen, had already suggested that such a body may have been ejected from Jupiter some time more than 4,000 years ago and that such a scenario may have occurred as this body passed close to the Earth, around 1,500 BC and again around 700 BC, accounting for the catastrophes he so ably documents.

So it now seems that Velikovsky was right, but for all the wrong reasons. We may forgive him, for he was not in possession of the latest scientific data. Which brings us back to the Maya.

The Birth of Venus

Their calendar began in 3,113 BC ('more than 4,000 years ago'). This date was known as the 'birth of Venus'. The sun's magnetic field is known to have reversed at that time which suggests it was this magnetic reversal that twisted the planet Venus upside down on its axis. Venus is closer to the sun than the Earth (see *Appendix one*) so it could well be that this reversal, although not strong enough to tilt the Earth, was successful in shifting Venus. True, Venus is the only planet in the solar system that spins on its axis backwards, (it is actually spinning in the right direction, but because it was turned upside down it is now relatively spinning in the wrong direction).

The surface of Venus is super-hot, more than 500 degrees centigrade both on its night-time side and its daytime side (proving that the temperatures are not caused by the sun's rays but emanate from the surface of the planet), suggesting Velikovsky's eddy currents are alive and kicking (due to magnetic misalignment of Venus and the sun) as he predicted, and further, that the same could have happened in the past on earth causing oceans to boil and ice-caps to grow during the final phases of the occurrence which may or may not have been accompanied by polar wander, polar shifts or magnetic reversals.

He also researched many accounts of a cataclysm documented by many races 'more than 4,000 years ago' when the planet Venus lit up the sky so brightly it was able to cast shadows on earth, which is what you would expect if the carbon dioxide polar caps of Venus were to wander to a new position 90 degrees from where they started, as the reflection of sunlight bounced off the highly reflective Venusian poles towards Earth. The planet may since have settled between 90 and 180 degrees from its original axial orientation.

So was this the 'birth of Venus'? The 'new' Venus? And given that a magnetic reversal took place at that time a new fertility cycle began, what better time to commence a calendar than when a civilization is born? Could this be why the Maya calendar commenced in 3,113 BC?

Velikovsky was almost there. The birth of Venus was not a chunk of Jupiter after all, it was all down to the sun's reversing magnetic field. As for the events of 1,500 BC and 700 BC when 'his' protoplanet passed Earth: perhaps these were indeed caused by the passing of other unrelated comets. Recent events on Jupiter, when comet Schumacher smashed into the planet, have shown this to be a real possibility.

So in 1989 I began to study the Maya, beginning my journey in Palenque, their greatest ceremonial centre far away in the jungles of Central America. This was the home of the Temple of Inscriptions, one of the finest Mayan monuments, the burial place of their priest-king Lord Pacal who died around 750 AD. It turned out to be a truly remarkable adventure. Imagine my amazement when I learned that my discoveries about the sun and how its cycles affect life on Earth had all been discovered before by the Maya more than 1,250 years ago. They had even carved these discoveries into the tombstone of their leader and hidden it beneath an ancient pyramid. I saw their gods, I marvelled at their intelligence, I witnessed their skill, their wealth and their power and I wondered, how did they know? What super-human minds encoded all of this information into one single picture?

This was the mystery of the Maya.

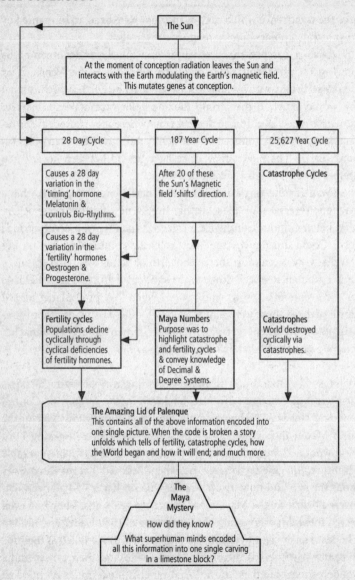

The Sun

At the moment of conception radiation leaves the Sun and interacts with the Earth modulating the Earth's magnetic field. This mutates genes at conception.

28 Day Cycle

187 Year Cycle

25,627 Year Cycle

Causes a 28 day variation in the 'timing' hormone Melatonin & controls Bio-Rhythms.

Causes a 28 day variation in the 'fertility' hormones Oestrogen & Progesterone.

After 20 of these the Sun's Magnetic field 'shifts' direction.

Catastrophe Cycles

Fertility cycles Populations decline cyclically through cyclical deficiencies of fertility hormones.

Maya Numbers Purpose was to highlight catastrophe and fertility cycles & convey knowledge of Decimal & Degree Systems.

Catastrophes World destroyed cyclically via catastrophes.

The Amazing Lid of Palenque This contains all of the above information encoded into one single picture. When the code is broken a story unfolds which tells of fertility, catastrophe cycles, how the World began and how it will end; and much more.

The Maya Mystery

How did they know?

What superhuman minds encoded all this information into one single carving in a limestone block?

Fig 4 Comparison of recent scientific discoveries with the knowledge of the Maya.

CHAPTER TWO

The Lost Tribes
of Meso-America

First of all we need to look at the origins of the Maya. At some time, between 10,000 and 11,000 years ago, the polar caps were much larger and the sea level 36 metres (120 feet) lower than today as more of the world's water was piled high into glaciers. It was at this time that Asiatic peoples hiked across the frozen land bridge thought to exist between Asia and America to populate Alaska.

This was the time of plenty when the woolly-haired mammoth, musk oxen, caribou and Arctic hare ruled the great plains and seal, sea lions and great shoals of fish filled the ocean. Anthropologists suggest that the first hunters were probably one or two families who chased the roaming herds from Asia into America to commence the first settlements of what would later become Eskimos, precursors of the American Red Indian (although the Red Indian from the earliest times has been known to be racially mixed and could quite possibly have arrived independently by sea from Indo-China).

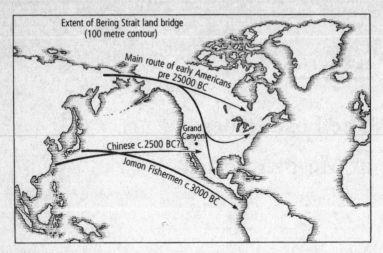

Fig 5 The Bering Straits. A land bridge was thought to have existed more than 10,000 years ago, joining Asia to America.

But very little is known of these earliest of settlers on the North American continent. Some believe they migrated southwards into Mexico. What is known is that by 6,000 BC corn was cultivated which tied growers to one area of land. As they settled in one place to harvest their crops, they began to produce tools and pottery, previously too cumbersome for their nomadic lifestyles. Certainly, archaeological digs show pottery fragments to be much more plentiful from 1,500 BC onwards.

Peoples naturally began to group into villages, not just because more hands eased the burden of harvesting, but also for protection and by 1,000 BC the Olmec began to emerge as the first Middle American civilization. Various groups are then seen to emerge through Middle (Meso) America which includes Mexico, Guatemala, Belize, Honduras and Nicaragua (although the region is defined not so much geographically as culturally by the history and origin of the peoples that inhabit these areas, and this classification tends naturally to exclude Nicaragua from our enquiries).

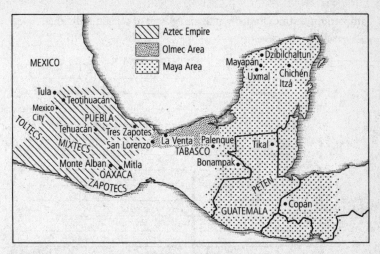

Fig 6 The tribes and towns of Middle America, 1,200 BC – 1,600 AD.

The first of these groups were the Olmec, creators of a highly influential civilization that flourished along the Gulf of Mexico, in an area which has now become the states of Tabasco and Vera Cruz. Very little is known about the Olmec, although they are thought to have subscribed to a hierarchical structure occupying both urban and ceremonial centres. The most notable of these was San Lorenzo, which flourished between 1,200 and 900 BC and the sites of La Venta and Tres Zapotes, from 900–500 BC. They are best known for their carvings of colossal basalt heads found scattered around the region, their blue jade serpentine carvings, the possible introduction of the Mexican calendar system and their use of numerical symbols, which they used for the chronicling of astronomical data.

It is not known why the Olmec disappeared, although it seems that some tragedy befell them around 700 BC (a fly-by date for Velikovsky's comet). Despite this, and the decline in their numbers, their influence lived on, carried forward to several places which preserved the unique Olmec style. At the site of Kalminaljuya, in Guatemala, the community built an important town on the borders of what was to become the land of the Maya. In one tomb a corpse surrounded by sacrificial companions testifies to the wealth and power of certain individuals over a lower class.

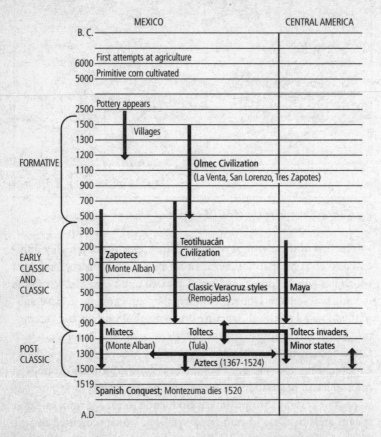

Fig 7 Time scale diagram showing the lost tribes of Middle America.

In Izapa, just across the Guatemalan border, an art style bearing Olmec influence flourished for three or four hundred years after the decline of La Venta. This new style was more complex: their *stelae* (bas-relief statues) and carvings for the first time could be seen carrying bat masks, possibly depicting the Bat god – god of Death – and wind-masks, perhaps representing Ehecatl god of Wind, providing early evidence of god-worship not previously confirmed, except further north in the valley of Mexico. There, at Cuicuilco (900–350 BC), was evidence of a much earlier settlement whose medicine men had built a circular sacred house from slabs of rock, the walls of the structure sloping in like a hut. Inside the slabs have been carved with several figures, most notably that of a rattlesnake which may have been the earliest known depiction of the god Quetzalcoatl, 'the Good god', and outside, a small carving of a squatting old man carrying a dish on his back, possibly the first representation of the Fire god Xiuhtechutli, was found.

But it seems that all their worship of the gods had come to nothing. This sacred temple was built upon over the years to form one of the first pyramidal structures before a volcanic eruption around 350 BC razed it to the ground. Rubble thundered over the pyramid and the original stone circle was buried under volcanic ash. Then the volcano Xictli exploded and spewed out a great river of lava which roared, crackling with fire, to engulf the now three-tiered pyramid, and with it the town of Cuicuilco.

Now appears a gap in the history of the peoples during which time the god-worship cult became more and more important throughout Mexico. From its first tenuous foothold at Cuicuilco it re-emerged to seize centre stage and dominate and preoccupy the lives of the peoples in the plains of Mexico, at Teotihuacan. At about the same time, 500 BC, settlements began to develop in the west of Mexico in the valley of Oaxaca. There the summit of the massive hilltop of 'Monte Alban', or 'mountain of white blossom', was carved into plazas, and the first platform buildings began to rise. This phase of development was undoubtedly Olmec-influenced and by 100 AD Monte Alban had become the ceremonial centre of the Zapotec, who carried forward known worship of the Bat god and other deities.

Fig 8 Teotihuacan, city of priests and temples. Teotihuacan was a magnificent, abandoned ruin, the capital of civilization that lasted 1,000 years, but declined and vanished in the eighth century AD. The city stands on a plateau 2,300 metres (7,500 feet) high. It was designed on a rigid grid pattern spreading out from either side of its main thoroughfare, the Avenue of the Dead (1), which is 2.5 kilometres (1.5 miles) long and 44 metres (145 feet) wide. This processional route links the Square of the Moon (2), with its Pyramid of the Moon (6), to the Citadel (3), the religious centre of the city. This is a sunken enclosure containing the temple of Quetzalcoatl, the Plumed Serpent (4). Towering 66 metres (216 feet) over the sacred Avenue of the Dead and the city itself are the two pyramids of the Sun (5), and the Moon (6). The aristocrats and leaders of the city and the priests lived in the centre near the great pyramids. To the east of the Avenue of the Dead was another group of palaces (7).

To the west was the most beautiful of the priestly palaces, Quetzalpapalotl, the Palace of the Butterfly-Bird (8). The houses in this part of the city were large and contained many rooms, all opening out on to patios. Many were built, like the pyramids, of a red volcanic rock mined locally. Volcanic deposits of obsidian, a glass-like rock harder than flint which could be shaped into tools and weapons and luxury artefacts, gave Teotihuacan its main industry. Although the part of the city shown here mainly contains houses of the priests and aristocracy, elsewhere in Teotihuacan there was little social segregation. Excavations show that houses of varying social classes stood side by side. At its largest, Teotihuacan covered about 20 square kilometres (8 square miles). Then, in the fifth century AD, building stopped. By AD 600 its still-growing population was between 125,000 and 200,000, but within 100 years Teotihuacan had fallen into total obscurity.

Teotihuacan

The magnificent stone city of Teotihuacan, 15 miles north of today's Mexico City, rose up suddenly around 200 BC.

For some reason the god-worship cult continued, now with a new fervour. As though fighting against time itself, the Teotihuacanos built massive pyramids comparable to those of Egypt, which rose out of the dusty plains and towered into the sky. Small pyramids, ornate pyramids, stepped pyramids, carved pyramids. They worshipped the gods, the stars and the planets. They carved their idols in solid rock and all this before 50 BC, before the invention of the wheel and the days of the horse.

We do not know what name they gave to their buildings, although the Aztec who appeared on the scene a thousand years later settled for the names of the largest as the 'Pyramid of the Sun', and 'the Moon'. And for them the main precinct was to become 'the Way of the Dead'.

At its zenith Teotihuacan embraced 20 square kilometres (7 square miles) of intense development. The city was divided into sections with areas for artisans, and merchants, and ceremonies. Its influence was to spread to all parts of Meso-America through trade with neighbours, and somehow the Teotihuacanos understood, like their neighbours the Maya, that the sun affected fertility.

We can trace the development of the city from their clay figurines and textiles. During the first phase these are delicate and fragile. Phase two shows more realism and more elaborate clothing made from more sophisticated fibres, while phase three is almost exclusively preoccupied with god-worship. By the time of Teotihuacan four, the gods are depicted with less enthusiasm and prominence as their culture declined.

Phase three, the phase of the gods, saw the emergence of the Rain god Tlaloc, who ruled the clouds. He was summoned to bring sweet rains to the hot and dusty city, together with the Corn god, the Wind god and Quetzalcoatl, who represented the morning star Venus, and several goddesses. The only writing of the Teothihuacanos concerned calendrical symbols which showed a preoccupation with time and the counting of time, as though they somehow knew that the midnight

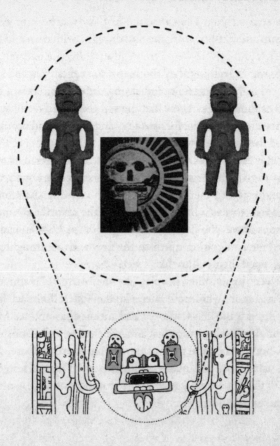

Fig 9 Archaeological artefacts found in Teotihuacan: carving of the skeletal head of the Sun god Tonatiuh inside the sun's rays. Tonatiuh was usually shown with his tongue extended indicating that he gave breath, or life. Here the skull seems to suggest the opposite, that he brings death. The 'solar baby' carving (either side of the Sun god) carries the mark of the sun on its stomach and a 'sad' mouth. The Teotihuacanos understood that the sun was killing them by causing a fall in fertility levels (see Appendix four).

The lower part of the illustration shows a section from the tomb lid of the King of the Maya which tells, amongst other things, the same story using iconographic symbolism.

hour was approaching. They were the first sky-watchers, preoccupied with the sun and fertility, with rain and drought, with corn and famine, whose beliefs and culture were a tremendous influence on later peoples like the Maya. Everything they did seems to suggest that the sun was killing them through infertility radiations, drought and infant mortality. It was as though they knew that the sun controlled fertility, that its radiations were responsible for astrology and ice ages and drought. But how could they have known?

The fact is that by 440 AD the sun had started to reverse its magnetic field. By 627 AD the magnetic field bottomed out to a 3,000 year minimum and by 750 AD the Teotihuacanos, who lived in the mountains, were dead (*see Appendix five*). The story was the same the country over. The glorious Maya who lived in the jungles of the Yucatan had by 750 AD started their migration north to the Lowlands as drought and infertility gripped their culture like a vice.

There were many other peoples like the Mixtec (Chichimec) and Zapotec, and more who came later, like the Toltec, Totonac, Tarascan or Aztec. But it is the Maya, whose name means 'illusion', that I want to examine in detail. This is not just because they were the most knowledgeable, nor just because their achievements in architecture, carving, painting, astronomy and mathematics surpassed all the rest, but because all of the evidence suggests that they understood the world much better than we do today.

Note – Naming of the Gods of the Maya

Because more is known about the gods of the Aztec than any of the other tribes, Aztec names are used throughout. This at first may disturb the true scholar, but it should not. In order to understand the message of the Maya we need to dispense with the concept of time. Once this has been done, the labels of the gods become unimportant. This is essential if we are to move forward and decode the secrets of their language.

In addition, many westerners find the Aztec names difficult to pronounce and even though Aztec names will be used where the use of such name is of importance, generic names such as the 'god of Rain' etc will be used when appropriate.

The Glossary of names, at the end of the book, gives an easy guide to pronunciation of the names.

CHAPTER THREE

A Stage for the Gods

By 500 AD the gods had established themselves at Teotihuacan ('the home of the gods') and they and their influence spread across Middle America quickly. The Maya, Zapotec, Mixtec, Toltec and Aztec in turn adopted and worshipped them and the gods themselves increased in importance and elevation.

For the Maya, Ku-Kul-Can, the feathered serpent, god of Goodness and Wisdom, was the highest of gods. He was to be worshipped by the later Aztec under the name of Quetzalcoatl and pushed aside in importance compared to the gods of War, Yaotl, the 'Bad god' who represented the North and Huitzilopochtli, the god of the South and Sacrifice. So the name of the god was changed during different periods, although they remained essentially the same deity throughout.

Fig 10 *Mask of Chaac on the Great Palace Sayil, Yucatan.*

Fig 11 *The God Huitzilopochtli as shown in the Aztec codex known as Telleriano-Remensis.*

For example, the Rain god for the Teotihuacanos was named Tlaloc. For the Maya the same Rain god was known as Chaac and for the Zapotec he became Cocijo, which at first is quite baffling for the student of mythology. Not only that, but gods could become the fathers of their father, and likewise daughters could give birth to their mother. At first this notion defies logic, but for the Maya and others it made good sense because there was no such notion as 'time'. The past would become the future and the future would become the past (*see Note at end of Chapter 1, p.32*).

The Maya believed this lifetime was a gift from the gods and Earth was known as 'the place of flower and song', summed up appropriately by the verse:

You tell me then that I must perish,
like the flowers that I cherish.
Nothing remains of my name,
nothing remembered of my fame?
But the gardens I planted still are young –
and the songs I sang will still be sung.

HUEXOTZIN, PRINCE OF TEXCOCO, 15TH CENTURY

Man was more than just a body to these Indians. He was spirit and like his gods he could and would transform himself upon death. Death was merely the casting off of a worn out body.

If the departing soul had led a good life then it travelled to one of the five paradises to savour the nectar of their gods. Those who died in battle or in sacrifice went to the paradise known as Tonatiuhcan, where lived the Sun god Tonatiuh, which lay to the East where the sun rose.

Women who died in childbirth went to the paradise known as Cincalco, the place of maize (corn) which lay to the West. Babies that died at birth went to the paradise of Tomoanchan, the place of our ancestors, where grew the suckling tree which carried 400,000 nipples instead of fruit. The dead babies would drink the milk from the nipples and in so doing receive enough nourishment to sustain them in the journey of reincarnation to Earth.

Two other paradises were known to exist but were not known destinations for the dead. These were Tlalocan, home of Tlaloc, the Rain god, which lay to the South where he lived with his consort the goddess of Water, Chalchiuitlicue ('the one who wears a jade skirt') and his friends the birds. The birds would sing sweetly and keep him awake so that he would send rain as often as possible.

Omeyocan was the home of Ometeotl, the original divine couple, the equivalent of Adam and Eve. It was from these two gods that all the others were born.

If they had led a sinful life, the departing souls would be escorted into the underworld carried in the arms of Lord and Lady Death, Mictlantechutli and Mictlantechutliuatl, who lived in the underworld of Mictlan, home of the dead. Once there they would meet the goddess of Filth, Tlazolteotl, the large house fly who ate filth. There she lived with her consort Ahuilteotl (he of filth and vices) whose friendly prostitute Ahuianime met his every need. Here the goddess of Flies would purge the sins of sinners in 'heart letting' ceremonies by listening to their confessions which eased the burden of guilt in their hearts. From this came the word purgatory, and the goddess herself become known by the more endearing name of the 'goddess of Hearts'. Once purged of sins, the sinners could reincarnate in the arms of Coatlicue, the Earth goddess, for another life and another opportunity to purify the spirit.

Fig 12 Lord and Lady Death, Dresden Codex.

Coatlicue was an emanation of the female side of Ometeotl and was the mother of all gods. She gave life and took life away and was therefore depicted with massive clawed hands and feet that could bring earthquakes, and hearts and bones that signified the giving and taking of life. Her earthquakes would shake the babies in their cradles and hence she became the guardian of the new born: the Earth Mother. Her face was formed from the heads of two serpents, that represented day and night, life and death.

Fig 13 Coatlicue, the goddess of Life and Death and the mother of the gods.

Like Ometeotl, the various gods were able to transform themselves into alter egos, give birth to other gods or appear as other emanations of themselves. Quetzalcoatl, for example, was also known as Tlahuizpantechutli, the god of Ice, who represented Venus in the morning. He was blinded by a dart which came from the sun and so wore a blindfold. His nickname was Twisted Knife after the ice crystals, or ice daggers, he represented.

Venus was known both as the Morning Star and the Evening Star because sometimes she would rise before the sun in the morning and at other times could only be seen after the sun had set in the West, depending upon her position in the sky.

As the Evening Star, Quetzalcoatl became Xolotol the dog who, it is said, once cried so much that his eyes fell out of their sockets and so like Twisted Knife became blind. This was not all bad, for it allowed Quetzalcoatl, in this disguise, to descend into the underworld and steal the bones that would make mankind in the fifth age of the sun, the age of the Jaguar. Only Xolotol could do this because his blindness allowed him to see in the darkness of Mictlan, where the bones of the dead were safely stored.

Lord and Lady Butterfly, Itzpapalotltotec and Itzpapalotltotechuatl, represented sacrifice. These two gods were picking flowers in the paradise of Omeyocan when they carelessly snapped a tree which gushed forth blood. The other gods were angry and threw obsidian rocks at them. Thus they became the obsidian butterflies who fell from grace and were associated with the disappearance of two stars from the sky, and hence could be associated with the twin star Venus.

Gods could transform themselves, and the sorceress Quilatzli, the green heron, was more able than most to transform herself into different things and so had many names: woman serpent, woman eagle, and woman warrior, amongst others. She is said to have accompanied the Mexica as they migrated to the valley of Mexico. Legend has it she was perched on a cactus in the disguise of a red feathered eagle when two warriors approached. They were intending to kill the eagle when she revealed her disguise as their sister. Once they recognized her, they decided against killing her.

In the beginning the original divine couple Ometeotl gave birth to Ehecatl, the god of Wind, who begat a son. He then merged with his son to form Quetzalcoatl the feathered serpent, the teacher of wisdom and goodness.

Ometeotl also gave birth to three more brothers, Xipe Totec (god of the Flayed), Yaotl, the Bad god and Huitzilopochtli who was associated with sacrifice. Another emanation of Ometeotl, this time the male side, was Xiuhtechutli god of Fire, the Old god. He represented Fire on Earth, as against Tonatiuh the Sun god – god of Fire in the Sky.

Fig 14 Ehecatl, god of Wind.

Again the picture becomes somewhat confused because Xipe Totec was the god of the Flayed and Sacrifice and Xiuhtechutli, was also associated with sacrifice; he carried a dish on his back upon which the sacrificed were cremated. Hence he was often depicted carrying two sticks which he could rub together to make fire. He also wore a protective metal helmet to protect his own head from the heat of the fire which he carried on his back. Similarly, he was the god of Fire in the Fireplace. Tonatiuh was the god of Fire in the Sky and Huitzilopochtli was sometimes depicted as Tonatiuh. If the Maya wanted to describe fire, or the East, or sacrifice, then either of these gods might be used at any one time. In addition, the gods would change according to the time of day, or night, they were pictured. Hence Tonatiuh changed names during the day. Other gods changed names depending on the time of the month, or season. For example, there were three goddesses of Maize – one to represent young green corn, one to represent ripe corn and another to represent old corn with dry brown leaves.

Coyolxiuhqui was the Moon goddess, who wore bells on her cheeks to represent the reflected gold of the sun. Her nickname was Jingle Bells and whilst she represented fertility on earth she was also associated with death, because she died every morning as the sun rose.

She crossed the sky together with her four escorts that represented the four faces of the moon: First Quarter, New Moon, Last Quarter and Full Moon.

Fig 15 Head of Coyolxiuhqui in greenstone. Mexican Civilization, National Museum of Anthropology and History.

So there existed a great pantheon of gods of which the above mentioned are only a few. We are led to believe that the peoples that worshipped these gods did so as much out of boredom as out of fear. But we will find that the message was much deeper than that. The gods represented a language of symbolism that could describe events in pictures or mythological belief. They could describe history, without the use of a dedicated language, to future peoples like ourselves, who might not understand the native Quiche of the Maya, or the Nahuatl of the Aztec, or even the Spanish of the conquistadors. The Mayas could use their gods to tell us that the world within which we find ourselves is temporal, that no such thing as time exists, that the world is a stage and we, like their gods, merely actors who can transform ourselves into different characters with each appearance, each incarnation on Earth.

Maya Numbers

Throughout history cultural traditions have been wiped out by conquering armies and political regimes, eager to impose their own beliefs upon defeated nations. Such loss of knowledge also occurs as a result of natural disasters and catastrophes on a massive scale, like that of the great flood in biblical times, and accounts for Velikovsky's 'collective amnesia'.

If a highly advanced people had knowledge of cataclysmic mechanisms that affect the Earth periodically, at predictable intervals spanning vast periods of time, it seems reasonable to suggest that they would wish to convey this knowledge to future generations. But how could any civilization communicate with another which would emerge perhaps 5,000 years later, given such collective amnesia? Languages would have been lost as nation conquered nation. Ideas and cultures would be wiped out and books burned through ideological succession. Technology would become a mere vapour in the passage of time through fire, flood and earthquake.

But life would go on and mankind would in time recover again to count the passage of time and the seasons on his ten fingers, carrying forward at least one basic skill from the past and with it a common denominator of advanced civilizations: numbers.

Little surprise then that early civilizations brought numbers to their gods, for by doing this their gods could express quantities, adding yet more significance to their accounts of their history and their prophecies. To accommodate this the Maya used the simplest of counting systems where a short bar represented the number five and a single dot represented the number one, greatly enhancing the scope of their iconographic vocabulary. So they had a 'message', of periodic catastrophe, and a 'system' of writing using representations of their gods, and another for counting, using the bar and dot. If we now put ourselves in their position what would be the best way to encode this important message to provide both its best chance of survival and of unambiguous decoding?

Today we have many ways, or 'systems', of encoding information: through musical vibrations on instruments, through dots and marks on musical scores, through printed characters in books and documents, on magnetic media on hard discs and floppy discs, on holes in paper tape used in Telex for codes used in electromagnetic transmission, Morse, Telex and Fax, visually in paintings, photographs, sculpture, architecture and even the layout of flower beds.

The methods of 'storage' are similarly various: paper, plastic disk, tape, light emitting diode, liquid crystal, CD (laser optics), concrete, marble and flowers to name but a few.

We take for granted these media that carry the information, and the encoding of the information itself which we struggled to understand in our childhood. For the illiterate the markings on this page are baffling. In the same way, without a computer the information on a magnetic disc does not exist, it is merely a piece of plastic. Without knowledge of the rules of the encoding nothing exists to be found. We also need to remember that the choice of encoding, and the method, depend upon the importance of the message. Important messages tend to be duplicated to ensure they are not missed or overlooked. We do this all the time today by perhaps confirming an important fax with a follow up letter, or by leaving a telephone message and confirming it in writing, increasing greatly the chances of our message getting through.

It was considerations such as these that persuaded the Maya to encode and duplicate their messages into their architecture, carvings, precious jewellery, paintings and their numbering system. These would stand the ravages of time whilst each simultaneously supported the message of the other, precluding ambiguity and increasing the certainty of eventual discovery, decoding and delivery.

In *The Mayan Prophecies* I showed why and how the Maya used cycles of time to convey messages of catastrophes. They used specific cycles of days with which to label periods of time. We, today, use cycles of 365.24 day periods, our year, together with 30.4375 days (an average) month, and 7 days, a week, to label one moment in time, which is measured from a starting date, in the distant past, of an important event. For example, 6 December 1997 tells us that 1,996 years 11 months and 6/7th of one week have elapsed since the birth of Christ.

Similarly, the Maya used cycles of 144,000 days, 7,200 days, 360 days and 20 days to measure time, and these were calculated from the birth of Venus in the year 3,113 BC. Not surprisingly the choice of these durations for cycles has confounded scholars for more than two centuries. Why use them at all, why not just have an accumulation of days from that distant point in 3,113 BC? Clearly something was missing. What was missing was the most important numbers of the Maya; this is a bit odd to say the least, because the Maya year was known to be 260 days long and they were known to have 'worshipped' the number 9, which never appeared in any numbering system but appeared just about everywhere else – in wooden peg calendars, in written records, astronomical tables etc.

From recent space-age research we know that our own sun spins every 26 days at the equator and every 37 days at the pole, resulting in a mutual cycle of 260 days which may be used to calculate magnetic activity on the sun and the radiation of particles from the sun which affect life on Earth (*see Appendices*). By including this very important number into the cycle series so that the series becomes:

144,000 + 7,200 + 360 + 260 + 20 and multiplying by 9,

we arrive at the sun-spot number of 1,366,560, the catastrophe period, which for the Maya was the birth of Venus.

What this shows is that the Maya did not wish the meaning of their cycles to be revealed except to the person who understood the scientific importance of the number 260, because it was the astronomical significance of the numbers 260 and 1,366,560 that was the message they wished to convey. As for the worship of the number 9, we will see how they developed an incredibly clever system of clues which they used within the encoding of the Temple of Inscriptions in Palenque, enabling a duplication of the same message in their architecture, as well as carvings and jewellery.

Those interested in Mayan Numbers should see the section of the same name in *The Mayan Prophecies*. There, I showed that the numbering system has several other levels which reveal that the Maya were aware of a decimal system even though they chose not to use one in their inscriptions.

CHAPTER FOUR

The Genius
of the Maya King

Palenque

Palenque nestles between the Maya highlands on the Pacific Coast and
the lowlands of the Yucatan to the North in the Gulf of Mexico. Its
magnificent limestone palaces and temples, monuments of one of the
world's greatest civilizations, stand as testimony to a people of genius,
misunderstood for centuries (*see plates 1, 2 and 3*).

In 1952, the greatest ever Mexican archaeological discovery was
made by archaeologist Alberto Ruz Lhuillier. After three years of
painstaking digging, using only picks and shovels, his team finally
cleared the rubble-filled stairway that ran down into the Temple of
Inscriptions in the ancient Maya city of Palenque. Moving away the
massive triangular monolith that blocked the entrance, he was confronted by 'an enormous empty room that appeared to be graven in
ice...the walls glistened like snow crystals...and almost the whole of
the room was filled with a great slab top of an altar...only the fact that
it was completely carved could be made out...'

Fig 16 *Map areas showing part of North and Central America.*

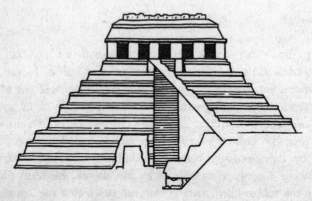

Fig 17 *Diagram showing secret stairway leading to the tomb of Lord Pacal (see also plate 5).*

How they celebrated their discovery, and the treasure trove, intoxicated by their own achievement. How clever they had been to find the four pairs of holes in the paving slab that lay on the floor of the temple, the uppermost floor of the pyramid. And then how ably they had lifted the slab off the floor with car jacks and blocks and tackle to scratch away the rock hard mortar base to reveal at first a single limestone step, and then another and another.

Fig 18 Cross-section view of the Temple of Inscriptions.

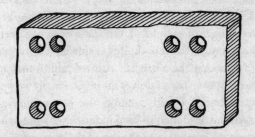

Fig 19 Holes in the paving slab on the floor of the temple.

Discovery followed discovery. Halfway down the steps the staircase greets a landing from which it turns to descend a second flight of steps ending at the foot of a stone and lime wall. Attached to the wall was a stone chest filled with 3 clay trays, 3 red painted shells, 11 jade pieces and a single pearl in a shell filled with cinnabar, all *peace offerings* (italics in this section refer to the orthodox interpretation followed by the general body of archaeology, guide books etc). Demolishing the wall they found themselves in a small square chamber containing the skeletons of 5 men and 1 woman, *sacrificed victims*, to the left of which could be seen a triangular stone door. On 15 June 1952, for the first time in 1,200 years, the tomb was opened.

In front of Ruz Lhuillier lay the covering of the tomb, a solid stone block weighing 5 tons that was completely carved all over with *a picture of the man in the tomb sitting on top of an earth monster, falling from this life into the next*. On top of the slab were some fragments of *a ceremonial belt* that carried three small human masks and *hatchet shaped pendants*. A number of earthenware goblets and plates were discovered, *probably left here filled with food and drink at the time of the burial*. Two stone heads were positioned on the floor, one of a *woman* and one of a man, *the man in the tomb*.

Removing the tomb lid they uncovered another *mummy-shaped* stone inner lid and removing this they discovered the bones of the man in the tomb who was aged about 40 when he died. The entire inside of the sarcophagus had been painted with red cinnabar and his face was covered by fragments of the green jade mask. He wore a crown of jade discs, *complicated ear hoops*, various necklaces of jade, jade bracelets comprised of individually strung jade beads, jade rings, one for every finger of each hand. One jade bead had been placed in each hand and one in the mouth. By his side lay 2 miniature jade figurines. And of course the 9 brightly painted figures that adorned the walls of the crypt were *the 9 Lords of the night*. Finally we must not forget the square stone boxed conduit, the *communications channel* which allowed the dead man to keep in touch with the living; this ran from the crypt up every step to the top of the pyramid.

So it was all over. Everything had been accounted for and the accolades followed as expected. The man in the tomb was a priest-king Lord Pacal who, if the inscriptions in the temple were to be believed, was born in 703 AD and died in 783 AD aged 80. Yet nobody asked any questions, such as:

- *Why did the pyramid have 9 levels (storeys) but only 5 staircases? Surely it would have been much simpler to have built a short staircase up every sloping level, but this was not done.*
- *Why did the 5 stairways amount to 69 steps?*
- *Why were there 5 porchways and 6 pillars at the top of the temple? Could these be in any way significant?*
- *Why 4 sets of double holes in the paving slab on the temple floor? Why not simply 1 hole in each corner to assist lifting?*
- *Why was the entire staircase filled with rubble and mortar, so that it took 3 years of digging to reach the tomb?*
- *Why were there 620 carved inscriptions in the temple?*
- *Why 26 steps down the first level of the inside staircase?*
- *Why 22 steps down the second staircase?*
- *What was the reason for the stone box containing the items at the foot of the stairs?*
- *Why were there 5 male skeletons and 1 female?*
- *Why was the door to the tomb triangular?*
- *Why were there 4 steps down, just after the triangular door?*
- *What was the meaning of the carving on the lid? and why had the corners been removed?*
- *Why was one corner missing from the sarcophagus?*
- *What did the 9 'secret codes' on either side of the lid represent?*
- *What was the significance of the 2 stucco heads on the floor? and why did 1 head have a 'high hairstyle' while the other had a low hairstyle? and why did 1 of them have 2 ears, but the other only 1 ear?*
- *What was the significance of the jade jewellery? Why did the jade mask have peculiar dot markings in certain areas?*
- *What did the other jade pieces represent?*
- *Why use jade for jewellery, why not gold?*

- *How come the bones of the man in the tomb show he died aged 40 whilst the inscriptions suggest a man twice his age?*
- *Why was the inside of the tomb painted with red cinnabar, the powdered form of liquid mercury?*
- *Why were 9 'Lords of the Night' painted on the wall?*
- *What was the true purpose of 'the communications channel'?*

It seemed to me that the investigation, far from being over, had not even begun! So, having knowledge of the sun-spot cycle, I took a fresh look at the mysteries of the temple pyramid.

Just before arriving at the Temple of Inscriptions you come to the Palace at the foot of which lies a tablet carrying 96 inscriptions. In *The Mayan Prophecies* I showed that there are 96 micro-cycles in the 187-year sun-spot cycle. The 97th I described as the 'rogue' cycle which causes an even longer cycle of 18,139 years. The 96 glyphs on the tablet represent these 96 micro-cycles of solar activity (*see Appendix one III*). At the same time, I showed how the sun-spot cycle is divided into 5 segments and these can be seen to correspond with the 5 doorways of the temple (*see Appendix one IV*).

The reason the Temple of Inscriptions pyramid has 9 levels is to emphasize the most important number of the Maya. The reason for 5 landings is to reinforce the number 5. At first this seems a little far fetched, but in a few minutes the reader will begin to realize that encoded into the pyramid is the numbering system of the Maya that points to the Birth of Venus number. In *The Mayan Prophecies* I compiled a numeric table which when used in conjunction with the Maya cycles threw up the Birth of Venus. It looked like this:

144,000	7,200	360	260	20 days
1	1	1	1	1
2	2	2	2	2
3	3	3	3	3
4	4	4	4	4
5	5	5	5	5
6	6	6	6	6
7	7	7	7	7
8	8	8	8	8
9	9	9	9	9 = 1,366,560 days
				(Sun-spot cycle)

Fig 20 cycles of days used by the maya

I arrived at this table through a mathematical inquiry into the revolutions of Venus against the base 360. The game of the Maya in the Temple was the game of numbers. All of the numbers in the table above are encoded as clues in the pyramid.

The first clue to this is the tablet of 96 glyphs, found at the base of the Palace building, that represented the 96 micro-cycles of the sun-spot cycle. This 'reflects' the enigmatic '69' steps of the Temple of Inscriptions – the numbers are reversed, 96 against 69. The next is the number of inscriptions in the floor of the temple 620, an anagram of the important Maya year of 260. Subtracting 260 from 620 gives us 360, the base number of the Maya counting system.

Now let us reconcile each of the numbers in the table with clues in the tomb. There are:

9	9	9	9	9
Steps at the bottom of the pyramid (outside)	Levels of the pyramid	Steps on the top stairway of the pyramid (outside)	Lords of the Night painted on walls of tomb	Codes on each side of the tomb lid

Fig 21

We can show that every other line of the table is also represented, for example just outside the triangular door, the entrance to the tomb, was the square chamber which carried the stone chest, together these contained:

1	1	1	1	1
	11 jade pieces in the stone chest	Pearl	Female skeleton	Shell

Fig 22

Similarly, there were 4 sets of double holes in the temple paving slab amounting to 2 2 2 2. There were also 2 heads on the floor of the tomb (and 2 jade figurines accompanying the bones of Lord Pacal, as well as 22 steps on the lower internal staircase which will be dealt with later).

The number of steps on the first section of the internal stairway is 26, the revolutionary period (in days) of the sun's equator. The number of sides to the door of the tomb was 3. And this was no ordinary door:

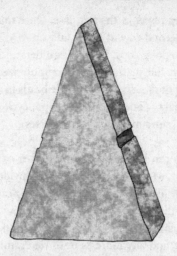

Fig 23 The triangular doorway into the tomb.

This was a journey into the mind (*see colour plate 7*).

Completing the row of 3s we have 3 clay trays, 3 red shells in the stone chest and three jade beads, one placed in each hand of the dead king and one in his mouth, and he wore a 3-tiered necklace.

There were 4 sets of double holes in the paving slab, 4 steps down into the crypt and 4 rings on the dead man's left hand, 4 rings on the dead man's right hand and 4 plugs in the sarcophagus.

There were 5 stair levels, 5 temple doorways, 5 ceiling beams inside the crypt, 5 sides to the sarcophagus, and 5 male skeletons outside in the square chamber. And talking of skeletons, the reason for 5 male skeletons and 1 female skeleton conveys the message that one was different from all other skeletons (men), or more loosely that the man in the tomb was different from all other men. This tells us that Lord Pacal was no ordinary man.

There were 6 pillars to the Temple entrance and 6 sides to the Lid of the Palenque. The remaining sixes, 666, are curiously missing but can be found in conjunction with 7s and 8s in the jade necklace found around Lord Pacal's neck (*see next page*): Examining the necklace we see that the three 6s, missing from the tomb, can be found only as a factor of higher numbers in the necklace. Once found, the 7s and 8s also appear. The second row of beads add up to 37, the revolutionary period of the sun's polar caps. The top two tiers add up to 71 which is a critical factor in the mathematical computerized calculation that leads to the sun-spot cycle period (11 (jade beads in stone chest) × 71 × 87.4545 = 68,302 days = one 187 year sun-spot cycle. After 20 of these, 1,366,040 days, the sun's magnetic field reverses).

The missing 6s can be found in the number of strips of 13 beads which provide 6+7, 6+7 and 6+7 which also provide 3 of the required 7s. The second row likewise shows a 7. The next 7 cannot be found except as a factor in the next level of numbers the 8s, 7+8 = 15 which can be found on the centre strip of beads and which takes us on to the 8s. At first we cannot find any more 8s until we examine the lower strip which runs 1 long bead followed by 3 round beads, then, 1 long bead followed by 3 round beads, then1 long bead followed by 3 round beads and once again 1 long bead followed by 3 round beads. This in Maya numbers is:

8   8   8   8

Before we finish with the bead necklace we need to reconcile the single oblong bead in the centre of the bottom row of the necklace and the 2 single oblong beads on the centre row, either side of the 7, which as yet have not been accounted for. Earlier when attempting to accommodate the first row of our number matrix, the 1 1 1 1 1, we included 11 jade beads found in the square chest as well as the 1 single pearl found in the sea-shell on a bed of cinnabar. These 3 remaining oblong beads on the necklace tell us that we have made a slight mistake: the 11 jade beads from the chest do not belong in the first line of the matrix after all but belong with the 71 in the necklace (11 × 71 × 87.4545 = one 187-year sun-spot cycle described above). Likewise the single pearl in the shell has also been incorrectly included into the matrix and this, we will see shortly, is another clue in the decoding of the Lid of Palenque itself (*see next page*).

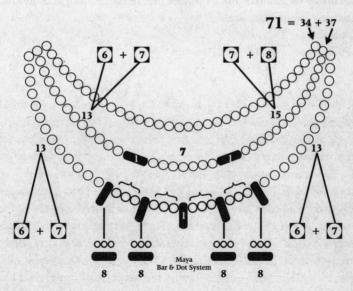

Fig 24 The mystery of the necklace – the sixes, the sevens, the eights.

So, the clues all point to a numerical matrix the conclusion of which culminates in 9 9 9 9 9. Taking 9 each of the Maya cycles and also 9 of the 260-day Maya years we arrive at the message of the Temple of Inscriptions: 1,366,560.

The sceptic might argue that 'if we looked hard enough then all of these numbers could have been found somewhere'. The point is, firstly, that we have not looked very hard at all, and secondly, you will be hard pressed to duplicate this matrix using other references inside the pyramid. The only exception might be the 2 figurines and the 22 steps mentioned earlier. But, like the beads we shall account for these in due course. Finally, another clue to the matrix can be found on the outside of the steps of the pyramid which supports our analysis (*see Appendix one v*).

And this is only the beginning because now we embark upon a journey inside the mind of man, through the triangular door and into the Amazing Lid of Palenque.

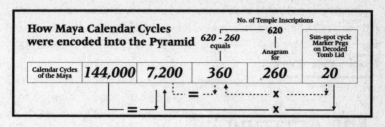

Decoding the Clues of the Pyramid and Temple of Inscriptions				
1 Pearl in sea-shell	**1** Female skeleton in ante-chamber	**1** Single long bead on necklace	**1** Single long bead on necklace	**1** Single long bead on necklace
2 Holes in paving slab	**2** Holes in paving slab	**2** Holes in paving slab	**2** Holes in paving slab	**2** Plaster heads on Tomb floor
3 Clay plates in stone chest	**3** Red shells in stone chest	**3** Sided Tomb door	**3** Jade beads (1 in each hand 1 in mouth)	**3** Tiered jade necklace
4 Steps down into Tomb	**4** Jade rings on left hand	**4** Jade rings on right hand	**4** Sets of holes in paving slab	**4** Cylindrical plugs in Sarcophagus
5 Pyramid stairway landings	**5** Temple doorways	**5** Male skeletons	**5** Ceiling beams	**5** Sarcophagus sides
6 Temple pillars	**6** Sides to Tomb Lid	missing **6** +	missing **6** +	missing **6** +
missing **7** +	**7** Necklace beads	**7** =13 Necklace beads	**7** =13 Necklace beads	**7** =13 Necklace beads
8 =15 Necklace beads	**8** Dash Dot beads ●●●	**8** Dash Dot beads ●●●	**8** Dash Dot beads ●●●	**8** Dash Dot beads ●●●
9 Bottom steps of Pyramid	**9** Pyramid levels	**9** Top steps of Pyramid	**9** Lords painted on Tomb walls	**9 / 9*** Codes on left / right sides of Lid

Decoding in relation to calendar cycles used by the Maya	9 x 144,000 +	9 x 7,200 +	9 x 360 +	9 x 260 +	9 x 20

= 1,366,560 days

9 of each of the Maya Cycles amounts to the sun-spot catastrophy period of 1,366,560 days.
The extra 9*, in the row of nines, is the final clue to the sun-spot number:
1+3+6+6+5+6+0 = 27; 2+7 = 9*

Fig 25 How Maya calendar cycles were encoded into the pyramid.

CHAPTER FIVE

The Amazing lid
of Palenque

The limestone slab covering the tomb of Lord Pacal (*see plate 8*) weighs 5 tons and measures roughly 4 metres (12 feet) in length, 2 metres (7 feet) in width and just under 30 centimetres (1 foot) in depth. Its top surface carries a picture of *the occupant of the tomb falling from this life into some afterlife region – while seated on top of an Earth Monster*, at least that is the official interpretation. A border carrying various motifs frames the central carving and, notably, two corners of the lid are missing – although this is not mentioned in any official literature.

In *The Mayan Prophecies* I showed how, by finding the missing corners, the surrounding border could be decoded to reveal secret instructions which enabled the central carving itself to be decoded. The purpose of this inquiry is not to repeat how the lid was decoded, but to reveal some of the decoded stories themselves, hidden within the lid.

In 1989 I decoded more than two hundred secret pictures hidden in the Lid of Palenque and arranged these into a logical sequence of around 40 different stories in two separate Volumes (*see Appendix nine*). Volume 1 shows the various gods of the Maya and describes their ancient mythology and traditions. Volume 2 builds upon this by showing

Fig 26 The carving on the tomb lid.

the gods in various roles. In this way the information in the lid unfolds and provides an account of the afterlife which awaits mankind.

Significantly, the sacred book of the Maya, the *Popol Vuh* (the 16th-century version) begins and ends with these few words: 'The [original] *Popol Vuh* cannot be seen anymore…it has been hidden from the searcher and the thinker'. This lid was hidden beneath a pyramid, in the jungles of Central America. The steps leading to the tomb were filled with mortar and rubble and yet a paving stone at the top of the pyramid provides holes by which the paving slab may be lifted to expose a stairway below. So those who buried the lid, inside the tomb, within the pyramid, at the bottom of a rubble- filled stairway <u>wanted</u> the tomb to be found <u>but</u> made sure that only a 'team' of diggers, with resources that would last the course – three years of digging – would succeed. In other words they made sure on the one hand that the tomb was safe from gangs of grave-robbers, yet on the other, accessible to authorized diggers, such as the government of the day.

In the same way the decoding of the lid was not obvious. It required a great deal of thought before I was able to break the code. It was hidden from the thinker, but not from the 'determined' thinker familiar with sun-spot cycles, catastrophe cycles and fertility cycles. The Maya made sure that the person who would eventually crack the code would, and must, first understand these before revealing what you are about to see. The reason for this will become clear later.

The Secret Pictures of the Amazing Lid of Palenque (Vol II)

I discovered the secrets of the lid by making a plastic photocopy of a drawing of the design (on acetate) and placing this on top of the original drawing. When the two are placed on top of each other, and manoeuvred, the story of the afterlife begins:

The Physical Death of Lord Pacal

Two stucco heads were found on the floor of the crypt. One shows Pacal as a younger man with a low hairstyle and only one ear, the other as an older man with a high hairstyle and, more correctly, with two ears. The younger one also carries what appears to be a defect crack just above the nose bridge and the older one carries a curious circle between the right eye and nose.

Fig 27 Two stucco heads of Lord Pacal found on the floor of the crypt.

These are clues which help decode the secret messages hidden within the lid. I must re-emphasize that our purpose here is not to decode the pictures but to examine a few of the already decoded pictures taken from *The Amazing Lid of Palenque, Vol 2*, which is available in several public libraries (*see Appendix nine*).

Firstly the two acetates are taped (fixed) together into position (for this particular series of scenes).

Next an iconographic representation of a tiny bat face with tiny open wings emerges from the confusion of lines and this is the first scene of Lord Pacal dying (*see Fig 28 below*). Just above this a larger bat with open wings (in black) emerges as Scene 2, The Approaching Bat.

Scene 2
Approaching Bat
(Approaching Death)

Fig 28 The Physical Death of Lord Pacal, Scene 1: Distant Bat (Approaching Death) Scene 2: Approaching Bat (Approaching Death).

Erasing these two scenes, a third bat fills almost all of the picture, as though only inches from the tip of the observer's nose, with its wings enfolded around the sides of the observer's head. This is Scene 3, the Landing Bat (*see Fig 29*).

Fig 29 The Physical Death of Lord Pacal, Scene 3: Landing Bat.

The Bat represented death for the Maya, hence this series represents the approach of death, or dying.

Scene 4 (*see colour plate 9*) shows the occupant of the tomb wearing the Landed Bat mask across his face, although here, to improve resolution of Lord Pacal's face, the mask is coloured in orange and yellow, instead of black, which would obscure the lower face. Notice also the baby bird that sits on top of Lord Pacal's head. This bird carries a chain in its beak upon which hangs a conch shell, the mark of the wind, and Quetzalcoatl.

The message from The Physical Death of Lord Pacal, Scene 4 is therefore that death came to Lord Pacal who was reborn as a baby Quetzalcoatl bird, or that upon death Lord Pacal became Quetzalcoatl (*see also plate 6*).

Earlier we came across the four Tezcatlipocas, the first four gods who represented the four corners of the sky. Yaotl represented the North, Death and Darkness; Xiuhtechutli represented Fire, the East, Rebirth and Sacrifice; Huitzilopochtli represented Purification; while Quetzalcoatl epitomized Goodness. These four gods now feature in the following scenes to help us understand the meaning of the hidden pictures.

The orientation of the acetates is now shifted slightly and again taped into various positions. The next position shows Scene 5 (*see plate 10*) of this series with Lord Pacal slipping away into death with eyes closed. On his head stands the Great Bear, Yaotl, god of Darkness, digging his two hands into two outwardly facing skull profiles, which rest upon Pacal's head.

Notice also that Yaotl holds a chain between his teeth from which hang two conch shells, the mark of Quetzalcoatl, whilst from his neck hang the four twisted ribbons of the measuring cord, confirming his status as one of the four Tezcatlipocas, an emanation of Quetzalcoatl.

At the same time, in the lower part of the picture, the Bat god flies toward the reader with outstretched wings, carrying the Messenger of Death, who has a skull for a face and a black cloak and hat. Now the face of Pacal becomes 'stressed' between these two forces of death: one from Yaotl at the top and one from the Messenger at the bottom. As a consequence the head of Pacal begins to split around the nose bridge. The stucco head showing the nose bridge crack is the clue to Scene 5: Pacal now begins his journey from this world to the next.

Scene 6 (*plate 11*) shows again the face of Lord Pacal in a more advanced stage of decay as the death process ensues. The clue to this scene is the circular mark on the older stucco head that emphasizes the squinting nature of the facial expression. Pacal is startled and opens his eyes to squint in shock as he sees a maiden emerging from the crack between his eyes.

At the top of the scene crouches the stooping figure of Xiuhtechutli, the god of Fire, the giver of life, in flames, with the conch shells and measuring chord hanging from his mouth and neck. The maiden emerges from the splitting skull of Lord Pacal with her heels either side of his mouth, her backwards falling body covering the nose, and her head rising from the crack on the nose bridge itself. Pacal is awakened, and startled by the emerging figure, and his eyes open wide with surprise. The presence of Xiuhtechutli, above, suggests that the emerging maiden comes to bring new life.

The Spiritual Rebirth of Lord Pacal

A single pearl resting in a sea shell filled with cinnabar was found leading to the tomb and as we have already seen a heavy jade mosaic mask covered the face of the corpse inside the sarcophagus. These two items are clues to The Spiritual Rebirth of Lord Pacal, Scene 1 (*plate 12*) which shows Tezcatlipoca Quetzalcoatl (the baby Quetzal bird) holding a jade mask in his beak as he lifts away from the corpse. The removal of the mask enables the release of the soul of Pacal, seen immediately below the rising bird, with eyes closed (formed from the converging elements of the measuring cord). Hence the heavy burden of life is lifted from the dying man.

At the same time, the maiden who emerged and startled Pacal in the last scene now falls backwards and kicks open her legs to give birth to a pearl which falls from the mouth of the now dead skull of Pacal. The pearl then becomes two 'solar babies'. The pearl in the shell hence represents the seed of a new life, a new beginning on a distant shore; while the solar babies represent rebirth of twins in the South, the paradise of Tomoanchan. These will suckle the nipples of the suckling tree and be reincarnated on Earth. This scene therefore suggests that a choice exists for the dead between purification and salvation of the soul or rebirth on Earth.

The pearl is also resting in a bed of cinnabar, the powdered form of liquid Mercury which is a very important disclosure. The message here reads that without (the planet) Mercury birth and rebirth cannot take place. This confirms the hypothesis in Appendix I that it is this movement of Mercury that causes the sun's equatorial region to rotate faster than the poles. This differential rotation is the underlying cause of sunspots, infertility cycles and catastrophe cycles. This is why the entire inside of Lord Pacal's sarcophagus was also painted with cinnabar, to re-emphasize the importance of Mercury.

Scene 2 (*plate 13*) shows the now 'featureless' Lord Pacal as his new self in heaven. There is no nose, because he does not need to breathe and so the nasal cavity, along with the rest of his face, is bedecked with jewellery which hangs from the 'skull cap', which now seals the top of his skull. His lips too are sealed and he smiles with inner peace, joy and bliss. Falling from his lips is a baby suspended from a pendant. The jade pendants scattered around the lid in the tomb are clues to this and the next few scenes.

We can now introduce the jade figurine (*plate 14*) which accompanied Pacal in the sarcophagus. Notice the bun of hair on the figurine which is depicted as a butterfly on the head of Pacal in this scene. This butterfly forms the torso of Huitzilopochtli who, as an emanation of Tonatiuh, represents a new day. In Volume 1 of *The Amazing Lid of Palenque* (not shown here) Lord and Lady Butterfly appear in a scene that depicted purification and sacrifice.

This scene therefore suggests that Pacal found purification through sacrifice. But the figurine gives us another clue: look at the gesturing hands at different levels – one is lifting up while the other is falling lower. This is a clue to the scene that follows.

Scene 3 (*plate 15*) shows the baby hanging from Pacal's lips on a pendant. At the top the young 'chick' Quetzalcoatl pulls upon a large pendant from which hangs another baby. The baby is 'mummy' shaped corresponding to the shape of the inner sarcophagus. Inside this baby figure is another rising in the same direction. Inside the second are two solar babies heading downwards in the opposite direction toward the underworld.

The meaning of this scene is not altogether clear in itself. Quetzalcoatl was represented by the twin star Venus and therefore Quetzalcoatl in this scene may be depicted as the vehicle by which the spiritual babies rise in the sky (pulled up by the chick) and also by the twin solar babies travelling to the underworld. The scenes that follow suggest that this may be a reasonable interpretation.

Quetzalcoatl Creates Mankind for the Fifth Age of the Sun

Legend tells that when the fourth creation of man came to an end Quetzalcoatl was given the job of descending into the underworld to steal bones for the men of the fifth age, which he had been ordained to create. To do this he assumed his role of Xolotol (Venus in the Evening) the blind dog who could see in the darkness of Mictlan, the place of the dead.

Scene 1 (*plate 16*) shows a V-shaped bat with massive head in the lower foreground of the picture. Lord of Death kneels to stare at the viewer and steer the bat. Standing upright behind him is his wife, Lady Death, who carries a basket filled with two twins who can be seen suckling the twin stars above, Venus.

The scene therefore tells how Quetzalcoatl ventured into the underworld to steal the bones to make mankind.

Scene 2 (*plate 17*) shows the bones materializing from the underworld and forming into babies.

Scenes 2 and 3 are not the most persuasive of this series but have been included because scene 3 introduces the character Tlachueyal, the giant who lived in the underworld: Yaotl (the god of the North and Darkness) was generally perceived as a malevolent character but when appearing as Tlachueyal he was a positive force performing good works like those of a 'caretaker'.

In Scene 3 (*plate 18*) the giant is seen with legs apart, formed by the overlaid border code patterns, tugging on another baby which hangs from another pendant. This baby, though, is clearly different from others we have seen so far because on its forehead is the mark of the bat, suggesting that this baby is 'physical' or flesh, rather than a spiritual rebirth. The mark of the bat tells us that this physical baby is born to die. So it emerges from the underworld, helped by the giant.

The giant Tlachueyal will feature in an important scene later on and this is the reason for inclusion of Scenes 2 and 3 here.

Tlazolteotl Goddess of Filth or Goddess of Hearts

Tlazolteotl was depicted as a house fly that lived in the underworld, who devoured filth. Together with helpers she would round up sinners and bring them before priests to confess their sins. As they confessed so their hearts would be 'lighter' and so she became known as the goddess of Hearts. This purging process inspired the notion of Purgatory, a stopping off place in the underworld for sinners.

In this scene (*plate 19*) we see in the foreground a large heart shape, forming the face of a house fly in full flight toward the reader. The fly carries on her back the twins representing Quetzalcoatl flying through the underworld as Xolotol. The heads of the twins are cradled by a bat of death.

Reincarnation on Earth

The next scene (*plate 20*) shows the twins in the arms of Coatlicue (the Earth goddess and patron saint of babies) suckling and holding her many nipples as her torso appears like the suckling tree.

The message here is that the twins are reincarnated on earth.

Completion of the Cycle

In this scene (*plate 21*) the two halves of the central peg and loop motif coalesce to 'square the circle', and in doing so provide a cross-section representation of the sun. The magnetic loops along the vertical axis complete themselves as do the horizontal half loops at the top and bottom centre of the square. Counting the marker pegs and horizontal loops, we have 20 magnetic loops or 'sun-spot cycles' which amounts to $20 \times 68,302 = 1,366,040$ my computerized sun-spot calculation, which for the Maya was 1,366,560 – the birth of Venus.

If we recall, there is another clue in the temple that points to this scene: the bones of Lord Pacal in the tomb were analyzed and scientifically verified as those belonging to a man aged 40. But the inscriptions at the top of the stairs say that Pacal was born in 703 AD and died in 783 AD suggesting that he was <u>twice</u> (× 2) that age.

Both the bones and the lid design contain an error of a factor of 2. The message to be conveyed is hence that the written figure is twice that which can be seen (in the age of the bones, or in the number of marker pegs on the lid).

These two 2s must necessarily be positioned together rather than separately as 2, and 2, because one 2 refers to a clue (the age of Pacal's death set at 80 in the inscriptions) at the top of the stairs and the other (2) relates to the clue at the bottom of the stairs (in the tomb). It is the staircase that separates the clues and hence the staircase which carries the 22-step clue.

The Story of the Fifth Age of the Sun

Many of the composite pictures we have seen so far have comprised of several layers of pictures, like the Approaching Bat series where layers require 'peeling off' before the one beneath can be revealed and understood. The Story of the Fifth Sun also employs this technique and has therefore been 'peeled' into two layers.

Scene 1a (*plate 22*) shows two bats. The bats represent death and their <u>positions</u> are very important in regard to the Scene 1b which rests beneath.

Scene 1b (*plate 23*) is the penultimate scene of the performance and the entire cast of the play appear on stage together in front of the audience. At the very bottom, just above the 'five sun' markers, we see the face of Xiuhtechutli of the East (formed from the patterns in the overlaid borders) carrying the sacrificial dish on his head. This dish doubles as the open mouth of Huitzilopochtli of the South, who is pinning down Xiuhtechutli beneath himself. But standing on top of Huitzilopochtli's outstretched arms is Yaotl in three different guises, the great bear, the giant Tlachueyal, and the owl (of the night). Tlachueyal is holding up a jaguar by the back paws as the jaguar in turn holds high the bones from the underworld which are carried in the mouth of Xolotol the blind dog, an emanation of Quetzalcoatl.

Referring to Scene 1a (*plate 22*) and the positions of the bats, we note that the lower bat renders both Xiuhtechutli and Huitzilopochtli dead because they both carry the mark of death, the bat. Similarly the three representations of Yaotl are covered by death suggesting that Yaotl is similarly dead. This leaves only the jaguar, the fifth age of the sun in which we are presently living, alive. He shows that he has been success-ful in carrying forward the bones from the fourth age to make mankind in the fifth age and this was done with the help of Quetzalcoatl, in his guise of Xolotol.

The message of this scene therefore reads that the age of the fifth sun is the age of the jaguar, created by Quetzalcoatl, with the help of Xolotol, which he won after conquering the other Tezcatlipocas to rule all of the skies.

The two main characters on the Amazing Lid of Palenque are the Bat god, who represented death, and the Sun god (Tonatiuh as Quetzalcoatl) who represented life. Scene 2, The Story of the Fifth Sun (*colour plate 24*) shows Tonatiuh the Sun god with tongue out giving 'life' or 'breath' riding astride an exhausted bat that takes a bow. But the bowing bat himself carries a bat on his forehead.

The message here is that the bat is dead and Tonatiuh the Sun god lives on in the fifth age of the sun, the age of the jaguar.

A common theme begins to emerge from these 'Maya Transformers'. The stories are told using their gods as characters as though in a 'play', and in keeping with this the cast appear on stage at the end of each per-formance to take a bow before the audience. We have just seen this in the case of the Lid of Palenque and it happens also in the Mosaic Mask, as we shall see in the next chapter and the Mural of Bonampak.

CHAPTER SIX

The Mosaic Mask
of Lord Pacal

The priest-king Lord Pacal was worshipped by the Maya as Quetzal-coatl, the bringer of knowledge and teacher of wisdom, the arts, the calendar and all good things. Quetzalcoatl (the plumed serpent) fea-tured prominently in Meso-American culture before, during and after the classic period of the Maya in Palenque. Among his many manifes-tations he was Ehecatl (god of Wind).

Legend has it that Ometeotl (the original God – the divine couple) created Ehecatl with a single breath. Ehecatl then went on to give birth to a son, 'Son of Ehecatl'. The father (Ehecatl), and son, then merged to form a single identity of a magnificent feathered snake Quetzalcoatl.

The two most widely used marks that depict Quetzalcoatl are the 'bird mask' and the cross-sectioned 'conch shell', that represents the 'jewel of the wind'. The bird was associated with flight and the wind. The wind in its turn was associated with evaporation of the waters from rivers that snaked through the jungle. Hence Quetzalcoatl be-came associated with a feathered snake that controlled the wind and separated the sky from the Earth. The clouds formed through evapo-ration and likewise linked Quetzalcoatl with Tlaloc the Rain god.

Fig 30 The god Quetzalcoatl (Kukulcan-Yucatan Maya), the plumed serpent and inventor of all great things such as writing, painting and the calendar.

Quetzalcoatl also represented the spirit in the sky and the snake that represented the Earth, the physical side of life.

Quetzalcoatl hence epitomized the complete being of spirit and flesh and a combination of earth (snake), air (bird) and water (clouds).

Quetzalcoatl ruled the Western quadrant of the sky whilst his brothers, Yaotl ruled the North, Xiuhtechutli ruled the East and Huitzilopochtli (associated with Tonatiuh, the Sun god) ruled the South.

The *Popol Vuh*, sacred book of the Quiche Maya, tells the story of these first four gods, the four Tezcatlipocas:

Fig 31 Sculpture of Quetzalcoatl from the Museum of Anthropology, Mexico City.

Great were the descriptions and the account of how all the sky and Earth were formed and divided into four parts; how it was partitioned, and how the sky was divided; and the measuring cord was brought, and it was stretched in the sky and over the Earth, on the four angles, on the four corners [the four cardinal points] as was told by the creator and the maker, the Mother and the Father of life, of all created things, he who gives breath and thought, she who gives birth to the children, he who watches over the happiness of the people, the happiness of the human race, the wise man, he who meditates on the goodness of all that exists in the sky, on the Earth, in the lakes and in the sea...

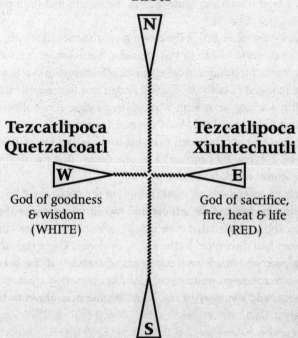

'Two Faces'
God of darkness, the night, & death
(BLACK)

**Tezcatlipoca
Yaotl**

**Tezcatlipoca
Quetzalcoatl**

**Tezcatlipoca
Xiuhtechutli**

God of goodness
& wisdom
(WHITE)

God of sacrifice,
fire, heat & life
(RED)

**Tezcatlipoca
Huitzilopochtli**

God of day 'Tonatiuh'
(BLUE)

The Measuring Cord

Fig 32a The Four Tezcatlipocas.

Lord Pacal's face, in the Tomb of Inscriptions was covered with a green mosaic mask made from more than 200 individual pieces of jade that had been fixed to a wooden mould, long since perished. Archaeologists painstakingly reconstructed the jigsaw of jade to produce a life-sized mask. The staring eyes were made from shell and obsidian, a type of volcanic glass, and in the mouth had been placed a jade bead (*see plate 25*).

At first they marvelled at their own reconstruction skills which had given a new lease of life to this treasured heirloom of a once great Mayan leader. I too admired the exquisite workmanship that had clearly been required in both the original design and the reconstructed article. But looking at it with a more inquisitive eye, following my decoding of the Amazing Lid of Palenque, I noted some curious marks on the mask which suggested that this too, like the Lid of Palenque, might be a 'Maya Transformer', a simple design that transforms into many pictures when decoded.

I noticed several sets of 'marker dots' on the mask: three below the right eye, one beneath the left eye and two in the region of the right eyebrow and suspected that these may be 'orientation markers', just like the ones I had discovered in the Lid of Palenque. Using the same decoding process, I made two colour transparencies of the mask and placed one upside-down upon the other. As I suspected, pictures began to emerge, and the story of the Four Tezcatlipocas began to unfold.

Decoding the Mosaic Mask

Scene 1 (*see plates 26 and 27*). Aligning the three rivet markers beneath the right eye, a bat can be seen. As we know, the bat represented death for the Maya. In this depiction the bat holds a bead in his mouth, just like the skull of the deceased Pacal, suggesting either that Pacal was dead or that Pacal brought death. But the tongue of the bat is fully distended, emulating the distended tongue of the Sun god Tonatiuh, who was 'the Giver of Life'. So the man in the tomb may have been responsible for both giving and taking away life. Beneath the tongue a diamond shape depicts the four corners of the sky, North, South, West and East, suggesting Pacal ruled the heavens.

Scene 2 (*plates 28 and 29*) shows a cross-legged human figure with outstretched wings and the head of a bird representing the feathered side of Quetzalcoatl, the plumed serpent. The arms of the seated figure are seen to be holding up above his head a slumping anthropomorphic figure which has 'two faces'. The lower face of the two resembles a bear like creature, while the other face is more human in form.

Mythology tells the story of how Quetzalcoatl (god of Light) fought his adversary Yaotl (god of Night). Yaotl fell from the sky into the sea below. Upon hitting the water he turned into a tiger whose bright eyes were said to make up the stars in the constellation known as the Great Bear. Yaotl's nickname was Two Faces, because of his qualities of darkness and deceit. This scene therefore gives the account of how Quetzalcoatl triumphed over Yaotl.

Other orientations of the two pictures produce more scenes:

Scene 3 (*plates 30 and 31*) depicts a snake with wings on its forehead. This represents the serpent side of Quetzalcoatl, following on from Scene 2 which showed the feathered side. This then confirms the feathered snake interpretation of the composite designs.

Scene 4 (*plates 32 and 33*) shows a human head wearing a helmet. Covering the nose and mouth of the face sits a full human figure in a meditative cross-legged posture.

Xiuhtechutli was god of the East and Fire (who walked upon the Earth, as opposed to Tonatiuh the god of Fire in the Sky) and was usually depicted wearing a helmet. He formed the divine dish in which sacrificed victims were placed when thrown into the fire during ceremonies. This scene therefore suggests sacrifice, perhaps of the man in the tomb.

On 8 December 1996 I scanned this scene into a computer in preparation for inclusion in this book. Increasing the brightness and contrast, the head of a young boy, previously hidden, emerged from the shadows below. The boy wears a feathered hat and has the forked tongue of the snake, identifying him with the god Quetzalcoatl. His nose is feline in shape, depicting his alter ego the jaguar, king of the land of the Maya. A bat pendant with open wings covers his mouth. Its head is that of Lord Pacal, the man in the tomb.

One scene in the Mosaic Mask depicts the massive face of the Bat god minus the ears. Remember that some 'complicated jade ear hoops' were found in the sarcophagus. When these are positioned around the composite bat, the picture is complete. But on turning this scene upside-down, the man (Lord Pacal) rises to take a bow to the audience (*plates 35 and 36*).

So here we have a jade mask covering the face of a man in a tomb, buried beneath a pyramid in the rainforests of Central America. It conceals a strange story suggesting that the man on the one hand was the giver of life and yet on the other took life away. It tells us this man was the feathered serpent who fought evil to rule the sky and that his opposite number is sacrifice. Yet no human being could have encoded so much incredible information into this jade jigsaw puzzle. So who, or what, did?

Before we answer this let us examine more evidence from the extraordinary Maya.

Jade

It is interesting to examine why the Maya favoured jade in preference to other materials to encode their secrets. Clearly the mask had to be 'precious', and yet not so precious (gold) that it might have been melted down. Secondly the mask contains a secret map showing the location of an undiscovered tomb in Palenque, the entrance to which is concealed by two large stone slabs. The mask also contains instructions on how these stone slabs must be moved in order to gain access to the undiscovered treasures, hence stone (jade) was a necessary part of the design. Finally, the refractive index of jade corresponds to the

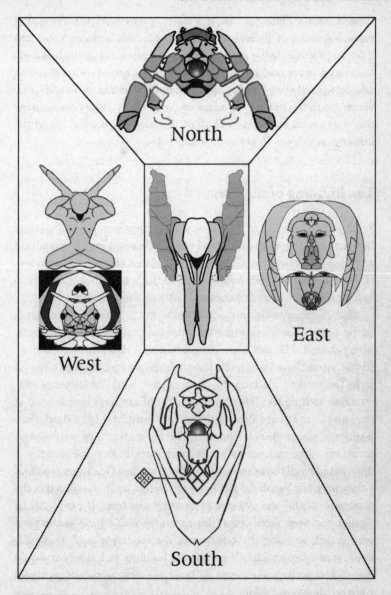

Fig 32b The Four Tezcatlipocas. Mosaic Mask of Palenque decoded.

Golden Ration PHI 1.618 (*see Appendices seven and eight*). The actual refractive index of individual fibres of jade falls between 1.600 and 1.627. In practice, owing to the aggregate nature of the individual crystals, only a vague reading around 1.618 can be achieved. Note, also, that 1.618 lies exactly two-thirds (.666) of the way between 1.600 and 1.627, which seems to confirm the intent of the Maya to convey the message that they understood PHI and all of the laws that control life in the universe, which we do not understand today.

The Building of the Pyramid

Taking a cross-section of the Pyramid of Inscriptions, it becomes clear that the sarcophagus of Lord Pacal was first lowered into its foundtion and then the carved Lid of Palenque was placed on top at ground level. The Pyramid was then built on top. The lid is far too large and heavy to have been introduced to the tomb after its construction.

That the interpretation of clues found in the pyramid is correct is borne out by considering the construction programme which must have followed. The ante-chamber containing 6 skeletons, 5 male and 1 female, would have taken some time to build after placing the 5-ton lid in its final resting place on the sarcophagus (using conventional construction techniques). These skeletons could not have been buried at the same time as Lord Pacal and therefore must have been dead when positioned inside the ante-chamber. This means that their purpose was to convey some message or information, namely that one skeleton is different from all the others, as we deduced earlier. One thing is certain – they were not 'sacrificial victims'. Lord Pacal's body was placed in the tomb and the lid was slid into place at ground level. If the sacrificial victims had been sacrificed at this time they would have had to been refrigerated, awaiting the building of the lower pyramid, triangular door, ante-chamber etc. Using normal building techniques it would have taken perhaps five years to build the first 15 feet of pyramid. Clearly this was not done.

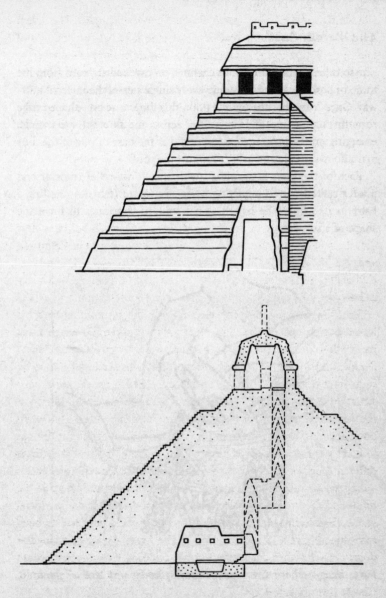

Fig 33 Cross-section side view of pyramid from centre line of stairs.

The 'Psychoduct'

The so called 'communications channel' or 'psychoduct' runs from the tomb of Lord Pacal and travels up every single step of the internal stairway. Once it reaches the temple floor, this limestone box-shaped tube runs through a line of inset stones across the floor of the temple, emerging on the outside of the pyramid at the base of one of the four main doorway columns which support the roof.

Each of the piers is decorated with stucco bas-relief (mortar and plaster carved panel) depicting a life-size figure (female) cradling a baby in its arms. The baby's spinal column continues to form the shape of a serpent.

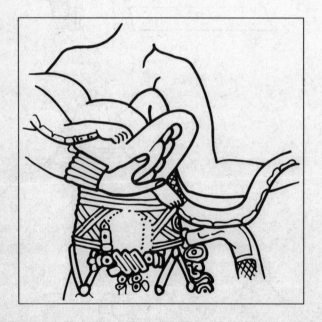

Fig 34 Design in bas-relief on pillars showing female with 'divine infant'.

Some sources believe that the duct allowed Lord Pacal to communicate from the tomb with the world of the living . Whilst this might be an appealing interpretation, its function was more likely that of a ventilator to vacate the tomb below of moisture and hence prevent damage to the contents of the tomb from flooding.

Palenque is not the only city which holds secrets of the Maya. Having decoded the Lid of Palenque and the Mosaic Mask, I turned to the books of the Maya, looking for more clues to help decode their treasures.

CHAPTER SEVEN

Stories of the Quiche

i. The Popol Vuh

'The *Popol Vuh* cannot be seen anymore...the original book written long ago, existed, but its sight is hidden from the searcher and the thinker.' So begins the *Popol Vuh* (p.79, University of Oklahoma Press edition – UOP), holy book of the Quiche tribe of the Maya. 'And this was the life of the Quiche, because no longer can be seen the book of the *Popol Vuh* which the kings had in olden times, for it has disappeared.' So ends the *Popol Vuh* (p.235 UOP).

At the beginning of the 18th century a Dominican monk, Father Francisco Ximenez, lived within the confines of a convent located at Chichecastenango in the mountains of Guatemala, which is about 200 miles up the River Usamacinta from the site of Palenque. He was a wise and virtuous man who had won the confidence of the Indians with his attempts to convert them to Christianity and in return they related stories of their own traditions in their native tongue of Quiche.

It comes as no surprise, given his intimacy, contact, and proximity with the Indians, to learn that it was he who accidentally stumbled upon an old manuscript, hidden behind a group of loose stones in the thick whitewashed walls of his parish church, at Santo Tomas Chichecastenango. The crumbling pages of the manuscript had been written in Quiche by an Indian, whose name is not known, around 1550, in an attempt to set down the ancient traditions of his people. This document told of the 'earlier book' which had been lost and was probably written down from memory by the author versed in the history of the Maya.

Father Ximenez translated the document into Spanish under the title *Historias Del Origen de los Indios esta Provincia de Guatemala*, which was later republished in 1857 in Vienna by Carl Sherzer, a European explorer, who had chanced upon the book buried beneath a pile of dust and cobwebs in the library of the University of San Carlos, Guatemala, three years earlier.

In 1861 another European explorer, Charles Etienne Brasseur de Bourbourg, published his own French translation in Paris entitled *Popol Vuh, le Livre Sacre et les Mythes de l'Antiquité Americaine, avec les Livres Heroiques des Quiches*, which also contained a facsimile of the original Quiche text.

A Spanish version of the book, prepared by Adrian Recinos, was released in Mexico in 1947 and later translated into English by Delia Goetz and Sylvanus G. Morley, who suggest in the introduction that it seems unlikely the 'original book' said to have been 'lost' (p.18,19 UOP), could have been a document of set form and permanent literary composition.

But the *Popol Vuh* was the book of prophecies and the oracle of the kings and lords. It goes on to say: '…and the Kings knew if there would be war, and everything was clear before their eyes; they saw if there would be death and hunger, if there would be strife'(p.19 UOP). Hence the *Popol Vuh* was the book of the past, the present and the future.

Like the original *Popol Vuh*, the Lid of Palenque contains prophecies that tell, for example, of the migration of the Mexicas (the story of Quilatzli – the Green Heron) to the valley of Mexico, as well as the gods of War which the Aztec would adopt in due course. These depictions, prophecies and predictions were possible because those who 'wrote' the Lid of Palenque were 'gods', the first of creation, which is also mentioned in the *Popol Vuh:*

> They were endowed with intelligence; they saw and could see instantly far, they succeeded in seeing, they succeeded in knowing all that there is in the world. When they looked, instantly they saw all around them, and they contemplated in turn the arch of heaven and the round face of the Earth. The things hidden [in the distance] they saw all, without first having to move; at once they saw the world, and so too, from where they were they saw it. Great was their wisdom...

In regard to the passing away of the four founding fathers, the book continues: 'We are going away [to die] we have completed our mission here...' Then Balam-Quitze (Sweet Laughing Jaguar) left the symbol of his being: 'This is a resemblance which I leave for you. This shall be your power...' He left the symbol, whose form was invisible because it was 'wrapped-up' and could not be unwrapped: 'The seam did not show because it was not seen when they wrapped it up...' (pp.204, 205 UOP)

Another manuscript, the *Titulo de los Senores de Totonicapan*, provides more information about this 'bundle of majesty'... 'this gift was what they feared and respected'... 'The gift was a stone, the stone of Naczit (Quetzalcoatl)', suggesting that the stone of Quetzalcoatl may in fact be the Lid of Palenque which was 'wrapped up' (encoded) and never 'unwrapped' (decoded) because nobody had seen it 'wrapped' (p.205 UOP).

The *Popol Vuh* continues, about the death of the first four founding fathers:

> They had had a presentiment of their death, they counselled their children. They were not ill, they had neither pain nor agony when they gave their advice...they were not buried by their wives nor by their children, because they were not seen when they disappeared...leaving their children on the mountain at Hecavitz...they remembered their father's gift (the stone of Naczit)...great was the

glory of the bundle to them. Never did they unwrap it but it was always wrapped and with them…(p.204,205 UOP)

Later, the book goes on to tell how their three sons retraced their fathers' footsteps by journeying to the East, and how, when they arrived in the East, they received the investiture of the kingdom from Quetzalcoatl. He gave the insignia of his kingdom and all its distinctive symbols to '…those [three men] who went to the other side of the sea to receive the paintings of Tulan, as they were called, *in which they wrote their histories…*'(p.209 UOP)

This is interesting because the Toltec were said to have carried their paintings to the East from Tula around 750 AD, following the migration of the peoples during the great eighth century decline of the Maya homelands. Historian Oidor Zorita claims that paintings of the Quiche existed 'in which they preserved the stories of ancient times around 750 AD, but their whereabouts today are unknown'.

I had heard of secret paintings of the Maya which they had left in a sacred place in the depths of the jungles not far from Palenque. Could these secret paintings be the ones spoken of by Oidor Zorita? Could they be the paintings which preserved the stories of ancient times and, if so, would they teach me more about the mighty Maya?

ii. The Mural of Bonampak

Bonampak is a Maya city on the Usamacinta river, close to Palenque, which shared in the flowering of the classic Maya around 750 AD.

One of the first accounts of the 'City of Painted Walls' emerged in 1946 from the American conscientious objector Carlos Frey, who was living the life of an exile in the forests of Chiapas with his wife, a Lacondon Indian. On two occasions, in consecutive Februaries, Frey had noticed the Lacondon pack their bags with copal incense, stain their tunics with red dots, and disappear into the forest for several days on an annual pilgrimage into the jungle.

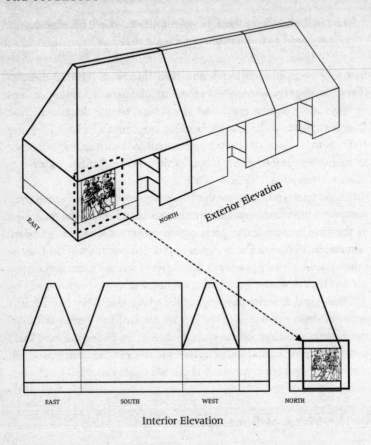

Fig 35 The Temple at Bonampak. Every face of every wall and ceiling in the three rooms of the Temple is adorned with brightly painted murals. (The area box-framed is decoded in this chapter.)

His persistent enquiries eventually revealed the purpose of the journey which was to a place of secrecy, forbidden to strangers, off limits to women and free from the destructive blade of the bushman. Gaining their confidence, he was eventually invited along to join in the incense-burning rituals in the temples, where he first came across the paintings that covered the walls.

In the same year another explorer, Giles Healey, stumbled upon Bonampak while gathering information for a film documentary on the Lacondon Indians. He made careful investigations of the temple which revealed gaily painted frescoes blurred by the build up of limestone on the walls and it was his reports, to a wider audience, which stimulated interest in the site.

Secrets of the Mural

There are many wall paintings in the 'Temple of Paintings' and we shall decode just one small section found on the north wall of the first room. The official interpretation of this painting is that it depicts a *group of dancers wearing fantastic disguises – a crab complete with claws, a cayman, and sea monsters – which perform as part of a ceremony*, circa 500–800AD. (This interpretation, of course, presents the orthodox view that the Maya were less intelligent than ourselves.)

After decoding both the Lid of Palenque and the Mosaic Mask, I had learned to search for 'decoding epi-centres' – clues that suggest that a particular design may be a decodable transformer. Examining the Mural of Bonampak, a typical epi-centre becomes quickly apparent, that of a cross within a circle resembling a cross-section view of the magnetic fields of the sun. So, using the same technique as before, I began to decode the Mural of Bonampak.

Fig 36 overleaf Mural from the first room of the Temple of Paintings, Bonampak.

Fig 37 overleaf A circle with a cross can be seen as a major feature of the design of the Mural.

But before we move on, we need to return to Maya mythology which will provide the information to assist us interpret the composite designs.

Xipe Totec

Xipe Totec was the first son of the original divine couple, Ometeotl (Hunab-Ku). His colour was red and he represented the eastern quadrant of the sky. He was thus associated with fire and like Xiuhtechutli, the god of Fire (on Earth), could be identified as the one who carried 'two sticks', which he used to rub together, to make fire.

His original name was Tlatlauhqui Tezcatlipoca, (Red Smoking Mirror), and he was known and worshipped by the Tlaxcaltecas and the Huejocinas as Camaxtle. He was also a deity of Zapotlan Xalisco and known more widely throughout Meso-America as Xipe Totec, 'Our Lord of the Flayed', or 'he who has an extra skin', or 'he of the foreskin'. This name was derived from his association with time, spring, and rebirth; the new growth of leaves on the trees, the shedding of the skin of the snake and hence a new cycle of fertility, freshness and hope.

It appears that the positive meaning of Xipe Totec was lost to the Aztecs and later peoples, who instead interpreted his benevolent symbolism as the malevolent literal skinning, or flaying, of sacrificial victims.

Each of the Meso-American deities can be recognized by the attributes ascribed to them. Xipe Totec was seen to be wearing the skin of a flayed victim. The skin would hang loosely about his person like a waistcoat, whilst the arms would be slipped over his own arms. Often the hands of the flayed victim would be seen drooping, like gloves, from his wrists. He wore a hood with tassels upon his head, and was said to have long plaited hair and gold ear caps. He also wore a green knee-length skirt and was often depicted with a poppy-headed chalice within which he carried the seed of fertility, and renewal.

Fig 38 A depiction of Xipe Totec, Our Lord of the Flayed, from the Borbonic Codex 14, here wearing the skin of a flayed victim whose hands hang like gloves from his wrists. He was the god of Spring and Rebirth. One of his emanations was Camaxtle the god of Hunting. Mock wars would be held in celebration of Xipe Totec and all that he represented. Participants would dress in garments resembling skin whilst others would wear clothes representative of the season. Spring would be the victor and winter the vanquished. The mock battle was followed by a tour of the houses of the village where a collection was made in the name of Xipe Totec, in much the same manner as we do for the Harvest Festival or Thanksgiving in the West today.

Camaxtle

Camaxtle was an emanation of Xipe Totec and was the god of Hunting. His name has been translated as 'he who wears breeches'. Legend tells how, in year 1 Tecpatl, after the flood, Camaxtle went up to the eighth sky and created four men and a woman whose job it was to find food for the sun. But as soon as they were created they fell into the water, died and returned to the sky.

Seeing his first attempt fail, Camaxtle banged his great staff against a rock in the eighth sky and from it burst 400 Otomi Chicimecas, precursors of the Mixtecs. He appealed to the higher gods to allow the Otomi Chicimecas to visit the Earth so that they could kill the barbarians and offer them as food for the sun. The gods granted Camaxtle his wish and sent the beings down to Earth where they landed on the branches of trees and were fed by eagles. The natives, drunk on cactus liquor, discovered them, brought them down from the trees and killed them, all except for Ximue, Mimich and Camaxtle himself, who had joined in, disguised as a Chichimeca.

In the year 4 Tecpatl, a loud noise was heard in the sky and a two-headed stag fell out of it. Camaxtle caught it and gave it as a god to the people of Cuitlahuac who fed it on rabbits, snakes and butterflies. The stag was said to give the people super-human strength to defend themselves and in 8 Tecpatl 47, Camaxtle won the war he had started with a neighbouring tribe, due to the good fortune and added strength of the stag which he carried with him. But the war continued until 1 Acatl 66 when Camaxtle lost the double-headed stag and his strength and as a consequence, he was eventually defeated. Then he met his wife Chimalma, who begat 5 sons.

A wooden sculpture of Camaxtle, in the Museum of Anthropology in Mexico City, shows him with long hair and a large headdress, wearing arm bracelets and carrying his hunting bow and three crossed arrows. Under his arm he carries a bag made from rabbit pelts. In his other hand he carries a basket of food. He wears breeches and sandals and white stripes are painted on his body.

The Tlaxcaltecas would celebrate the god of Hunting from 17 November, the first day of the month of Quecholli, dressing in new clothing and hunting in the woods, mountains and lakes for jaguar, rabbit, deer, wild boar and other creatures. Those who had been successful paraded through the town with black rings around their eyes and mouths, eagle-feathered headdresses and designs painted on their legs with white clay. The festival was followed by eight days of dancing and feasting.

Chimalma

Chimalma (the one who carries the shield) was the wife of Camaxtle who reportedly swallowed a *chalchihuitl* (precious stone of jade) and became pregnant without the stone touching her insides.

Another account of Chimalma by historian Ignacia Bernal, suggests she was also the second wife of Mixcoatl, the man who conquered the valley of Mexico, who came across her during one of his military sojourns into Morelos. She came out to meet him, laying down her buckler and casting down her arrows and pouch on to the ground, and stood before him, naked and embarrassed without her skirt and tunic. Seeing her, Mixcoatl fired arrows just above her, as she bowed her head. The first arrow flew above her head, the second skimmed her ribs, she caught the third in her hand and the fourth passed between her legs. Mixcoatl turned and left and at the same time Chimalma fled and hid in a cave.

After finding more arrows Mixcoatl returned but could not find Chimalma and so instead abused the women in the local village of Cuernavaca until they agreed to look for her.

Again Mixcoatl went to look for her. This time she came out and stood in his path, again standing naked in her shame, her arms folded across her chest. Again she placed her buckler on the ground. Again Mixcoatl fired his arrows to no avail. Then he took her, lay with her and she conceived.

Mixcoatl was later murdered by one of his captains who seized the throne of Cuthuacan and Chimalma fled to Tepoxtlan where she gave birth to Ce Acatl Topilzin Quetzalcoatl, who became the King of Tula.

Decoding the Mural

(*See plate section*)

Scene 1 (*plate 37*). Placing the solar epi-centre on top of its transparent facsimile and rotating the two, a composite picture emerges that shows a human figure dressed in a green striped skirt.

His chest is formed by the two-headed stags of Camaxtle. He carries two sticks to show his association with fire and above his head is his poppy-headed chalice within which he carried the seed of fertility and renewal – all marks of Xipe Totec, Lord of the Flayed, Lord of the Foreskin, who was associated both with fire and Camaxtle, the god of Hunting.

Scene 2 (*plate 38*). The birth of Xipe Totec. Here two midwives comfort the mother of Camaxtle as she gives birth to her son. The head of Camaxtle, the double-headed stag, is represented by the emerging head with two set of complementary antlers or horns in the lower centre of the scene. The large stag's head fills the composite picture above. The head is itself adorned with another skeleton of a second stag's head. The stag licks the head of the female in labour, suckling and comforting the mother during the painful process of birth.

Scene 3 (*plate 39*). The young (playful) Xipe Totec. The young Xipe Totec here swings by his hands and arms in an upside-down crouching posture. The mark of the stag can be seen on his lower back whilst his hood, with tassels, and plaited hair flow as he moves.

Scene 4 (*plate 40*). Lord of the Flayed, Lord of the Foreskin. Here Xipe Totec is depicted as Lord of the Foreskin. His second skin which he wears and his enormous penis in the foreground, confirm his attributes.

Scene 5 (*plate 41*). Xipe Totec, the youth. Here the youthful Xipe Totec is easily recognized emerging from the flames of the fire with which he is associated and as the Lord of the Skin, wearing a second skin around his body and arms. The hands of the second skin can be seen hanging from his wrists. He pulls himself away from the flames using the two sticks which point to the double-headed stag, below, which represents Camaxtle.

Scene 6a (*plate 42*). The hunting scenes – the deer. The festivals that took place in honour of Camaxtle involved the hunting of deer and other creatures. The deer here is flanked by two stags heads, confirming that Camaxtle, the god of Hunting (an emanation of Xipe Totec) is the central subject.

Scenes 6b and 6c (*plates 43 and 44*) depict the pig and the jaguar.

Scene 7 (*plate 45*). Chimalma, wife of Camaxtle and Mixcoatl. Camaxtle married Chimalma, the one who wore a shield. She begat him five sons and was said to have become pregnant upon swallowing a jade bead, which never touched her insides. Here pregnant Chimalma can be seen seated with knees apart wearing a shield upon her chest.

Scene 8 (*plate 46*). Chimalma also married the warrior Mixcoatl. Mixcoatl chanced upon her in the woods. She was naked and stood before him, hands folded upon her chest, in shame. He fired arrows. The first flew above her lowered head. In this scene Mixcoatl chances upon Chimalma. His enormous lowered head, eyes staring to the viewer, can be seen to dominate the foreground whilst Chimalma stands behind, naked, covering her breasts with her folded arms and hands. The lowered head of Mixcoatl relates to the arrow that missed Chimalma as she lowered her head as he fired.

Scene 9 (*plate 47*). Xipe Totec as Camaxtle making his first curtain call. This penultimate scene shows a character holding two sticks either side of his neck. He wears a green skirt, the mark of Xipe Totec and has stag's legs, showing that he is both Camaxtle and Xipe Totec. This scene introduces the final scene of the series.

Scene 10 (*plate 48*). The final curtain for Xipe Totec and Camaxtle. In this, the final scene, of this epicentre series, Camaxtle (the one with sticks either side of his neck) with stag's legs and wearing the green skirt of Xipe Totec, makes a bow (curtsey) to signify the end of the performance. The two stags, in the audience, offer rapturous applause.

The story of Xipe Totec and Camaxtle is just one of the stories contained within the Mural of Bonampak. There are many others. The mural shows that the paintings of the Maya, just like their sculpture (Lid of Palenque), jewellery (Mosaic Mask and necklace) and architecture contain hidden messages about their history and ancient traditions. This puts paid to the notion that the Maya were a violent and barbaric people. Indeed before the murals at Bonampak were discovered in 1946, the orthodox view had been that they were passive and peaceful. But the pictures of battle scenes eventually swayed orthodox opinion into believing that the Maya were much more warlike and barbaric, like the later Aztec.

Having decoded just one of the scenes from the mural, we are led to question the assumption that paintings of battles portrayed elsewhere in the temple actually depict battles at all. This seems to suggest that the pre-1946 interpretation of the Maya, as a peaceful people, is as true today as it was then.

As we saw in the last chapter, it was the *Popol Vuh*, the sacred book of the Maya, which first hinted of hidden secrets locked away in the treasures of the Maya, when it spoke of the original version as 'hidden from the searcher and the thinker'. It continued, saying that the book had been 'wrapped up' (encoded) by the early forefathers, in a stone – the stone of Naczit (Quetzalcoatl).

Fig 39 Murals from the Temple of Bonampak showing warlike scene. Given the results of decoding of the mural from the first room of the temple, it is unlikely that the scene represents what it appears to depict.

Lord Pacal's tomb was hidden from the searcher for 1,250 years. Even today the contents of the tomb and the pyramid continue to mystify scholars unfamiliar with all the evidence which I have put before you. It becomes clear that the Maya succeeded in concealing their secrets safely, out of the reach of the thinker.

It was these clues that prompted my investigation into the perplexing design on the tomb lid, with its missing corners. Is this the stone of Naczit, the stone of Quetzalcoatl, the highest god of the Maya?

It is certain that our overall picture of the Maya and their message to mankind becomes clearer with every artefact decoded. Each decoding leads on to yet another and we question where this super knowledge of the Maya could possibly have come from. Who was the man in the tomb?

For our next clue we turn again to the sacred books of the Maya.

CHAPTER EIGHT

Ancient Lands and New Revelations

The Paris, Dresden and Tro-Ano Codices

Around 1547, in an effort to eradicate 'pagan beliefs', the Spanish clergy set about destroying all traces of indigenous Indian culture. The first archbishop of Mexico, Juan de Zumarraga, boasted of destroying 500 temples of the native Indians, along with 20,000 idols, and countless books during his period in office, including the entire contents of books and paintings on show at the Painting Academy of Tetzuco.

Fray Diego de Landa, another Spanish bishop, took it upon himself, with fervent zeal, to condemn the spiritual and peaceful Maya, alongside their successors, the militaristic Toltec and bloodthirsty Aztec. In a single night, in the northern Yucatan town of Mani, south of Merida, de Landa assigned the written treasures of the Maya, their precious paper-bark books, to a communal bonfire. What had taken years to compile and generations to preserve was reduced to smoke and ash in seconds.

Later, a Spanish priest Father Jose de Acosta was to comment:

To a teacher of Christian doctrine, all of it seemed like witchcraft and black magic, and the books were burned, but afterwards not only did the Indians regret it but also the Spanish, who were curious to fathom the secrets of that land. The same has occurred in other things and since our men deemed everything superstition, they have lost the records of ancient and occult [secret]matters they could have profited from.

From now on, knowledge of the Maya would grow from three remaining books which somehow miraculously escaped the fate of the rest. These were the *Paris Codex*, the *Dresden Codex* and the *Tro-Ano Codex*.

The *Paris Codex*, also known as the *Codex Perez*, (and *Codex Peresianus*), a name which had been scribbled into the margin of one of the pages, was discovered in a wastepaper basket in the Library of Paris in 1859 by Leon de Rosny, a botanist and Japanese linguist. This 11-page document gives a brief account of Maya history.

The longer *Dresden Codex* surfaced in 1939, when an unknown seller handed the manuscript to Johann Christian Goetze, director of the Dresden Library in Germany, who passed it to librarian Ernst Forstemann. After years of study, Forstemann concluded that the book was preoccupied with the Maya cycles of time, 144,000, 7,200, 360 and 20 day periods. He also detected the frequent appearance of the Maya 'zero' mark, and the 'super number' of Venus, 1,366,560. Using these, he was able to set a start date for the Maya calendar of 3,113 BC. Other pages covered Mayan prophecies and ceremonies, solar eclipses and stories of Quetzalcoatl.

Fig 40 The 'zero' mark as recognized by Forstemann.

In Madrid, in 1864, the French researcher and journalist Charles Etienne Brasseur de Bourbourg became acquainted with a professor of palaeography at Madrid University, Jean de Tro y Ortolano, who revealed an old family document of divination known as the *Troano Codex*. Three years later these 70 pages were identified by Leon de Rosny as a missing part of another 42-page codex entitled the *Cortesianus*, found in Estremadura, Spain and together the two parts become known as the *Tro-Cortesianus Codex*.

Before setting sail for America in 1845 Bourbourg had decided to study theology in Rome and his subsequent accession to the priesthood, together with his newly acquired title of Abbé Brasseur de Bourbourg, allowed access to records which would otherwise have been impossible. It was in Guatemala that he first came across the *Annals of the Cakchiquels* and the *Popol Vuh*, both of which, in 1861, he translated into French. Publication in France of the *Popol Vuh* enabled access to a collection of documents in the archives of Joseph M. A. Aubin, professor of the Ecole Supérieure of Paris, from which he gathered enough information to compile a four-volume publication entitled *Histoire des Nationats Civilisées du Mexique et de l'Amerique Centrale*, the most comprehensive account of Central American History so far produced.

His next success was a translation of *Relacion de las Cosas de Yucatan*, written by Bishop de Landa in an attempt to conceal his occupational excesses.

The Lost Land of Mu

The successes of Bourbourg were followed by those of the son of a French naval commodore, Augustus le Plongeon. Years of exploration of the Maya and life in the Yucatan had persuaded le Plongeon that the Maya had practised mesmerism, induced clairvoyance and used 'magic mirrors' to predict the future. But his ideas were unacceptable to orthodox archaeologists who scorned his views.

Le Plongeon further suggested that the Maya had sailed westward from Central America to develop civilizations in the Pacific, and then onwards, across the Indian Ocean and Persian Gulf to Egypt. To substantiate this he compared many examples of Mayan and Egyptian architecture, writing, and beliefs, which extended to sun-worship. His interpretation of the *Troano Codex* suggested that several pages were devoted to the ten lost countries of the mythological Island of Mu:

> The year six Kan and the eleventh Muluc, in the month of Zac, there occurred terrible earthquakes which continued without intermission until the thirteenth Chuen. The country of hills and mud 'the Land of Mu' was sacrificed. Being twice upheaved, it suddenly disappeared during the night, the basin being continually shaken by volcanic forces. Being confined these caused the land to sink and rise several times and in various places. At last the surface gave way and the ten countries were torn asunder and scattered into fragments; unable to withstand the force of the seismic convulsions, they sank with their sixty-four millions of inhabitants eight thousand and sixty years before the writing of this book.

A supporter of Le Plongeon was the Englishman James Churchward who believed that the lost continent of Mu, referred to in the *Troano Codex*, was indeed in the Pacific. For his part, Churchward had his own persuasive evidence to substantiate the previous existence of Mu and this consisted of sketches of some ancient Naacal stones he had discovered years earlier in a monastery in Brahmaputtra Tibet, whilst working as an intelligence officer for the British Government as a member of the Bengal Lancers. A local priest, skilled in deciphering the stones, told him they were written in the original language of mankind and recorded the geology, history, religion and the final catastrophe that befell the Muvians who came from the Pacific.

Churchward believed that Mu once measured 18,000 square miles and that the Muvians exploited technologies surpassing our own. These, he believed, included an understanding of anti-gravity, which enabled the movement of large objects and the construction of colossal buildings.

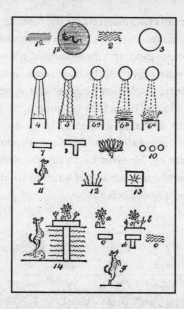

Fig 41 One of Churchward's sketches of the Naacal Tablets showing the creation of life on Earth, earthquakes caused by overheating of the land mass, release of subterranean gases and the sinking of the land itself.

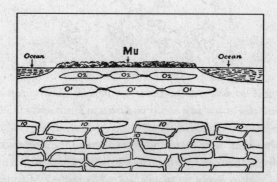

Fig 42 Churchward's theory showing how the release of subterranean gases undermined, and led to the sinking of, Mu: gases trapped between rocks expand when heated. The ground above heaves as gases escape causing the land above to resettle and subside beneath the ocean.

He says that the tablets explained how overheating of the land mass occurred due to an increase in solar radiation, and that this caused the release of subterranean gases and the sinking of Mu.

Such accounts were supported by later research from other 'drawings' found on tablets discovered by American mineralogist William Niven who had collected thousands of mineral samples and tablets whilst excavating in the valley of Mexico in the 1920s. From Niven's tablets Churchward concluded that Muvians inhabited the plains of Mexico 10,000 years BC. He went on to suggest that this colony had been sent from Mu to carry the sacred writings of Mu as far afield as south-east Asia, India and Tibet.

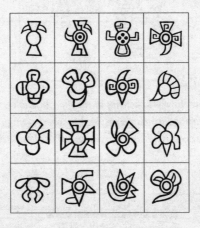

Fig 43 Some of the designs on Niven's tablets from the plains of Mexico which Churchward said he had seen earlier on tablets in a monastery in India.

Churchward became increasingly involved with his research and in 1930 published *The Lost Continent of Mu*, which was followed in 1931 by *The Lost Children of Mu*, in 1933 by *Sacred Symbols of Mu* and in 1934 by *Cosmic Forces as They Were Taught in Mu*, which established him as the leading authority on the subject.

The name Mu was borrowed from the German naturalist Ernest Haeckel who, in the 1870s, coined the term in an effort to solve the puzzle of the habitat of the lemur monkey found in Madagascar, Africa and India, each of which are separated by vast stretches of water.

Fig 44 The ring-tailed lemur is the most familiar member of the lemur family whose distribution caused such consternation among 19th-century scientists. Related to humans and monkeys, lemurs live mainly in Madagascar but may also be found in Africa, India and the Malay archipelago.

If the evolutionist, Charles Darwin had been right, then the lemur should have evolved in only one of those places, meaning, conjectured Haeckel, that a land mass once joining them together must have since sunk beneath the waves of the Indian Ocean, taking with it the first of mankind, the 'Le-Mu-rians'. It was Alfred Wegener, whom I mentioned in Chapter 1, with his theories in the 1950s of continental drift, who solved the riddle of the distribution of the lemur by pointing out that a land 'bridge' had not existed, but that all of these countries were once 'joined-together' as part of Pangaea-land (*see Fig 1*). This notion of deluvian destruction, wiping out the earliest progenitors of the human race, appealed to Churchward who borrowed the name 'Mu' to describe his own ideas, which more and more persuaded him that this original homeland lay in the West – a departure from the popular notion that the lost continent of Atlantis, which lay to the East in the Atlantic, was the birthplace of man.

From the Naacal and Niven tablets he concluded that the lost continent of Mu extended across the Pacific from the island of Ladrones in the West, Easter Island to the East, Hawaii to the North and Tonga to the South. These islands, he maintained, are the last remaining evidence of a once thriving civilization which sank beneath the waves around 10,000 BC: 'It was a Garden of Eden resplendent with colourful birds and lush vegetation where the ten tribes all lived together peacefully, the brown the white and the yellow. They built magnificent temples of stone and sailed the oceans of the world, leaving behind their inscriptions.' (Churchward, *The Lost Continent of Mu*)

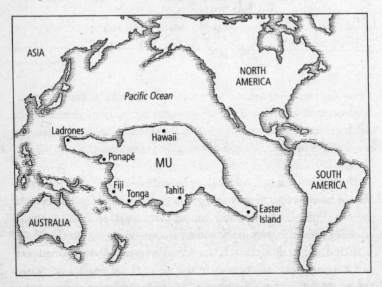

Fig 45 Churchward believed that the present-day islands of the Pacific are the last remaining vestiges of a once great land called Mu.

In support of his theory that Muvians sailed westward to India he compared ancient scripts found on Easter Island to those found in the Indus valley of India which he showed to be amazingly coincident. He also showed similarities between the writing found in Greece, Chaldea, Babylonia and Persia, suggesting that all these came from Mu.

Fig 46 Comparison of scripts from the Indus Valley (left) with those from Easter Island (right).

The Naacal tablets, sketched by Churchward in Tibet, also told that Atlantis, a mere colony of Mu, lay to the East, stretching from the Americas in the West to the Mediterranean, and of a global communications network centred in Mu, through the Yucatan in Mexico, Atlantis, and Egypt in the East, and India, Asia and Egypt to the West. The tablets go on to tell, says Churchward, that the Egyptian god Osiris was born in Atlantis around 20,000 BC and was educated in Mu. Returning to Atlantis he became a priest and taught a religion of love and simplicity.

It was Thoth, the deity of scribes and knowledge, said to have given mankind the art of hieroglyphic writing, who carried this religion to Egypt 4,000 years later. The indoctrination again reappeared as the teachings of Moses, in the old testament, and later as those of Jesus. The founding fathers of Lower Egypt, Churchward believed, came from Mu as opposed to those of Upper Egypt who came from the Yucatan via Atlantis.

A race of white settlers, said to have colonized the sub-continent of India, were thought to have originated 'from the East' in the area of the Pacific Islands, around 13,000 BC, and moved on with their cuneiform texts, which shared similarities with the Tibetan tablets, to Babylonia. The ancient Indian holy books the '*Vedas*', he said, likewise originated in Mu and travelled via Naacal in Tibet to the ancient Brahmins in India.

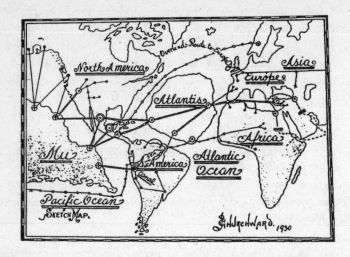

Fig 47 Churchward's routes of communication from Mu.

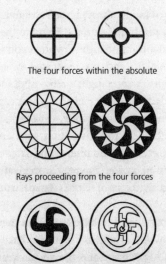

The four forces within the absolute

Rays proceeding from the four forces

Fig 48 Ancient cosmological symbols from Churchward's Naacal tablets which he compared with Niven's from the valley of Mexico.

In his book *Mysteries of the Mexican Pyramids,* Peter Tomkins comments:

> Churchward maintains that the Naacal tablets he was shown in Tibet contain religious concepts and a cosmology of a very high order. He says the civilization which produced the tablets was in no way primitive, even though some of the workmanship of the tablets appears crude. According to his interpretation their knowledge of the cosmic forces of 'energy' was remarkable, and the tablets were the exposition of the knowledge of a profound science, 'which is only dawning on the scientific world of today, and which has not been learned or mastered by modern man'.

Compare, for the first time ever, these cosmological symbols with those showing the sun's magnetic structure and schematics of the solar wind in Appendix one of this book.

Churchward believed, quite rightly, that the symbols represented the sun, although at that time he had no scientific justification for doing so, and the sun in its turn represented God the creator. The tablets tell how 'in the beginning', the universe was pure 'soul' energy, or 'spirit' and that man, at creation, was given cosmic forces under control of the soul, and that when the soul leaves the body 'upon death' it carries the cosmic energy back to the creator. These teachings epitomized love for the creator as the heavenly father. Our investigation will soon arrive at the same conclusion as Churchward's but from a totally independent analysis which brings together the knowledge revealed in the decoded messages of the Lid of Palenque, modern scientific understanding and ancient teachings of the world's religions to produce an overall appreciation of the meaning of life.

The first parts of this book told us about catastrophic evolution of our planet, together with a causal mechanism that enabled an understanding of how such catastrophes come about. We then learned that the ancient Maya were aware of all of this knowledge.

Churchward would have us believe that these secrets were handed down from Mu, generation by generation, but periodic catastrophes must, if we recognize Velikovsky's 'collective amnesia' theory, limit this handing-down process to relatively short 'inter-catastrophic' periods of (judging from present-day written accounts) 5,000 years or so. This cuts short, periodically, the perceived linear intellectual ascent of man carried over from Muvian times some 15,000 years ago.

Others have questioned how the super-knowledge which enabled the flowering of the Egyptian and Maya periods was carried forward. And this is where the problem lies: because the knowledge was alive and well in Mu does not necessarily mean the knowledge <u>came</u> from Mu. Because mountains exist, it does not mean that they were built up from millions of years of sedimentation – they arose through catastrophic-geological upheaval and intervention. In the same way the intellectual ascent of man has not been uniform and gradual, it has been punctuated from 'outside', it seems, on several occasions, and again we are limited to the sacred writings going back only 5,000 years or so.

The Supergods

The Amazing Lid of Palenque (Volume 1) tells us there are various destinations for the dead (in the story of The Paradises) and of periodic physical destruction (in the story of The Four Previous Ages). It tells us how this destruction comes about: through infertility cycles inspired by solar activity, increases in infant mutations, drought through mini iceages and catastrophic destruction through pole tilting adjustments of the Earth's crust and axis, in response to a variable solar magnetic field.

Volume 2 (*see Chapter 5 and plates 9–24*) tells us that a choice exists between purification of the soul through sacrifice, or alternatively a journey through the underworld, and purgatory, before rebirth on Earth. It tells us of a better place, and a worse one than Earth, and that each of us is born of the one God who created himself along with the universe. It teaches us that I am you and you are me, that night becomes day as certainly as day becomes night; life follows death as certainly as death follows life.

Clues in the Temple of Inscriptions tell us that the man in the tomb was no ordinary man, while the Mosaic Mask tells us that he gave life, and took life away. We learn that the numbering system is built into the Mayas' pyramid and that the duration of the sun-spot cycle is contained in the lid as well as in the pyramid, just in case we missed it first time around. And we learn from their use of jade that the Maya understood better than we do how the universe works. They have shown us in their art and their decoding system that the mind of Lord Pacal was far superior to that of his contemporaries who were not involved with the 'wrapping up' or 'encoding' of the information, and far superior to the mind of modern man. When he died he became one with the highest God through purification and sacrifice which makes us ask: 'Who was this man who left behind these living miracles'?

Similarly, many races have spoken of spiritual teachers. In olden times a man called Jesus was said to have performed 'miracles'. They say he could walk upon water and heal the sick by the laying on of hands and stories say that in one single day he fed 5,000 people with the food from one basket. He walked among his own people and spoke of a God not of this Earth and he preached purification through love and sacrifice, which would lead to rebirth after death, and an everlasting life. And they say that when he died he rose from the tomb and from a mountain ascended to 'heaven'.

This was in our own year of zero, 2,000 years ago. This man Jesus was said to have been born through an 'immaculate conception' without a physical, biological 'father'. They say he was the son of God.

Five hundred years before this the Indian holy book, the *Bhagava-Geeta* (The Lord's Song), tells the story of a man called Krishna who claimed to represent the living God who created the universe. He too could perform miracles and spoke to the prodigy Arjuna, on the battlefield of Kurekshetra thus: 'Whenever spirituality decays and materialism is rampant, then O Arjuna, I reincarnate myself…I am reborn from age to age…He who realizes the divine truth concerning my birth and life is not born again; and when he leaves his body, he becomes one with me.' (BG, 4:7–9)

These teachers, from 'outside', from 'somewhere else', have visited recent civilizations, bringing over and over again the super knowledge
known by the Muvians, Atlanteans, Mayans and others which enabled
the flowering of the great civilizations and the evidence suggests they
came specifically to teach us of the higher spiritual and scientific orders.

I have chosen to call these visitors 'Supergods', because they brought
their super knowledge to mankind, and because they were not from
this planet. That these visitors are 'related' became apparent while decoding the Mosaic Mask of Palenque. Was it just coincidence that the
composite picture of the god of the East, Xiuhtechutli, looked very
similar to depictions of a stained glass representation of Christ? Was it
just coincidence that the cross-legged figure covering the nose and
mouth of the Christ-like face resembled the praying Buddha of India?

And why was the number 666 missing from the tomb of Lord Pacal?

The book of Revelations, in the Christian Bible, tells of the revela-
tion which appeared to St John, a disciple of Christ. It prophesies a future apocalypse and global destruction.

Few can agree on the true meaning of the undoubted allegory of the
book, which is both strange and mysterious. Chapter XIII tells of a
beast that rises out of the sea. The beast has seven heads and ten horns
and 'upon his heads the name of blasphemy' and continues 'here is wisdom, let him that hath understanding count the number of the beast:
for it is the number of a man; and his number is six hundred threescore
and six...' (666).

Once we understood the intellectual game of the Maya, in the
Temple of Inscriptions, we were invited to count. We counted firstly
11111, 22222, 33333, 44444, 55555, 66...the number of the beast, of blasphemy, is missing from the Temple of Inscriptions at Palenque. But
then we began to count the beads on the necklace from the neck of
Lord Pacal (see Chapter 4). Only when we began the count did the
numbers 666 appear, not as themselves but as part of the number 13,
which occurred in three sections of the necklace. Then the numbers
777 and 888 appeared in the necklace and then the 9s were found
elsewhere: 'Let him that hath understanding count the number of
the beast.'

The expression 'Let he that hath an ear, let him hear' appears no less than eight times in Revelations, and we recall that one of the plaster heads of Lord Pacal found on the floor of the tomb had one ear missing: 'Let he that hath an ear, let him hear' (*see Fig 27*).

Revelations continues by telling of an angel that came to 'seal the servants of God':

> And I saw another angel ascending from the East, having the seal of the living God: and he cried with a loud voice to the four angels, to whom it was given to hurt the Earth and the sea, saying 'Hurt not the Earth, neither the sea, nor the trees, till we have sealed the servants of our God in their foreheads.' And I saw the number of them which were sealed; and there were sealed an hundred and forty, and four thousand of all the tribes of the children of Israel. (Rev VII 3,4)

It goes on, 'And it was commanded them that they should not hurt the grass of the Earth, neither any green thing, neither any tree, but only those men which have not the seal of God on their foreheads...' (Rev IX, 4).

Look again at The Physical Death of Lord Pacal, Scene 4 (*Fig 49 below*). Look again at his forehead, and count the number sealed: 144,000.

Like all composites, the picture is made up of two halves which are 'reflected' either side of the centre line of the drawing. It is therefore not possible to show the number 144,000 from left to right and again (the mirror image) from right to left. To overcome this, 1440 is written from left to right. The mirror image of 1440 can be seen from right to left. The missing two zeros (in Mayan notation, an oval embellished with three lines) are shown above this number.

It seems that the man in the tomb at Palenque had much in common with the other Supergods – Jesus, Krishna and Buddha – and that he brought the same message and the same super-knowledge which has powerfully influenced the intellectual ascent of man since time began.

Fig 49 The Physical Death of Lord Pacal, Scene 4, showing the number 144,000 on Lord Pacal's forehead.

Plate 1 (top) The Temple of Inscriptions at Palenque rests on top of a nine level pyramid. The central stairway is broken into five sections comprising of 9, 19, 19, 13 and 9 steps each (total 69). The temple walls are carved with 620 inscriptions, hence the name. The temple has 5 doorways, and 6 columns support the roof.

Plate 2 (left) Map of the Yucatan peninsula. Maya culture flourished in Southern Mexico Guatemala, Western Honduras and El Salvador. Palenque was one of the major ceremonial sites of the Maya, reaching its zenith around the time of Lord Pacal, aound 700 a.d.

Plate 3 (above) The Palace at Palenque. A tablet carved with 96 glyphs was found at the bottom of the stairway.

Plate 4 (right) Tablet of 96 glyphs.

Plate 5 (below)   Staircase inside The Pyramid of Inscriptions at Palenque. A square stone ducting travels the length of the stairway from the tomb below, to the Temple of Inscriptions above.

Plate 6 (right)
Turquoise and Jade inlaid mask of Mixtec design showing the mouth covered with a bat mask and the high hairstyle of Quetzalcoatl, as depicted in 'The physical death of Lord Pacal' Scene 4, in the decoded Lid of Palenque. The high hairstyle is also featured on one of the stone heads found in the tomb.

Plate 7 (left)
This skull, of unknown origin, was presented to the Spanish Conquistador Cortes by the Aztec King Montecezuma in the 16th century.

Plate 8   Inside the Tomb of Lord Pacal.
The tomb roof was supported by five ceiling beams. The carved tomb lid
has two corners missing. The sarcophagus below has one corner missing.
The man in the tomb wore four jade rings on each hand, carried a jade
bead in each palm and one in the mouth. He wore a three tiered jade
necklace and a jade mosaic mask. Two stone heads, representations of
Lord Pacal, were positioned on the stone floor. Jade pendants were
found scattered over the tomb lid. Nine 'Lords' were painted on the
walls of the tomb.

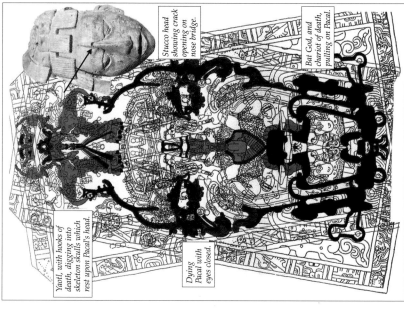

Yaotl, with hooks of death, digging into skeleton skulls which rest upon Pacal's head.

Stucco head showing crack opening on nose bridge.

Bat God, and chariot of death, pulling on Pacal.

Dying Pacal with eyes closed.

Plate 10 (right) The Physical death of Lord Pacal, *Scene 5.*

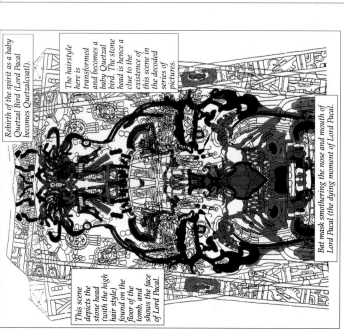

Rebirth of the spirit as a baby Quetzal Bird (Lord Pacal becomes Quetzalcoatl).

The hairstyle here is transformed and becomes a baby Quetzal bird. The stone head is hence a clue to the existence of this scene in the decoded series of pictures.

This scene depicts the stone head (with the high hair style) found on the floor of the tomb, and shows the face of Lord Pacal.

Bat mask smothering the nose and mouth of Lord Pacal (the dying moment of Lord Pacal).

Plate 9 (above) The Physical death of Lord Pacal, *Scene 4.*

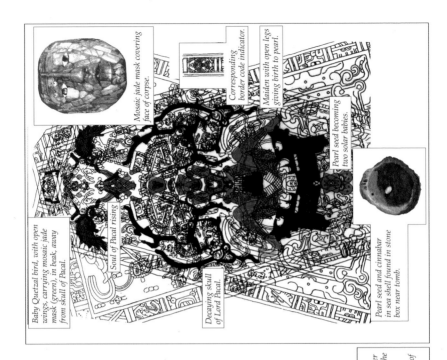

Mosaic jade mask covering face of corpse.

Corresponding border code indicator.

Maiden with open legs giving birth to pearl.

Baby Quetzal bird, with open wings, carrying mosaic jade mask (green), in beak, away from skull of Pacal.

Soul of Pacal rising

Decaying skull of Lord Pacal.

Pearl seed becoming two solar babies.

Pearl seed and cinnabar in sea shell found in stone box near tomb.

Xiuhtecuhtli 'Giver of life'.

Maiden falling backwards on heels.

Stucco head showing squint.

Plate 11 (above) The Physical death of Lord Pacal, Scene 6.

Plate 12 (right) The Spiritual rebirth of Lord Pacal, Scene 1.

Note: The 'Corresponding border code indicator', referred to in Plate 12, Scene 1 (right), appears in several scenes. Every story in 'The Amazing Lid of Palenque Vols. 1 & 2' has a corresponding border code indicator (denoting just one of the scenes from each particular story) to inform the decoder of the existence of the story, which can be found once the inner area of the lid has been decoded using acetates. These 'border code indicators' are themselves decoded portions of the border pattern which circumscribes the Lid of Palenque. The decoding process is explained in detail in 'The Amazing Lid of Palenque Vol. 1' and again, briefly, in 'The Mayan Prophecies'.

Plate 13 (left)
The spiritual
rebirth of Lord
Pacal, *Scene 2.*

*Baby Quetzal bird
tugging on baby
pendant*

*Pacal
rising
through
different
levels.*

*Itzpapalotl-
totec 'Lord
Butterfly', god
of sacrifice
and
purification.*

*Huitzilopochtli,
god of the South
and god of the day.*

*Featureless
Pacal bedecked
in jewelled
refinery.*

*Baby pendant
hanging from
smiling lips of
Pacal.*

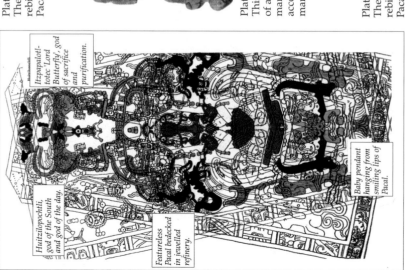

Plate 14 (above)
This jade figurine
of a bearded white
man (Quetzalcoatl)
accompanied the
man in the tomb.

Plate 15 (right)
The spiritual
rebirth of Lord
Pacal, *Scene 3.*

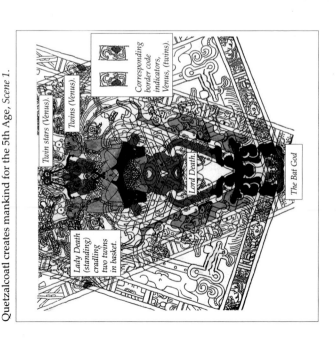

Plate 17 (right)
Quetzalcoatl creates
mankind for the 5th
Age, *Scene2.*

In this illustration the combined acetate arrangement has been rotated 180°.

Plate 16 (below)
Quetzalcoatl creates mankind for the 5th Age, *Scene 1.*

Twin stars (Venus).

Twins (Venus).

Corresponding border code indicators, Venus, (twins).

Lady Death (standing) cradling two twins in basket.

Lord Death.

The Bat God

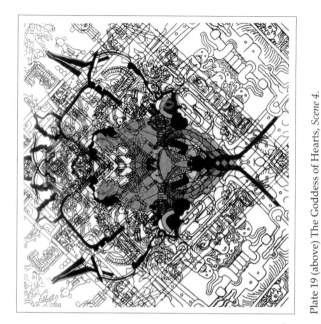

Plate 18 (left)
Quetzalcoatl creates mankind
for the 5th Age, *Scene 3.*

Plate 19 (above) The Goddess of Hearts, *Scene 4.*

Tlacauhueyal
(The Giant).

Bat.

Baby on
pendant.

Note: The two figures to the left are half the size of other Lid of Palenque illustrations.

Plate 20 (top left)
Reincarnation
on Earth.

Plate 21 (lower left)
Completion of the
Cycle.

Plate 22 (below) The
story of Fifth Age of
the Sun. *Scene 1a.*

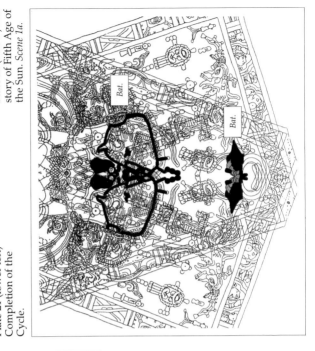

Bat.

Bat.

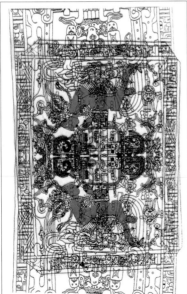

Plate 23 (left)
The story of the
Fifth Sun, *Scene 1b*.

Plate 24 (above)
The story of the
Fifth Sun, *Scene 2*.

Within the image (Plate 24, left):

Bones, fetched
from the
underworld to
create
mankind in
the 5th Age.

Xolotol, the
monster dog,
helper of
Quetzalcoatl.

The Jaguar,
ruler of the
5th Age.

Note: Here the God of the
North, Tezcatlipoca Yaotl,
appears in his three guises;
the Bear, the Owl of the
Night and Tlacahueyal the
Giant.

Giant

Ozti

Yaotl; God of
the North.

God of the
South
Huitzilopochtli.

Xiuhtechutli;
God of the East.

Within the image (Plate 23, right):

Tonatiuh; the Sun-God.

Bat

Dying bat

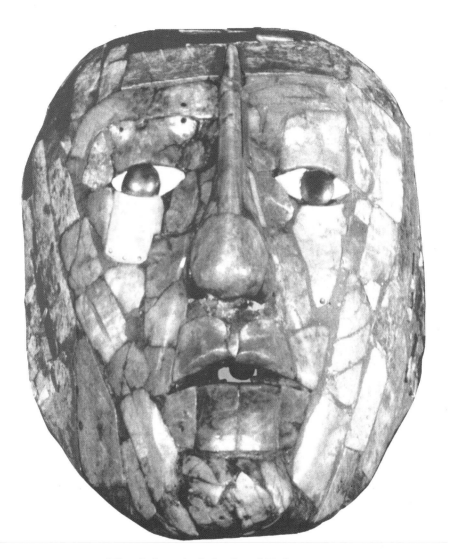

Plate 25 The Mosaic Mask of Palenque

This jade mosaic mask covered the face of the man
in the tomb. Note the three dots beneath the right
eye, the two vertical dots above the right eye, the
single dot to the right of this pair and the single
dot beneath the left eye. These are all orientation
markers as explained in the main text.

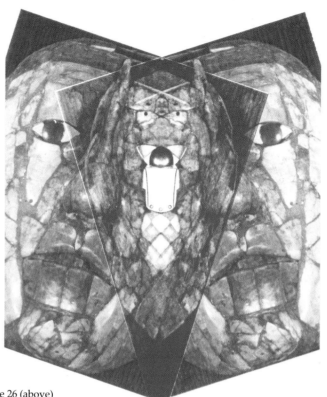

Plate 26 (above)
Composite Mosaic
Mask transparency
arrangement, the
Bat God, one of
many which now
follow.

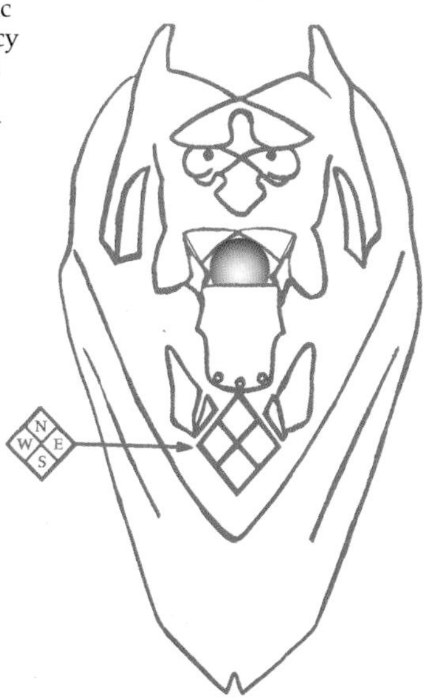

Plate 27 (below)
The Bat God,
composite
sketch.

Plate 28 (above)
The Man with
wings, composite.

Plate 29 (below)
The Man with
wings, composite
sketch.

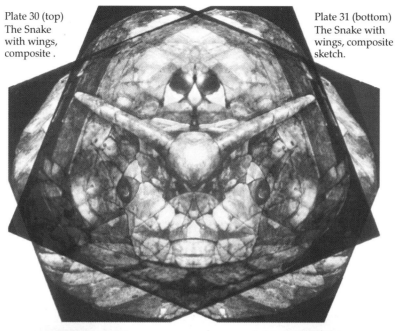

Plate 30 (top)
The Snake
with wings,
composite .

Plate 31 (bottom)
The Snake with
wings, composite
sketch.

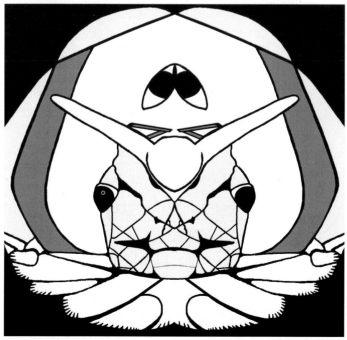

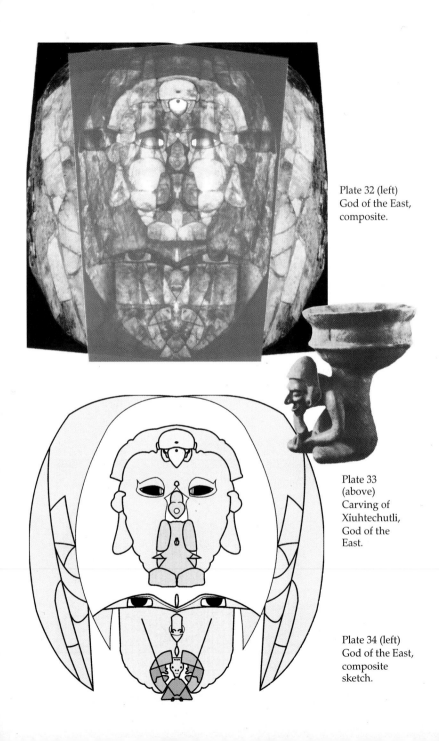

Plate 32 (left)
God of the East, composite.

Plate 33 (above)
Carving of Xiuhtechutli, God of the East.

Plate 34 (left)
God of the East, composite sketch.

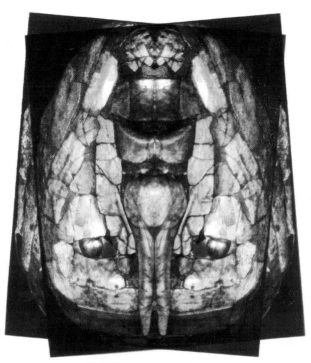

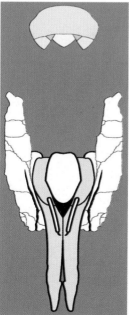

Plate 35 (above)
The Man
with wings,
composite.

Plate 36 (left)
The Man
with wings,
composite sketch.

Plate 37 The Mural of Bonampak, *Scene 1*: Xipe Totec, like Xiuhtechutli, was the God of the East, fire, and sacrifice.

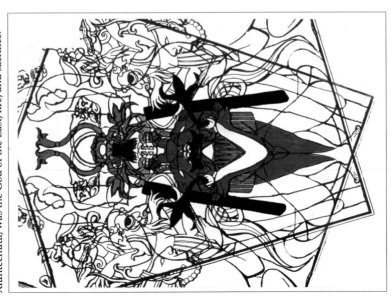

Plate 38 The Mural of Bonampak, *Scene 2*: The birth of Xipe Totec.

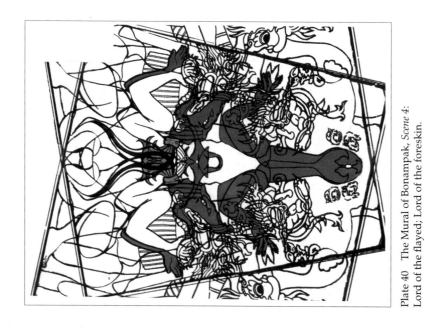

Plate 40 The Mural of Bonampak, *Scene 4*: Lord of the flayed; Lord of the foreskin.

Plate 39 The Mural of Bonampak, *Scene 3*: The young (playful) Xipe Totec.

Plate 42 The Mural of Bonampak, *The Hunting Scenes. Scene 6a:* The deer.

Plate 41 The Mural of Bonampak, *Scene 5:* Xipe Totec the youth.

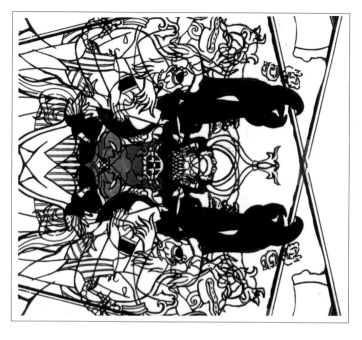

Plate 43   The Mural of Bonampak, *Scene 6b*:
The Pig.

Plate 44   The Mural of Bonampak, *Scene 6c*:
The Jaguar.

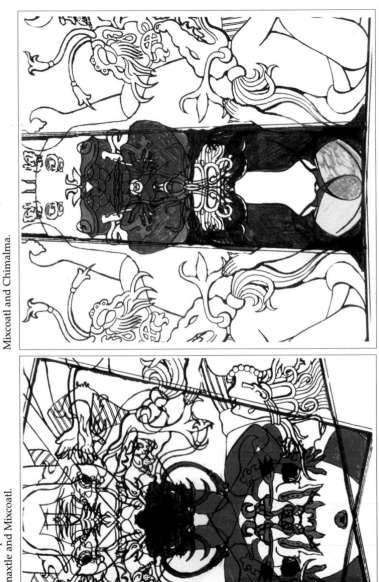

Plate 45 The Mural of Bonampak, *Scene 7*: Chimalma, wife of Camaxtle and Mixcoatl.

Plate 46 The Mural of Bonampak, *Scene 8*: Mixcoatl and Chimalma.

Plate 47 The Mural of Bonampak, *Scene 9*:
Xipe Totec as Camaxtle; the first curtain call.

Plate 48 The Mural of Bonampak, *Scene 10*:
The final curtain call; Xipe Totec as Camaxtle bows to the audience (two stags),
who applaud the end of the performance.

Plate 49 (below) 17th century miniature from Rajasthan:
In between cosmic cycles Vishnu, an earlier incaration of Krishna, rests between the serpent of infinity below and the Garuda bird above. The Garuda bird was a sun-god, a vehicle of divinity which evolved into a creature half eagle, half man.

PART TWO

CHAPTER NINE

Supergods and Miracle Men

THE MIRACLE MAKERS

	500–420 BC BUDDHA Buddhism (Asia) Book: Dhammapada Derivation: Brahman Books	703–743 AD LORD PACAL Quetzalcoatalism Central Americas Book: Popol Vuh Maya Transformers

TIME →

	1700 BC	6 BC – 26 AD
Holy Trinity {	Brahma Vishnu LORD KRISHNA Siva Brahmanism India & Ceylon Books: Vedas, Mahabarata, Bhagava Geeta	JESUS Christianity Europe & Middle East Book: Bible Derivation: Jewish Books

Fig 50

Many peoples cherish their stories of a spiritual leader who walked among them preaching the word of God while others, like the Jews, await the coming of their Messiah as prophesied in their holy books. These peoples believe that a super-intelligent 'organizing energy' is responsible for creating the universe, and that the purpose of the spiritual teachers in coming to Earth was to enlighten mankind with esoteric knowledge which answers the age-old questions of existence, such as why we are born and why we die.

The teachings suggest that man is more than just a physical creature comprised of flesh and bone, a product of chemical coalescence, of genetic material donated by two similar biological entities. They suggest that a life 'energy field' envelops each human being so as to make the individual more than the sum of its physical parts and that these two separate parts, the 'physical' and the 'spiritual', together become the 'being'.

The biological side of the creature displays a 'personality' which changes through 'time' to age and react to its environment – this is the 'personality' of the physical being. The spiritual energy enveloping the biological entity, if we are to believe the teachings of the spiritual teachers, is unchangeable and unaffected by time. The soul does not age, it is said merely to move, to 'transmigrate' into the body of a creature, or into an inanimate object. This is the 'individuality' and thought to be a part of the 'creative energy' of the universe.

Within this framework of understanding, biological parents imagine their offspring as having originated from themselves, but although this is true of the flesh, the soul is an old soul, a tiny piece of God. Hence offspring all tend to look like each other – clones of their biological parents – but behave very differently from each other (and from their biological parents): each 'individual' and each different.

The 'super-knowledge' of the holy teachers suggests that the 'soul' takes on a physical body in this physical world in order to 'purify' itself, to raise its energy level and, providing it does this during its physical lifetime, return to the creator upon physical death to rest in equilibrium and peace for eternity. The alternative 'spiritual' view is that if the soul does not achieve perfect purification during its Earthbound lifetime, it will return again for another try, which is the popular notion of 'reincarnation'.

But this 'overview' fails to convince the majority of humans to patronize and embrace the teachings, largely because the explanation fails to answer the more down-to-earth questions of 'If there is a God, and the soul is part of God, why should it need to be purified?' and 'If God is perfect to begin with, why didn't he make all souls perfect and purified in the first place?' These are only the first stumbling blocks. The super-teachers go on to tell us that in order to achieve purification we must make sacrifices, a case of 'bread today and jam tomorrow', which has never been an effective political motivator. If we lived forever then perhaps the notion would be more appealing, but time, or the lack of it, precludes serious consideration for the 'average' person preoccupied with the demands of everyday life.

Each of the super-teachers brought the same general message to Earth, sometimes emphasizing a different aspect of the knowledge, but the Maya, through Quetzalcoatlism, go further than the other schools by rationalizing the goal of purification through sacrifice. They, in common with the others, believed in the overall organizing creative energy: each of us is a part of that energy, meaning that 'I am you and you are me'. In addition, the Maya possessed a philosophical insight that explained away the 'irrationality' spoken of above in the overall plan. They explained, quite simply, that the day becomes the night and the night becomes the day. At first this is quite straightforward and seems unremarkable, but taking it one step further, what is good becomes bad and what is bad becomes good.

To explain further: 'the worst day in our life' conjures up all sorts of feelings. The first is fear that a moment like that should ever recur; but then gratitude and relief that we have emerged from that moment. How much happier we are today than on that awful day and how relieved we are to have escaped and survived that awful moment in our lives.

Similarly, when we remember the happiest day of our life, we think how wonderful it was and feel miserable that today cannot be like that day. So we see that what was bad becomes good, and what was good becomes bad. Happiness turns to unhappiness just as unhappiness turns to happiness; the day becomes the night and the night becomes the day; rain follows sunshine as surely as sunshine follows rain.

Sacrifice at first appears as penance, difficult and tortuous, attracting few followers. In the Hindu holy book, the *Bhagava-Geeta*, the teacher Lord Krishna supports this view saying:

> Hear further the three kinds of pleasure. That which increases day after day and delivers one from misery, which at first seems like poison, but afterwards acts like nectar – that pleasure is pure, for it is born of wisdom. That which is at first like nectar, because the senses revel in their objects, but in the end acts like poison – that pleasure arises from passion. While the pleasure which from first to last merely drugs the senses, which springs from indolence, lethargy and folly – that pleasure flows from ignorance. (BG, 18:36–9)

Later we will examine how the physical and spiritual worlds can be reconciled and rationalized, allowing us a better understanding of our presence and purpose in life. Firstly we need to look at the super-teachers who brought the same message over and over again, throughout the ages. Let us examine these four Supergods.

Brahminism and Hinduism

It was around 1,500 BC that Indo-Aryans invaded India from the north-west to conquer the Indus Valley. During the next thousand years Aryans pushed south-eastwards, expanding into the Ganges Valley along Northern India establishing Sanskrit (Brahman), an ancient Indo-European language and culture.

The Brahman sacred books, the *Vedas*, are among the oldest to have survived the ages. One of these, the *Rig-Veda*, the book of hymns, spans 10 volumes which date from around 1,200–800 BC and contain some 1,017 hymns. Because the books do not refer to earlier texts, they are thought to originate some time after the earlier Old Testament of the Exodus. Indeed the mention of 'writing' is specifically excluded until the time that the Laws of Manu appear around 500 BC. (These amounted, in a simplistic sense, to a codification and consolidation of Brahman thought).

The *Vedas* (Divine Knowledge, breath of the creator) were the work of the Aryans, produced previous to their entering India, and handed down from generation to generation, inspiring a group of sages known as Rishis. At first there were four *Vedas*, all highly technical and voluminous, which later formed the body of Hindu literature known as the *Puranas*. For those incapable of understanding this level of teaching the Hindu book the *Mahabarata* was written and this contains the famous epic poem of the *Bhagava-Geeta* which was followed by the *Vedanta-Sutra*, a summary of all Vedic knowledge, and lastly was again simplified in the *Srimad-Bhagavatam*.

Although the Brahman *Vedas* are ancient, they appear fully developed and therefore must have been preceded by a period of growth. They tell of a pantheon of 33 gods that arose around 1,500 BC to epitomize the perception of the Brahman who worshipped the powers of Nature. These gods could be reached, or influenced, through prayer, praise and actions. Some are thought to represent deified ancestors who acquired immortality through acts of virtue, or as a gift from the Fire god Agni.

The gods are at times seen at war with one another, as in the Maya pantheon, and had powers to punish or reward mortals. The gods of Heaven and Earth, the Mother and Father of gods were Dyaus and Prithivi who between them created the rest of the Vedic pantheon, juxtaposed Heaven against Earth and generally preserved the cosmic order.

Brahma (holy ghost or spirit) was one aspect of the holy trinity together with Vishnu (the son, flesh) and Siva (the father). The beautiful goddess Satarupa was formed from half of Brahma's own self and he became incestuously intoxicated with her beauty, his eyes following her every move, which leads to the depiction of Brahma as having four heads, facing in the four directions.

Aditi was the archaic Mother goddess, wife of Brahma who gave birth to six offspring among which were the sons Mitra and Varuna, gods of the Day and Night, who were said to have mounted a chariot which carried them to the sky allowing them to see all the things in Heaven and Earth.

Two sons of Dyaus and Prithivi were Indra and Agni. Indra was the god of Weather (Rain) and guardian of the Eastern Quadrant of the Sky while Agni was the god of Sacrificial Fire, born in wood as the life force of trees and plants who emerges when wood is rubbed together, like Xiuhtechutli and Xipe Totec of the Maya, and his colour in the South Eastern Quadrant of the Sky is likewise red.

Surya and Savitri personified the sun under different phases while Soma was the deification of the sacred yellow drink, the hallucinogenic drug, and guardian of the Northern Sky. Drinking Soma immortalized the gods for a thousand years.

Ushas was the beautiful goddess of the Dawn described as 'she that wakes the sleeping with a smile and cheerfulness', goddess of the Sky, said to have the sun as her lover, which is similar to the Mayan view of Venus, goddess of the Dawn, who never leaves the side of the sun.

Vishnu, as one of the three creator gods (of the trinity) dated from much earlier than the others, at around 1,700 BC. He was said to be reincarnated ten times as Matsya, Kurma, Varcha, Narashima, Vamana, Parasuma, Rama, Krishna, Buddha and Kalki. He is the preserver of the world who rules history through time and *karma* (the law of action and reaction) during his many incarnations and is depicted with many heads and four arms holding an array of accessories including a conch shell and prayer wheel (the conch shell was also the mark of Quetzalcoatl, the highest god of the Maya), together with a discus, the mace of authority and a lotus flower. He is also seen wearing the sacred stone Kausrabha around his neck.

Ideas of immortality and a later life do not appear on the scene until the ninth and tenth books of the *Rig-Veda*. Heaven was guaranteed for those who sacrificed, those who have died in battle and those who had 'bestowed thousands of largesses'. In the tenth book of the *Rig-Veda* he who injures his worshipper is consigned to the lower darkness whilst in the ninth Soma is seen to hurl the hated and irreligious into the abyss.

The 121st hymn of the tenth book of the *Rig-Veda* is surprisingly like the creation passages in the *Popol Vuh*:

In the beginning there arose the source of Golden light – He was the only born Lord of all that is. He established the Earth, and the sky; who is the God to whom we shall offer our sacrifice?

He who gives life, he who gives strength, whose blessing all, the bright gods desire; whose shadow is immortality, whose shadow is death. He who through his power is the only King of the breathing and awakening World. He who governs all man and beast. He whose power these snowy mountains, whose power the sea proclaims, with the distant river – He whose regions are, as it were, His two arms.

Thus do we have, in the oldest of Vedic texts, a series of conceptions of deities associated with the powers of nature similar to those of the Maya.

Krishna

Krishna was the eighth incarnation of Vishnu, the second aspect of the threefold godhead (Brahma, Vishnu, Siva), born through an imma-culate conception when his mother, Devaki, was 'overshadowed' by Vishnu. His birth at Mathura on the bank of the river Yamuna was announced by the appearance of a bright star in the heavens. The name of Krishna has its root in the Sanskrit word meaning 'rubbed-on' or 'the annointed one'.

Like Lord Pacal, Jesus and Buddha, Krishna taught that purification of the soul comes from sacrifice, from abstinence in this transient world of illusion; that the qualities of the body – ignorance, purity and passion – fetter the spirit and hinder proper discrimination between right and wrong. He taught that purified souls would upon death join God in Heaven, while the unpurified were destined to return to Earth once again to seek salvation.

Like Jesus, Krishna was said to have been put to death on a tree and to have risen again.

Krishna's teachings are lucidly expressed in the *Bhagavad-Geeta* (the Lord's Song), part of the epic poem of the *Mahabarata*, which provides in its teachings a path of salvation for the spiritual aspirant in the discourse between the prodigy soldier Arjuna and Lord Krishna, who appears to help Arjuna during his hour of need on the battlefield at Kurukshetra.

Fig 51 Sanjaya tells the king of the events taking place many miles away on the battlefield of Kurukshetra.

The ancient story begins with the blind King Dhrtarashtra sitting in his palace many miles from the battlefield of Kurukshetra, where his sons' armies are about to fight his nephew's, the Pandavas. The king is anxious about the outcome of the battle because the location of Kurukshetra is a holy place which would favour the pious Pandavas rather than his own sons.

He summons his secretary Sanjaya, who has spiritual vision, to describe the events taking place on the battlefield. Sanjaya tells the king how the two armies are poised to charge against each other and then, as though time is stopping or slowing down (as is often said to happen during such moments of trauma), the leader of the Pandavas, the soldier Arjuna, is overcome with despondency at the thought of killing his relatives who stand before him: 'Rather would I content myself with a beggar's crust than kill these teachers of mine...' (BG, 2:5)

Fig 52 The despondency of Arjuna (standing) accompanied by Lord Krishna his spiritual guide, creator of the universe…'my whole body trembles…my bow is slipping from my hand…'

Lord Krishna, an incarnation of the highest of gods, the creator of the Earth, then descends to accompany Arjuna on his chariot as it stands between the armies. Krishna begins to describe to Arjuna his true purpose in life and the reason for his being on the battlefield at that moment. During the discourse Krishna explains the meaning of life and death, and the purpose of the universe. This is the beginning of the *Bhagava-Geeta*.

Arjuna's lamentations are due to 'illusion' (*Maya*). He is identifying his relatives with their bodies, thinking that if he kills their bodies he will be killing their very selves. Krishna explains the difference between the body and the soul. The body is merely a temporary home for the soul. The soul occupies many bodies before, during and after its present incarnation, 'as the soul experiences in this body, infancy, youth and old age so finally it passes into another. The wise have no delusion about this...' (BG, 2:13)

The advice which follows is both deeply philosophical and pragmatic. In teaching Arjuna about the senses:

When contemplating the objects of our senses [attractions in the physical world] a person develops 'attachment for them' [desire]. This leads to frustration [because we can never acquire all that we desire] frustration leads to anger, anger to delusion and delusion to self destruction...(BG, 2:62 & 63)

Then, in one of the most revealing extracts, Krishna suggests that he is reincarnated on Earth whenever his presence is needed: 'Whenever spirituality decays and materialism is rampant I reincarnate myself...' (BG, 7:4)

Here Krishna refers to his original self (Vishnu) and his ten reincarnations on Earth and for the first time we are introduced to his ninth incarnation, the Buddha, founder of Buddhism around 430 BC in India. Buddha is said to have been born at Kapilavastu near Gorakhpur around 496 BC and to have died at Kusinagara around 419 BC. We will look at him in more detail later on.

For the first time we have a mention of 'God' visiting Earth twice, once on the battlefield as Lord Krishna and the next as Buddha. The dates of the literature of course exclude those teachers who followed later such as Christ and Lord Pacal. But here is the first evidence of a return visit of a teacher who came to Earth to explain the purpose of life.

The *Geeta* continues by stating that all creatures should be treated equally (BG, 3:18), recognizing that the true 'self' is not the physical personality that we perceive but a part of 'God' the creative energy (BG, 9:4–7).

Our biggest enemies, it seems, are the five physical senses (BG, 4:39) and these are described appropriately by the following illustration: the Vedic hymns compare the physical body to a chariot driven by five horses which represent the five senses of Sight, Smell, Sound, Touch and Taste. The reins of the chariot represent the mind.

The driver is the intelligence and the passenger is the spirit (soul). The message is that one must, with the help of intelligence, control the mind and senses, otherwise they will pull one, like wild horses to ruination and cause suffering to the soul. We must learn to rein-in our senses as a tortoise withdraws its head into its shell and renunciate (give up) actions because all action can have only three possible outcomes – good, bad, or partly good or partly bad (here appears the recognition as in Maya belief that good will become bad and bad will become good, therefore all actions have consequences and should be avoided). Where actions cannot be avoided, for example where duty is involved, then the fruits of the action should be surrendered. In so doing the living soul 'leaves no trace' which means no actions will result from the being and hence no reactions, no *karma* and no suffering.

This is a difficult concept to come to terms with but once grasped provides the ultimate in enlightenment.

Krishna describes the three qualities that make up the human 'nature' as Purity, Passion and Ignorance (BG, 14:5). Each being is 'controlled' during this lifetime by one of the qualities more than the others. Where purity is prevalent in the nature of the individual upon death, the soul passes on to the pure regions in the heavens to experience a period of bliss before returning to Earth to engage in 'fruitful' activities (BG, 14:9). When passion prevails the soul is reborn among those who love activity (BG, 14:7). When ignorance prevails the soul returns to the wombs of the ignorant commensurate with his consciousness. If that soul has acquired the consciousness of a dog then it will return again as a dog (BG, 14:8).

At first the quest for purity appears to be an honourable pursuit. But 'pursuit' it is and as such constitutes an 'action' which must again result in a reaction (*karma*), and suffering. Only when the soul transcends the qualities completely can it escape the suffering of *Karma* on this physical Earth, which can only be achieved through the sacrifice of desire and unequivocal love of the creative energy, both in its Godly form and fragmented form in the guise of living beings (BG, 14:26).

Krishna continues: 'Always think of Me [Krishna] worship Me and offer Me your homage. Thus you will come to Me without fail.

I promise you this because you are My very dear friend. Give up all varieties of religion and just surrender to Me. I shall protect you from all sinful reactions. Therefore you have nothing to fear...' (BG, 18:64,65)

The secretary Sanjaya continues his discourse with the king, expressing his foreboding as he explains he has good cause for concern because the Pandavas possess good fortune.

The soldier Arjuna goes on to victory in battle and, having done his duty without desire for gain, without fear or favour, he will experience no *karma*.

Karma

The notion of *karma* is familiar to the more spiritual Eastern peoples but little recognized by Westerners. It is the universal law of cause and effect. In the physical world it is said that for every action there is an equal and opposite reaction. Spiritually, *karma* is a fundamental law which strives to balance good actions against bad ones. As the nights equal the days so shall the days equal the nights. Implicit in this understanding is that ultimately all transgressions against our fellow man lead to reparations by the transgressor. The soul suffers for all the wrong actions inspired by the body and this soul suffering is carried forward to the next incarnation in the physical world. The soul hence suffers in the next life for transgressions in this life and likewise enjoys pleasures in the next life for good actions in the past; hence Krishna's advice to avoid all action.

In a practical sense reincarnation is reassuring in its ability to accommodate life's injustices by explaining why some, without any obvious merit, are born rich, healthy and privileged while others are born poor and sick. It also accommodates different levels of personal development such as gifted child prodigies and others who arrive in this life with highly developed abilities, without effort.

The Three Worlds and the Four Ages

The Hindu model of existence was founded upon the early Brahman *Vedas* and recognized the self as an individual piece of the Godly energy, the soul, which transmigrated between the physical and spiritual worlds. Choice was the deciding factor in the level of purification and hence determined the ultimate destination of the released soul.

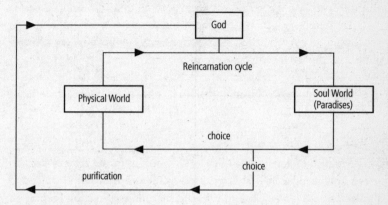

Fig 53 The three worlds.

For the Hindu there were three worlds: the God world, the physical world and the soul world, which facilitated a 5,000-year period of creation and destruction on Earth. This period was subdivided into four equal periods and as the cycle progressed, spirituality declined due to natural forces inherent in nature.

In the beginning the divine couple descended from the soul world and took on bodily form. The world was a beautiful and unpolluted place and the Golden Age, Heaven on Earth, ensued. Sadness had not yet evolved. The divine couple procreated and populated their homeland and enjoyed the fruits and harvests which the land yielded. After 1,250 years, the population had grown and their home became overfarmed prompting populations to migrate. This caused sadness as the single great family divided and 'tears' appeared, for the first time during the cycle.

The Silver age began and sustained the newly scattered peoples and although not quite as heavenly as the Golden Age, it provided well for the growing populations. By the end of the Silver Age the scattered peoples no longer remembered their roots and lineage and perceived themselves as different families and tribes. As each tribe developed

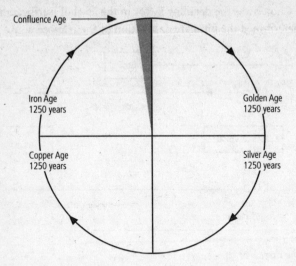

Fig 54 The four ages of life on Earth.

interests separate from their neighbour, their differences grew and by the time of the Copper Age trading had begun, replacing giving. Goods were exchanged for money. The rising population demanded greater sources of protein and animals were killed and eaten for the first time as land became owned, fenced and farmed.

Pollution and disputes grew during the Copper Age and within 1,250 years sin enveloped the Earth as resources began to accumulate inequitably in the hands of the rich. People stole; marriages broke down; people took up arms against each other; technology and science became the evil of the day. This is the Iron Age.

The scriptures *(Rig-Veda, Brahmanas, Mahabarata)* say that the present Iron Age (the Age of Kali), began with the death of Krishna, who is prophesied as returning on a white horse as the god Kalki to prepare the way for cosmic renewal after the planet is destroyed by fire and flood during the brief period known as the confluence age.

At the end of each cosmic cycle between the destruction of one age and the creation of another Vishnu sleeps on the serpent of infinity Ananta while above he rides through the air as a Garuda bird (*see plate* 49). By meditating between these two Vishnu demonstrates the extent of his powers, between the feathers and the serpent. We will see that Buddha reached enlightenment with the help of the serpent Mucalinda. According to Christian literature, the fall of Adam and Eve was due to temptation by a serpent. Quetzalcoatl (Pacal) was the feathered snake.

Buddhism

The decline of Brahmanism, around 500 BC, stemmed largely from a gradual disillusionment amongst the educated Brahman who came to believe that the pantheon of Vedic gods were largely poetic imaginations bearing no relevance to truth or reality, and from the realization that the gods must have arisen from a common source, a single creative energy.

So they began to develop a theological literature, the *Upanishads* and *Puranas* which were to become the foundations for the Hindu books the *Mahabarata, Bhagava-Geeta, Vedantra Sutra* and *Srimad-Bhagavatam*, mentioned earlier. These books of the later Hindu taught of both the unity of God and the immortality of the soul and although still heavily cloaked in myth and superstition, this new system of the Hindu would in time concern itself with the brotherhood of man; but not for another 800 years, after Buddhism had had its day.

Buddha believed that the individual soul, whilst suffering from past actions in this life, could at the same time be purified during this lifetime in preparation for the next. This allowed followers of all castes (social and religious levels of society), to work out their own salvation and elevate themselves from their present position in this life by escaping to settle on a rung higher up the ladder in the next, if they chose.

From 430 BC to 400 AD (around 800 years) Buddhism triumphed as the saviour of the people, but by 500 AD the tide began to turn as the modified version of mixed Brahmanism and Buddhism – Hinduism – replaced beliefs of the day. The new regime forced Buddhists to flee the land, taking refuge in China and Asia.

The exact dates of Buddha's life are not known and the best consensus places him in the fifth century BC, putting his death at around 420–400 BC. Sri Lankan records suggest he was born in Kapilavastu, between the Himalayas of Nepal and the river Rapti in the north-east of Oudh. In this fertile region the Aryan tribe of the Sakyas ('the powerful'), grew rice and maintained a close relationship with the nearby people of the Kosala (Oudh) to the south- west who were later to absorb them.

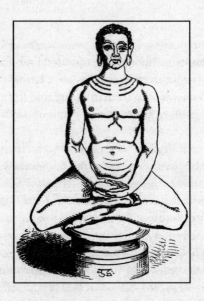

Fig 55 Seated figure of Buddha.

The Sri Lankan Buddhist accounts, written in Pali (the sacred language of Buddhism, an early modification of Sanskrit), refer to their founder as 'the enlightened one' (Buddha) or 'the exalted one' (Bhagava) and that 'a great teacher, Buddha, preached salvation and deliverance to the people…' (*Buddha*, Professor Oldenburg)

He appears to have married and fathered one son, Rahula, who became one of his disciples. Later, at the age of 29, Buddha left his home to become a wandering ascetic known as Gautama. As a deep feeling philanthropic philosopher he contemplated the states of old age, weakness, decay, and the horrors of sickness and death, and measured these afflictions of an imperfect world against the notion of a perfect creator; the resulting paradox would in time be overcome by the teaching of his own enlightened understanding.

Other records provide an account of his departure: ' The ascetic Gautama has gone from home into homelessness, whilst still young in years, in the bloom of youthful strength, in the first freshness of life. The ascetic Gautama, although his parents did not wish it, although they shed tears and wept, has had his hair and beard shaved and has put on yellow garments.' (*Buddha*, Professor Oldenburg)

Thus seeking spiritual enlightenment, freedom and deliverance, he travelled for seven years placing himself in succession under two notable teachers. Leaving them, without being satisfied, he travelled through the kingdom of Maghada, and arrived at the town of Uruvela. There in the beautiful forests he spent many years in self-discipline, repressing desires and aspirations awaiting spiritual enlightenment. Fasting, suppression of breath and other mortifications were all tried without success and it was at this time that five companions with whom he had travelled, abandoned him.

Finally, sitting beneath a Bo-tree (tree of knowledge) he contemplated for five weeks, during which time he was shaken by a storm. It was at this time that he was visited by the serpent Mucalinda, who provided protection by coiling himself round and fanning the canopy of his head above Gautama. (Compare Krishna's association with the serpent of infinity, Ananta and the fall of Adam and Eve due to temptation by a serpent; Queztalcoatl was known as the Feathered Snake. The tree is also associated with Krishna – he is said to have died on a tree; Jesus died on the cross; the cross is the central feature of the Lid of Palenque, featured as the Suckling Tree, said to have 400,000 nipples.) After five weeks he passed through successive stages of abstraction until he became enlightened about the transmigration of souls and the four sacred truths:

1) *Suffering envelops the world.*
2) *Its cause is 'desire' and 'attachment'.*
3) *It can be overcome with Nirvana (extinction of desire, of suffering, of error, of ignorance), the 'eternal state'.*
4) *The way to Nirvana is through Buddhism.*

Buddha had become 'the awakened', he had achieved enlightenment.

> When I apprehended this, and when I beheld this, my soul was released from the evils of desire, released from the evils of earlier existence, released from the evils of error, released from the evils of ignorance. In the release awoke the knowledge of the released; extinct is rebirth, finished the sacred course, duty done no more shall I return to this world; this I knew...(*The World's Religions*, G.T. Bettany, p. 258)

For some time he remained near the tree of knowledge, fasting and enjoying the happiness of deliverance for, as the oldest narratives says, four times seven days. After this time he endured and overcame the temptation to enter into Nirvana immediately instead of preaching his doctrine to the world. He met a Brahman on his way who questioned him on his right to assume the title 'Brahman', and Buddha explained that the true Brahman has illiminated all evil from himself, purified his spirit, and conquered himself.

Returning to Benares, he preached to his former ascetic companions the doctrine of the 'middle way' between mortification and self-indulgence, which would lead to peace, knowledge and enlightenment and ultimately Nirvana by the eightfold path:

1) *Right faith*
2) *Right resolve*
3) *Right speech*
4) *Right action*
5) *Right living*
6) *Right effort*

7) *Right thought*
8) *Right concentration*

From this first sermon we learn firsthand of the early form of the Master's teaching and how he explained the nature of suffering:

> Birth is suffering; old age is suffering; sickness is suffering; death is suffering; to be united with the unloved is suffering; to be separated from the loved is suffering; not to obtain what one desires is suffering; clinging to life is suffering.
>
> This O monks is the sacred truth of the origin of suffering: it is the thirst for being which leads from birth to birth, together with lust and desire, which finds gratification here and there; the thirst for pleasures, the thirst for being, the thirst for power...
>
> This O monks is the sacred truth of extinction of suffering, the extinction of this thirst by complete annihilation of desire, letting go, expelling it, separating oneself from it, giving it no room...
> (Sermon to the monks at Benares)

Then he explained the eightfold path by which he had attained the supreme Buddhahood in this world and the worlds of gods. From this moment forth there would be no new births for him. He who walked in purity would end all suffering.

Buddha, like all the Supergods, preached and travelled with disciples. The five ascetics of Benares were the first converts to Buddhism and soon others began to flock around as they wandered separately, receiving the initiative and investiture from their Master and spreading the words of the new way: 'Go ye out, O disciples and travel from place to place for the welfare of many people, for the joy of many people, in pity for the world, for the blessing, welfare, and joy of gods and men. Go not in twos to one place...' rang in their hearts as they went their ways.

Returning to Uruvela Buddha converted a group of ascetics and their leader Kassapa after, according to the records, performing numerous 'miracles'. The whole group united and moved on to Rajagaha, the capital of Magadha and converted the king thereof, Bimbissara. The noble youths of Magadha rallied round and volunteered their hearts and minds to the new arrivals so much so that murmurings began concerning fears that the ascetics had come to take the children and make widows of their women.

Buddha's public life waxed and waned around the Indian seasons. The three rainy months necessitated a period of rest and retirement in or around the towns which he spent with devotees and ascetics. The rest of the year he travelled together with disciples through the kingdoms of Kosola and Magadha keeping clear of western Hindustan where Brahmanism enjoyed its stronghold.

Pleasant gardens were bequeathed to the new Buddha and his followers near the cities of Rajagha and Savatthi which provided places for eating, lodging and assembling. The Buddhist books tell of the gardens:

> Not too far from, nor yet too near to the town, well provided with entrances and exits, easily accessible to all those who inquire after it, with not too much of the bustle of life by day, quiet by night, far from commotion and the crowds of men, a place of retirement, a good spot for solitary meditation...

Here stood beautiful groves of trees, pools in which the symbolic lotus grew, and every convenience for meetings; and similar gardens flourished elsewhere, around and about, on a smaller scale.

Strangers came from distant lands to listen to Buddha's teaching as he wandered the streets accompanied by his begging bowl mendicants – this brethren of religious men, with shaven heads and yellow robes, who through choice, had given up property, family ties and vanity and chosen instead a life of chastity.

In relation to women Buddha was in some respects more liberal and in others less so than the Brahmans who confined their women to subordinate, servile positions and while Buddhism abjured intimate relationships with women, it did acknowledge their right to become lay adherents to the orders, analogous to nuns, who were strictly segregated from men. But wider experience, and wisdom, were in time to modify Buddha's view. His foster mother and his disciples together persuaded him that women too were capable of realizing the eight-fold path, although this liberalism was not without its set of rules which constrained and subordinated them to men.

Buddha commented that:

> From time to time an unsurpassed teacher is born into the world as a guide to erring mortals, a fully enlightened one, a blessed Buddha who thoroughly understands the universe, the gods and men and makes his knowledge known to others. The truth doth he proclaim both in its letter and in its spirit, lovely in its origin, lovely in its progress, lovely in its consummation; the higher life doth he make known, in all its purity and all its perfectness.

It was considered high sacrifice to accept the Buddhist doctrine; higher still to become a monk; while the highest of offerings was to obtain deliverance, and the knowledge that 'I shall not again return to this world'.

Fate and the Parable of the Hen

As with Brahmanism and Christianity, parables are found frequently in the higher orders of Buddhist teaching. Buddha believed that fate would deliver where fate could deliver and this is illustrated by the Parable of the Hen:

> Just as when a hen has eight, ten or twelve eggs, and the hen has properly brooded over them, properly sat upon them, properly sat herself around them, however much such a wish may arise in her heart as this, 'Oh would that my little chickens should break open the egg shell with the points of their claws, or their beaks and come forth into the light of safety'. Yet all the while those little chickens are sure to break the egg shell with the points of their claws, or their beaks and to come forth into the light of safety. Just even so, a brother thus endowed with fifteen fold determination is sure to come forth into

the light, sure to reach up to the higher wisdom, sure to attain to the supreme security. The lesson is that the result is quite certain, however much doubt the hen or the believer may have about it. (*Sacred Books of the East xi*, Professor Oldenburg)

It is interesting to examine 'the parable' as a way of teaching. This form of communication has proven to be an effective mechanism for maximizing retention of information and has hence found favour throughout the ages with the wise owing its success to the word-picture association which the story conjures in the listener and the fact that the mind is more comfortable with images than words. Images seem to settle in the mind whereas words seem to pass in and out of the mind. So, not surprisingly the great teachers have used either parables or, like Lord Pacal, pictures to convey their wisdom, because while knowledge may be conveyed, wisdom must be absorbed. Both parable and picture leave little room for ambiguity or misunderstanding.

And so Buddha says, 'I shall show you a parable; by a parable many a wise man perceives the meaning of what is being said'. His own preaching is compared to the physician's work, drawing poisoned arrows from wounds, and overcoming the venom with remedies. Like the lotus flower with its head on the lake and its roots in the mud, so the Buddhas are unaffected by life.

Which brings us to the Buddha's death as told in the 'Book of the great decease' which has been compared to a gospel. The book appears from an unknown source about a hundred years after the Buddha's death around the end of the fourth century BC and puts Buddha's age at that time at around 80. It tells of a final journey from Rajagaha, the capital of Magadha, to Pataliputta the future capital whose greatness he prophesies. On this journey he was attacked by a great illness which he subdues hoping to give a farewell address to the order. He tells Ananda that he has withheld nothing and that he no longer wishes to lead the brotherhood due to his ageing and illness: 'My journey is drawing to a close. I have reached the sum of my days, I am turning 80 years of age; and just as a worn out cart, Ananda, can only with much additional care be made to move along, so, methinks, the body of the Enlightened one can only be kept going with much additional care…' He advises his people to be a refuge to themselves and not look for any other, and above all, be anxious to learn.

In a final scene of his life, that of the last temptation, the tempter Mara appeared to him in a vision suggesting that it was time to die as all his objectives had been accomplished, but that he would be given another three months to live.

But Buddha chose instead to die, and on rejecting the right to live on, a mighty earthquake arose, awful and terrible, and the thunders of heaven burst forth, and when Buddha saw this, he broke out into his hymn of exaltation and then he summarized in conclusion his teachings to his disciples:

My age is now full and ripe, my life draws to its close:
I leave you, I depart, relying on myself alone!
Be earnest then, O Brethren! holy, full of thought!
Be steadfast in resolve! Keep watch o'er your own hearts!
Who wearies not, but holds fast to this truth and law,
Shall cross this sea of life, shall make an end to grief.

A few days later, seized with pain he arrived at Kusinagara where he passed away without complaint, his final words to the few disciples, 'Behold, now brethren, I exhort you saying Decay is inherent in all component things. Work out your salvation with diligence…' Then followed earthquakes and wild thunder.

His funeral was celebrated in Kusinagara with all the honour due to a king, wrapping his body in 500 layers of cotton wool and new cloth, enclosing it in two iron vessels, and finally cremating it on a funeral pyre made of perfumes. Legends say that neither soot nor ash was left but just the bones, which were divided into eight portions, over each of which a mound was made by the groups who had claimed them.

Jesus of Nazareth

Practically everything known about Jesus comes from the gospels (Greek for 'proclamations') which his followers Matthew, Mark, Luke and John set down after his death, and these form the basis of the New Testament in the Bible. There are other texts not quite so celebrated and one of the best known is the Gospel of Thomas, thought to have been written at the beginning of the second century.

As early as 63 BC the Roman Empire extended in the East as far as Palestine, a region of some 8,000 square miles supporting a population of around a million Jews. They became reluctant bed fellows of the mighty Roman armies that squeezed them financially to fund their massive projects of roads, bridges, aqueducts and buildings.

About 57 years later, in pursuit of taxes, ruler Caesar Augustus decreed a census be taken of the population to quantify the taxation possibilities and it was this census that set the would-be parents of Jesus on a 90-mile journey to the town of Bethlehem. His mother Mary was unmarried, but engaged to Joseph when she became pregnant through an immaculate conception. Visions and dreams persuaded the couple that the child should be born and reared within marriage and the couple agreed to continue into marriage fulfilling the divine orders.

Jesus was born in a lowly stable at the end of Joseph and Mary's 90-mile journey to Bethlehem, after following a bright star which appeared in the sky. This seems a common feature in the birth of the four super-teachers. If we recall, Buddha appeared as a bright star in his mother's womb and Quetzalcoatl was known as the brightest star in the sky, the twin star (planet) Venus.

Jesus' birth fulfilled many prophecies from the Old Testament days of Moses and he grew up the son of a carpenter spending his first few years exiled in Egypt, removed from the despot king, Herod.

By all accounts Jesus was a remarkable child with a liking for the Jewish scriptures, from the oral traditions that had sustained the Hebrews in the desert, to the laws of Moses and the stories of the patriarchs which eventually evolved into the first five books of the Old Testament, the *Torah* or *Pentateuch* (regarded as the core document of the Jewish faith). We are led to believe that he became increasingly pre-occupied with these as he matured, although his exact movements be-tween the ages of 12 and 30 are little known.

His life as a teacher, as opposed to that of a novice, seems to have be-gun after meeting his forerunner John the Baptist.

According to Luke he began his ministry around the age of 30, quickly acquiring a group of followers (disciples), and set off for Galilee, establishing a new ministry at Capernaum, a small Jewish lakeside town with a population of some 5,000 located between Damascus and Alexandria. He taught the laws of Moses, of the Old Testament, and the 10 commandments and began to make his mark as an unusual teacher and the people were astonished at his teaching be-cause he taught them as one who had authority, and not in the man-ner of the scribes.

Clearly his teachings were based upon the laws handed down from God to Moses in the Old Testament Book of Exodus, Chapter 20, which amount to the 10 commandments of the Christian faith:

> And God spake all these words saying:
> Thou shalt have no other God but me
> Thou shalt not make or bow down before any graven image
> Thou shall not take the name of the Lord in vain
> Remember the Sabbath and keep it holy
> Honour thy father and thy mother
> Thou shalt not kill
> Thou shall not commit adultery
> Thou shall not steal
> Thou shall not bear false witness against thy neighbour
> Thou shall not covet thy neighbour's possessions

The Christian ethos epitomizes and embraces love, sympathy and charity and raises all of mankind to a position of brotherhood, be-longing to one Father, God. But this love was not the sentimental sort, nor that found between two brothers willing to die for each other, it was this and much more. It is easy to inspire affection among like-minded people, but this man loved those unlike himself, those most distant, even the evil and the wretched and in so doing inspired a new ideal: 'A new commandment give I unto you,' he said 'that ye love one another, even as I have loved you' (John 13:34). A love that would, could survive ingratitude, evil conduct, and repudiation of God. This love would be spontaneously tendered to those who had done nothing to deserve it, to all those who had any spark of goodness. 'And who has not?' said Jesus for he asserted that the Father of all did not will that anyone should perish.

His perception was one of God the Father unseen, but all seeing, ever watchful over the actions of his children, mindful of both thought and deed. No other religion had brought the Father so intimately close to his children with equanimity for all, the good, bad and the thankless.

The belief that a final day of judgement would take place, at which the condition of the departing soul would be determined according to actions in this life, is perhaps the most salutary for Christians. The path to salvation was a spiritual one requiring little ceremony, no payments and no daily orders. Sins would be forgiven and forgiveness could alleviate the soul from the burden of guilt, allowing purification through inward truth. Sincerity in thought and deed was more important than mere 'acts' of charity.

The Parables

The teachings of Jesus often took the form of parables – stories which had meaning on two levels, literal and figurative. Generally they formed allegories which impressed a picture in the mind, which as we have already seen was the chosen form of communication of both Buddha and Lord Pacal.

The purpose of the parable was to inspire the listener to consider deeply the underlying issues and inspire change as a result. In Matthew 13:3–23 Jesus points out how different people react to hearing the word of God: 'Some of the sower's seed fell on the footpath, and were eaten by birds. Some fell on rocky ground and perished on the hot earth. Some fell on good ground and thrived to produce gain of a hundred fold'. The message being that those who accept the teachings of God yield astounding results.

Rabbi Moses Maimonides, the great Jewish theologian comments: 'Every time you find in our books a tale, the reality of which is repugnant to both reason and common sense, then be sure that the tale contains a profound allegory veiling a deeply mysterious truth; and the greater the absurdity of the letter, the deeper the wisdom of spirit.' (*Hidden Wisdom in the Holy Bible*, G. Hodson)

Christ openly states that some knowledge is purposely concealed when he says, 'he that hath ears to hear, let him hear' (Revelations 2:7,11,17,29; 3:6,13,22; 13:9). To his disciples he says, 'Unto you it is given to know the mysteries of God: but to others in parables; that seeing they might not see, and hearing they might not understand' (Luke 8:8–10).

The reason for such secrecy becomes apparent when he speaks the words: 'Give not that which is holy unto the dogs, neither cast ye your pearls before swine, lest they trample them under foot and turn again to rend you' (Matthew 9:6).

Author Roland Peterson in his book *Everyone is Right* adds: 'Certain knowledge can be destructive in the hands of those who are morally unprepared – destructive to self and others.'

Pausing briefly, could this be the reason why Lord Pacal chose to conceal his holy knowledge 'wrapped up' in the form of Maya transformers? Hidden from the archaeologists and the grave robbers? Hidden from the searcher and the thinker as described in the *Popol Vuh*?

Returning to Jesus, it was another gift, beyond that of the parable that caused his fame to spread: he could heal the sick with his bare hands, or simply with his will.

Like the other three Supergods, Jesus worked miracles, as described in the New Testament narratives. He appeared to overcome physical laws to achieve super-human results for his efforts and in addition to have a deep insight into the foundations of physical nature and the influence of mind over matter. Such an understanding was not of this world.

The Miracles of Jesus

There are many documented accounts of the miracles of Christ. Some concern benevolent acts of provision, for example at Canaat Galilee he turned water into wine simply to satisfy the needs of the wedding feast (John 2:1–11).

In the sea of Galilee he satisfied the needs of the fisherman: 'And when they had done this (as Christ had said) they enclosed a great multitude of fishes: and their net brake' (Luke 5:1–11).

On hearing of the death of his dear friend John the Baptist, Christ set out to the desert followed by the multitude. As night fell his disciples decided to send the multitude away so that they might eat, but Jesus said:

> 'They need not depart...give ye them to eat.' And they said unto him,
> · 'We have here but five loaves and two fishes,' he said 'bring them hither to me'. And he commanded the multitude to sit down on the grass and took the five loaves and two fishes and, looking up to heaven he blessed and brake, and give the loaves to his disciples and the disciples to the multitude. And they did all eat, and were filled, and they took up of the fragments that remained twelve baskets full. And they that had eaten were about five thousand men, beside women and children...(Matthew 14,15,21)

That night he was seen walking upon the sea and beckoned his disciple Peter to join him, but Peter began to sink saying 'Lord save me'. Jesus stretched out his hand and caught him and said to him, 'O thou of little faith, wherefore didst thou doubt?...' Then the people who were in the ship came and worshipped him saying, 'Of a truth thou art the son of God' (Matthew 14:23–44).

Other miracles involved the healing of the sick and these are numerous and well documented: at Capernaum Jesus healed Peter's wife's mother of a fever (Mark 1:30–1) and a leper of leprosy. He brought back a widow's son from the dead (Luke 7:11–17), and in the same hour 'He cured many of their infirmities and plagues, and of evil spirits; and unto many that were blind he gave sight'. These are but a few of the many miracles which followed at Nain, Gadara, Decapolis, Bethsaida, Tabor, Jerusalem and elsewhere.

The Christian View of Reincarnation

In Galatians (6:7) we read, 'Be not deceived; God is not mocked; for whatever a man soweth, that shall he also reap'. This remark implicitly recognizes the notion of *karma:* all sins must be paid for. For every action there is an equal and opposite reaction. He that brings love will receive love and he that comes in hate will experience hate. If we are to believe this then we must include reincarnation in our view of things because, clearly, not every bad person is repaid for his misdeeds in this life and therefore there must be another life of sorts where the penance, described as 'reaping', above, becomes payable.

Reincarnation is cited in the New Testament on several occasions, particularly so in regard to the origin of John the Baptist: Matthew, suggests John the Baptist, is the reincarnation of the Old Testament Elijah (Matthew 11:11–15). Again, later in Matthew, the disciples ask Jesus:

'Why then say the scribes that Elijah must first come?' and Jesus answered and said unto them 'Elijah shall truly first come and restore all things. But I say unto you that Elijah has come already and they knew him not, but have done unto him whatsoever they listed. Likewise shall also the son of man suffer of them', then the disciples understood that he spake of John the Baptist (Matthew 17:10–13).

In the book of John (3:13), Jesus states that 'no man hath ascended up to heaven, but he that came down from heaven', supporting the view of pre-existence. Researchers, have noted that although reincarnation is not generally taught in the Christian churches today, it was much more widespread in the early Church. The early Church fathers Origen, around 200 AD, and St Clement of Alexandria are cited as supporting reincarnation. Origen writes:

Is it not rational that souls should be introduced into bodies in ac-
cordance with their merits and previous deeds, and that those who
have used their bodies in doing the utmost possible good should
have a right to bodies endowed with qualities superior to the bodies
of others? The soul at one time puts off one body, which was necessary before, but which is no longer adequate in its changed state, and
it exchanges it for a second. (From *Contra Celsum* quoted in
Reincarnation by Head and Cranston).

St Gregory, the Bishop of Nyssa, wrote around 350 AD, 'It is absolute-
ly necessary that the soul should be healed and purified and if this
does not take place during its life on Earth it must be accomplished in
future lives.'

As the fame of Jesus and his teachings spread he become known as the
'King of the Jews'. But it was the Jewish clergy who themselves object-
ed, insisting he did not conform to their perception of the Messiah (the
anointed one) as prophesied in the Old Testament. After all, he was the
son of a poor carpenter, born in a stable, without the credentials to call
himself king. And how, they questioned, could this man Jesus say he
was the Son of God? This was blasphemy.

For their part, it seems that the Romans had no axe to grind on the
subject of Jesus, or religion, and were more concerned with maintain-
ing law and order and with it the uninterrupted flow of taxes. However,
Jesus' adversaries conspired to entrap him and the Jewish Sanhedrin
(71 member Jewish High Court) duly found him guilty of blasphemy
and handed him to the Romans for punishment. The Romans, unsure
as to what action to take in the circumstances, threw open the fate of
Jesus to a referendum where the consensus led to a punishment of
death through crucifixion (a painful ritual of nailing the condemned
to a cross to die slowly).

When he died he was taken to a tomb and laid to rest, whereupon
three days later he returned to life, so the scriptures say, to preach a final farewell to his disciples before ascending to heaven. It was this final
act of heavenly defiance and achievement which became a watershed,

Fig 56 Roman soldiers preparing Jesus for execution.

a turning point, for those who would read the story of Jesus. It became known that he suffered and died on the cross to educate mankind into the ways of the creator. The act of resurrection symbolized everlasting life. Death was rebirth, available to those who followed his teaching. He showed that everlasting life comes through sacrifice, that purification of the spirit could be achieved through love and forgiveness. He took away the sins of the world brought by the serpent in the Garden of Eden. Some say he was the greatest man that ever lived.

The World's Religions

Having looked closely at the four Supergods, we need to examine briefly the other world religions to discover whether the same characteristics apply to other founders of faith.

Islam

Of the many religions, Hinduism and Buddhism are rooted in Brahmanism and, as we have seen, Buddha was the ninth incarnation of Vishnu. Similarly, Christianity and Islam both have their roots in Judaism and so now we naturally progress to Islam, the religion of Muslims which has 600 million followers in the world today, second in numbers only to Christianity.

The holy book, the *Koran*, details the works of the Islamic prophet Mohammet (Muhammad) born of the Koreish family in 570 AD in Mecca, the centre of the Arab world. His teachings differ and may be distinguished from earlier accounts, passed down from the *Veda*s and *Torah*, in that his inspirations came to him whilst in meditative trances and were written down by followers to become the *Koran*. He did not live a life as a son of God or God, as did Krishna, Buddha, Jesus and Pacal. He was but a messenger.

There are many similarities connecting those earlier teachers whom we have so far discussed: Buddha was the ninth incarnation of Vishnu (Krishna), who performed miracles; Jesus performed miracles and Lord Pacal left us, in the Maya Transformers, 'living miracles' which are now beginning to unfold.

But the *Koran* does not assert that Mohammet worked any miracles, and only a few, which are incredible, have been attributed to him by his followers.

Quetzalcoatlism, epitomized by the Feathered Serpent, shares similarities with Krishna (Vishnu) who returns at the end of the age of Kali, the present age, to watch over the next Golden age and who, in-between-times, meditates between the serpent and the feathers of the

Garuda Bird (*see plate 49*). But Mohammet has no connections with feathers or serpents.

There are other major differences between the four Supergods and Mohammet. He had many wives and unlike the earlier pacifist teachers fought many battles in the name of religion. Having said this, his accomplishments were many: before his arrival Arabia had been overrun by idolatry, with an idol for every day of the year; there was human sacrifice to idols and cannibalism by worshippers; lust, licentiousness, gambling and drunkenness.

Mohammet's efforts resulted in the belief in one God and the emphasis on truthfulness, justice, kindness and charity and the prohibition of drunkenness and adultery. Islam's own view of Mohammet is spelled out clearly in the *Koran*: 'Mohamet is but a messenger, messengers (the likes of whom) have passed away before him' (III, 144, *The Meaning of the Glorious Koran*, M.M. Pickfall).

As for reincarnation, this is covered in the *Koran* in several places. In *Sura* (Book) III 27: 'Thou causest the night to pass into day, and thou causest the day to pass into the night. And thou bringest forth the living from the dead, and thou bringest forth the dead from the living.'

Sura II 28 states: 'And you were dead, and he brought you back to life. And he shall cause you to die, and shall bring you back to life, and in the end shall gather you unto himself.' *Sura* II 286 recognizes *karma*: 'Allah tasketh not a soul beyond its scope. For it is only that which it hath earned, and against it only that which it hath deserved…' And Chapter 25, *Sura Zakhraf Meccan* Verses 5–10–6: 'As the rains turn the dry earth into green thereby yielding fruit, similarly God brings the dead into life so that thou mayest learn…'

It should be mentioned that although reincarnation was recognized in the Islamic teachings it found little discussion with the masses. The emphasis was much more concerned with 'purity of action' and it was left to the Sufis, the mystical cult who claim to carry forward the esoteric principle of Islam, to promote its principles.

Confucianism

Confucius lived from 551–479 BC and has at least 600 million Chinese followers. He was more of a philosopher than a religious teacher and Confucianism may perhaps therefore be regarded as more of a philosophy. He did not claim to be an original thinker but instead set down practical rules to guide others in their ways from childhood onwards.

At the age of 34 he met Lao-tzu, an 85-year-old philosopher, founder of Taoism, keeper of the state archives and author of the *Tao-Te Ching*. Lao-tzu asked Confucius if he was aware of the Tao (the divine way) and Confucius replied he had sought the knowledge for many years. This prompted Lao-tzu to reply, 'This knowledge cannot be seized by pursuing it, it will come into your heart if you give it sanctuary there' (Lao-Tzu 'Interviews with Confucius in *World Religions*, G.T. Bettany).

Lao-tzu had also commented:

On hearing of the way, the best of men
Will earnestly explore its length.
The mediocre person learns of it
And takes it up and sets it down.
But vulgar people, when they hear the news,
Will laugh out loud, and if they did not laugh,
It would not be the way. (Lao-Tzu, Tao-Te Ching)

The way of Confucius was to spread wisdom through wise sayings, never claiming originality. Of his teachings he said, 'I am but a transmitter, and not a creator'; when asked about humanity he said 'Love men'; on fault-finding he comments, 'Excuse small faults'; on goodness he states, 'Better than one who knows what is right is he that loves what is right'; on God: 'Does heaven ever speak? The four seasons come and go and all creatures thrive and grow. Does heaven ever speak!'

This way of teaching had not impressed Lao-tzu who after his meeting with Confucius reported to a visitor that, 'those whom you talk about are dead, and their bones are mouldered to dust; only their words remain...put away your proud air and many desires, your insinuating habit and wild will. These are of no advantage to you…' He was making the point that the ceremony, reverence for antiquity, and self-righteousness apparent in Confucius were very much against the spirit of the 'quietism' and 'rationalism' of his own teachings in which he tried to keep himself concealed and unknown.

Another philosophical 'way' is that of Shintoism in Japan, a sort of hybrid between Taoism and Buddhism and another is that of Siza, professed by many middle-class Japanese.

Shintoism means 'the way of the gods' and may be described as animism, a belief that inanimate things, like trees, rocks, wind, fire, mountains and heavenly bodies have spirits.

Clearly there is little common ground here with our four founding fathers of religion, Krishna, Buddha, Christ and Pacal – the miracle-makers who brought super-knowledge to the world. Likewise other smaller religions, whilst no doubt of the utmost importance to those who subscribe to them, are not covered here in detail. For example, Jainism (similar to Buddhism) Zoroastrianism (which has its roots in the Old Testament) and its offshoot Parseeism, both of India, are sufficiently dissimilar to the four to preclude a wider discussion at this time.

Quetzalcoatlism

The Mosaic Mask of Palenque shows us that Lord Pacal was the feathered snake Quetzalcoatl. There is no doubt about this. He left us with his legacy of living miracles, the Mayan Transformers. And from the inscriptions in his temple, and dating of bones in the tomb, we know he lived between 703 AD and 743 AD, having died at the age of 40. So where did the knowledge come from that enabled the sophisticated rise of Teotihuacan, some 900 years earlier, about 200 BC?

A study of Aztec accounts of Quetzalcoatl suggests that the term Quetzalcoatl was also given to other esteemed rulers both before and after the time of Lord Pacal. The Aztecs believed that Ce Acatl Topiltzin Quetzalcoatl (the man) was a 10th-century ruler in Tula, the Toltec capital (about 50 miles from today's Mexico City). Records say that after this 10th-century incarnation Quetzalcoatl would again return in the 16th century. The 10th-century leader was described as 'tall, fair-skinned, bearded' and renowned as a wise teacher who lived in a 'precious house of jadeite, silver, feathers and white and red shells'.

This all sounds familiar, like the tomb of Lord Pacal, the Quetzalcoatl of 700 AD: the Temple of Inscriptions contained the jade mask showing Lord Pacal as a feathered snake; the stone chest at the bottom of the stairs to 'his house' contained three red shells, and one white shell filled with a single pearl in a bed of 'quicksilver', the common name of mercury. The inside of the sarcophagus was similarly painted in quicksilver. Which suggests that either the historical accounts are confused or that Lord Pacal did in fact reincarnate again in Tula 250 years after he had died in Palenque.

This suggests that he could well have had an earlier incarnation at Teotihuacan and it was these earlier teachings which enabled that mighty city, with its advanced knowledge, to rise and flourish.

There are further connections that we can make between our four Supergods which distinguish them from other prophets and teachers. For example, Ce Acatl Topiltzin Quetzalcoatl, the 10th-century ruler, was the son of Chimalma. The decoded stories from the Mural of Bonampak tell us that Chimalma became pregnant by swallowing a jade bead which did not even touch the insides of her body. Like Mary, the mother of Jesus, no physical father was involved in the conception of Ce Acatl Topiltzin Quetzalcoatl – it was immaculate, miraculous. Do these accounts tell us that Lord Pacal, the earlier Quetzalcoatl, was conceived like Jesus 'miraculously'?

Examining the Super-four

The ancient Brahmin *Vedas* dating from 1,700 BC set down the creation of the universe and in so doing describe how Lord Krishna, the 'universal creator', visited earth at the battlefield in Kurukshetra (the exact date of the discourse between Krishna and Arjuna is unknown).

The Hindu poem the *Mahabarata* also confirms the identity of Krishna as the god Vishnu, one of the holy trinity of gods. Vishnu is said to have been reincarnated 10 times, the 9th as Siddattha, the Buddha, around 430 BC. The mother of Buddha was called Maya, illusion.

As we have seen, the 5,000-year cycle of the Hindu is made up of four equal periods of time which are watched over by Vishnu. In between cycles he rests between a serpent and the feathers of the Garuda bird. He will be reincarnated as the god Kalki, appearing on a white horse, at the end of the present age of Kali.

Both Krishna (Vishnu) and Buddha (Vishnu) performed miracles. Jesus performed miracles and was born through an immaculate conception. They say he was the son of God, the embodiment of God who preached love and purification through sacrifice. They say he was the King of the Jews. They say he will come again.

Buried beneath a pyramid in the jungles of Central America lie the bones of Lord Pacal, King of the Maya. He left us with living miracles which tell us that he gave life and took life away, that he was the feathered serpent who ruled the spirit and the flesh, that he died through sacrifice. They say he will come again.

The four Supergods all brought a common message, that mankind has been created in order to 'purify the spirit' and that failure to do so will result in reincarnation and suffering in future lives. They all believed in the *karmic* principle that all transgressions against our neighbour must be paid for in full. All debts must be repaid either in this life or the next. We cannot hurt others and hope to escape.

So we need to pause for a few moments, and ask, 'Is somebody trying to tell us something?'

The more closely we examine these four teachers the more consistently remarkable their teachings become.

FIG 57 SUPERGOD BELIEFS AND TEACHINGS

Teachings	Brahminism and Hinduism	Buddhism	Christianity	Pacalism (Quetzalcoatlism)
The Supergods	Lord Krishna c 1700 BC	Buddha 500 - 420 BC	Jesus 6 BC - 26 AD	Lord Pacal 703 - 743 AD
Embodiment of God the Creator?	Yes Eighth Incarnation of Vishnu ('Son' in Hindu Holy Trinity, 'Father, Son & Holy Ghost').	Yes Ninth Incarnation of Vishnu.	Yes Son of God in Holy Trinity.	Yes The Highest of Gods. Embodiment of Creator God.
Immaculate Conception?	Yes	Yes	Yes	Yes
Association with a star?	Yes At birth bright star appeared in heaven.	Yes Bright star in mother's womb.	Yes At birth bright star appeared in heaven.	Yes Known as Quetzalcoatl 'The Twin Star Venus', brightest star in the heavens.
Association with light?	Yes 'I am light' (Bhagava-geeta). Depicted surrounded by bright light.	Yes Teacher of Enlightenment; became the 'illuminated one'.	Yes God is Light (Bible). Depicted with halo of light.	Yes Known as the Sun-God in various guises.
Association with Bird or Snake?	Yes Associated with Garuda Bird, half man -half bird and Serpent of infinity, Ananta.	Yes Reached Enlightenment with help of Serpent Maculinda.	Yes Fall of mankind (Adam & Eve) due to temptation from serpent.	Yes Was Quetzalcoatl, the 'Feathered Snake'.
Association with names?	Yes 'Krishna' means 'Annointed one' in Sanskrit. Taught that this life is illusion.	Yes Buddha is the next incarnation of Krishna, 'The Annointed one'. Mother's name is MAYA.	Yes 'Christ' means 'Annointed one' (Baptised) in Greek.	Yes King of the Maya (illusion) taught that this life is illusion.
Performed Miracles?	Yes	Yes	Yes	Yes Maya Transformers are living miracles.
Similar teachings?	Yes	Yes	Yes	Yes
(Love & Service to Humanity. Self control. Duty. God. Karma. Spirituality of man. Qualities to be gained and overcome. Purification of the Soul comes through sacrifice. Immortality of the Soul).				
Was method of teaching subtle or secret? (for the few, not the many).	Yes By Parables and allegory (enabling pictures in the mind) for true believers, but out of sight for non-believers.	Yes By Parables and allegory.	Yes By Parables and allegory.	Yes By Maya Transformers (hidden pictures showing stories).

Teaching	Brahminism and Hinduism	Buddhism	Christianity	Pacalism (Quetzalcoatlism)
Prophecied destruction?	**Yes** At the end of the Iron Age c 2000 AD. Purified souls will return to Earth in the next Golden Age.	**Yes** Indirectly subscribed to Hindu belief of 4 ages of creation.	**Yes** The Apocalypse in Revelations. The first will be last and the last will be first. The meek will inherit the Earth. 144,000 would not suffer. These can be recognised by the number 144,000 written on their forehead.	**Yes** World destroyed in cycles. Next Age begins in 2012 AD. The number 144,000 appears on Lord Pacal's forehead in the decoded Transformer. The Maya numbering system breaks down after 144,000 has been reached.
Belief in Reincarnation?	**Yes** Eighth incarnation of Vishnu. Epitomised by pantheon of Gods that changed roles.	**Yes** Ninth incarnation of Vishnu.	**Yes** Recognised but not taught.	**Yes** Told of in the decoded Lid of Palenque. Epitomised by pantheon of Gods that changed roles.
Association with tree?	**Yes** Said to have died on a tree.	**Yes** Enlightenment came while sitting beneath Tree of Knowledge.	**Yes** Died on Cross with Crown of thorns.	**Yes** Cross is the central feature on Lid of Palenque. The Suckling Tree, said to have 100,000 nipples, grew in the Paradise of Tamoanchan 'home of our ancestors'. Dead babies could suckle the 'tree of life' and gain the strength to reincarnate.
Existence of destinations for the dead? (Afterlife)	**Yes** Perfectly purified souls return to the creator in heaven. Almost purified souls reincarnate to Earth, in the next Golden Age. Impure souls reincarnate during the next Iron Age (the Age of Hell on Earth).	**Yes** Purified souls become one with the force of creation that pervades the Universe. The alternative is reincarnation and suffering.	**Yes** Purified souls join God the Creator in Heaven. Speaks of Souls who have lived on Earth before (Elijah). Impure souls may suffer and repent sins in Purgatory (the place where sins are purged).	**Yes** Perfectly purified souls return to God. Others journey to the paradises via the underworld and Purgatory and then reincarnate on Earth.
Resurrection or prophecy of return?	**Yes** Said to have risen again after death on the tree. Will return again as the God Kalki at the end of the present age.	**Yes** Although no resurrection, same as Krishna who, as Vishnu, will reincarnate as Kalki.	**Yes** After 3 days reurned to life. Prophecied to 'come again'.	**Yes** Reincarnated as Ce Acatl Topiltzin Quetzalcoatl, tenth century ruler of Tula.

The Reconciliation

Krishna, Buddha, Jesus and Pacal have told us of another way, of an all-loving God, of a paradise which awaits us, of an everlasting life. They have demonstrated, through their miracles, a super intelligence which they bring with each incarnation, each visit to Earth. They have given us a spiritual insight and shown us that if we do not choose the difficult path then we will again experience pain and suffering on this Earth.

At the same time we have been told, and shown by the decoded works of the Maya, that the Earth is periodically destroyed and everything comes to nothing. We might choose not to believe in reincarnation and yet time after time we have been enlightened about its ways. Yet is there anything more extraordinary about being born twice than being born once?

What are we doing here? What is it all about? Clearly, we need to reconcile the physical world with the spiritual world which our four Supergods keep telling us about. On the one hand we have physical destruction and on the other spiritual redemption. If we are to find answers to these questions which have perplexed thinkers throughout the ages, we must firstly seek to reconcile these two worlds and we can begin by asking: why would an ostensibly benevolent creator of the universe choose to destroy it physically every few thousand years? What purpose could the recycling of souls possibly be meant to serve? Why live, age and die at all if we are only to return for repeat performances over and over again?

CHAPTER TEN

Life, Death
and the Universe

All of the world's religions describe the creator 'God', as 'light'. God could also be compared to electromagnetic energy, a source which manifests as 'light'. They also seem to agree that God is love and hence, presumably, more God is more love; which must by definition be 'more good'. And we are told that 'God made man in his own image'. Man can only 'grow' through 'sacrifice' – man must sacrifice a piece of himself, a sperm, and woman must likewise sacrifice an ovum, before they can multiply. Similarly, the apple tree must sacrifice an apple if a new tree is to grow.

The only known mechanism of growth in our universe is therefore, sacrifice. Could it be, quite simply, that God must sacrifice a piece of himself before he can grow? But God, is energy and as Albert Einstein reminds us, energy cannot be destroyed, it can only be converted from one state to another.

This relationship is contained in his famous equation $e=mC^2$, which means that energy (e) may be converted to mass (m) and mass (m) may be converted to energy (e).When mass is crushed it results in the release of a great deal of energy, which may be calculated in relation to the speed of light (C). So, when a heavyweight element like Uranium is crushed, it results in a very large explosion, an atomic explosion.

Similarly, energy, when compressed, can be converted into mass, at least in a mathematical sense, which suggests that in the beginning an energy source existed, some of it broke away, and was converted into mass to form the universe.

Earlier, our search for a mechanism that explained astrology led to the Astrogenetic Theory which showed that both bio-rhythms and fertility are controlled by radiation from the sun. Our research into sunspot activity provided a mechanism of catastrophe cycles and physical destruction and then the decoding of Maya numbers and the Amazing Lid of Palenque showed us that all this had not only been discovered by the Maya more than a thousand years ago, but that they also went to incredible lengths both to conceal and to convey the knowledge as though it were in some way secret, meant for the few and not the many. But more importantly, the Lid of Palenque tells the spiritual story of how the soul, through purification, can either become one with the creator, or return to Earth to be reincarnated.

In order to find answers to the meaning of life we need first to reconcile the physical with the spiritual. We see in the physical world periodic destruction and regeneration. We see in the spiritual world either a permanent resting place of the soul or reincarnation on Earth, the possibilities of which are governed by choice. We need to question why this state of affairs exists at all. Why the physical and why the spiritual? Why would any benevolent creator periodically destroy that which has been created? To answer this we return to the nature of the creator.

The original creator was 'energy', spoken of in many teachings as 'light', or God the creator, who is spoken of as representing universal goodness, or love. The only thing better than this God must by definition be 'more good'. The objective of the original creator therefore must be growth. We saw earlier, using the analogy of the apple tree giving up the apple, that the only known mechanism for growth is through sacrifice. Therefore, we must begin with the original creator at a point where he sacrifices himself:

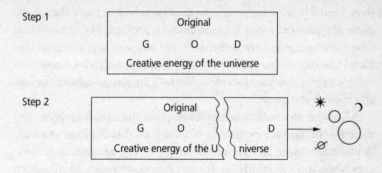

Fig 58

When the energy (e) shown on the right-hand side breaks away it is converted through the process known to modern scientists as 'The Big Bang' into mass (m), the physical universe. This includes everything from stars, planets, rocks, clouds etc., or as Albert Einstein expressed it: $e=mC^2$.

We now have on the one side creative energy and on the other side the physical universe, although no 'God growth' has been achieved, in fact, clearly, the size of the creative energy at this stage has diminished, but as we shall see this is only an intermediate temporary state of affairs which we accept as our model develops and becomes much more representative.

Because we now have a physical world we can recognize the concept of 'time'. With time we can recognize evolution. Through the process of evolution, chemical reactions take place on Earth whereby collections of living cells grow in complexity. These cells are capable of generating electrical charges, and as they become more and more complex so the electrical charges grow. In time the charges reach a level sufficient to attract and tear off another piece of creative energy. So as man evolves physically, at a given moment in the evolutionary process, he acquires a soul (*see Appendix four iii*).

Before we develop our model further, we need to note a distinction between the physical and metaphysical worlds. The rules of the physical world are quite simple: if I have £1 and you have £1 and we exchange them then I have £1 and you have £1. This seems to prove that in the physical world we cannot get something for nothing. The metaphysical world, though, is not the same: if I have one idea and you have one idea, I can give you my idea and you can give me your idea. I now have two ideas; you also have two ideas. We each are able to double our creative wealth at no cost.

All of the messianic teachers throughout the ages have promoted the ethos of 'love thy neighbour'. Could it be that if I love you I can double my 'voltage', my emotional energy? And might this creative energy when it is released from my decaying body, return to its source, thus satisfying the creator's objective of growth? This would reconcile the divine objective of growth with physical destruction and with the need to repatriate purified soul energy. Whenever physical destruction takes place, the purified souls would return to the creator. It thus makes sense to destroy the world periodically because the universal amount of love grows as a consequence. This is the Theory of Divine Reconciliation.

We have seen how physical destruction was accommodated through the sun's magnetic activity and now we must accommodate the notions of reincarnation on Earth that we learned from the Lid of Palenque. If loving purifies the soul then hating must damage the soul and this, within such a framework, must be avoided at all costs. Souls which have reduced their purity ('voltage') during their lifetimes must therefore be returned to Earth, upon 'death', for another try. But of course the reduced level of this purity must in the next incarnation attach to a physical body of a damaged or inferior kind (lower voltage). Hence the soul will suffer in the next life for the transgressions, the hate, in the former life. This notion of spiritual redemption fits in well with the notion of *karma*. These theories of Divine Reconciliation and Iterative Spiritual Redemption compare migration of the soul to that of a raindrop, which is born and perceived as an individual entity. Later it dies, and the raindrops coalesce into streams that become rivers that flow to the oceans, before rising again to fall as raindrops. In the spiritual world the soul energies have a choice either to purify themselves and grow and return to the creative energy or not to purify themselves and be reincarnated for a second try.

Theory of
Iterative Spiritual Redemption

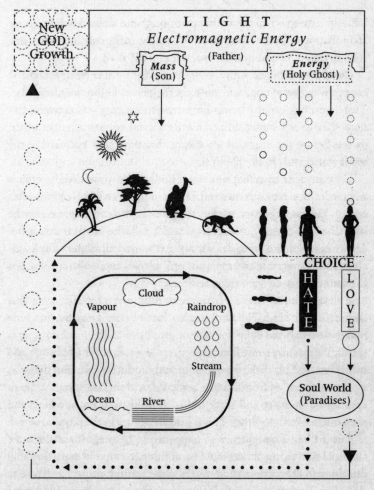

The journey of the Soul is analagous to that of a raindrop which is reborn many times. Purification comes through love and sacrifice. Purified souls return to the creator. As a result the creator grows. Bad Souls return to Earth, attempting purification once again.

Fig 59 Summary of soul theories.

TIME

Time speeds up when we are happy or busy and slows down when we are unhappy or bored, from which we might easily conclude that time is all in the mind and does not subsist in itself at all.

Clearly, time began with the Big Bang. Before this electromagnetic energy was everything, and nothing happened before anything else. There were no 'events'. It was only after the energy was converted to mass that 'things' appeared and events transpired, one after the other, or one before the other; which means that time does not exist in the spirit world, only in the physical.

Little surprise then that we cannot understand 'time' except perhaps when confronted by our own reflections in the mirror, which grow older with the passing years. We feel the same at 80 as we did at eight: the soul does not change...'weapons cleave it not, fire burns it not, water drenches it not and wind dries it not...It is eternal, all pervading, unchanging, immovable and most ancient' advises the *Bhagava Geeta*. For the soul there is no such thing as time.

And yet common sense tells us events must be arranged in a way that conforms with time. The mother gives birth to the daughter, and time makes sure that the daughter cannot give birth to the mother, or so it seems. We can take some flour, an egg, some water, sugar and butter and mix them together, bake for one hour and produce a cake. But the rules of time prevent us from placing some flour, alongside some sugar, an egg, a glass of water and some butter into the oven for one hour and then mixing them together. This is how things are in the physical world.

But if I had a daughter, who happened to be pregnant at the same time as I was 'dying' there would be nothing to stop my departing soul attaching to the foetus within my daughter's womb should it choose to do so. I would then be born as my daughter's son, she would be my mother. There is no limiting direction in the spirit world and this is what the Maya were trying to explain with their gods who begat their own grandmother (Coatlicue), and Quetzalcoatl, who was born of Ehecatl and his own son, along with many others.

We have seen how purified souls (who do not return to God) are reincarnated into a better body in the next life and they likewise benefit from 'time'; higher level soul energy appears capable of accelerating through the underworld during the afterlife to be reincarnated at an earlier time during the next 5,000-year cycle of creation. Instead of returning after 5,000 years to an Iron age, the age of hell on Earth, it could instead return after 3,750 years arriving in the next Copper age, or perhaps to the Silver or Golden ages. In the same way lower voltage souls would not only return to a defective body but would be reincarnated at a later moment in the cycle to suffer during a worse period during the evolutionary cycle.

This can be summarized using a model which shows the physical and spiritual sides of life (*see figure 60*):

On the left-hand side we note that periodic physical destruction is accommodated via pole-tilting mechanisms which provides a constant supply of bodies to which souls can attach and purify themselves. On the right-hand side the Theory of Iterative Spiritual Redemption reconciles the repatriation of souls to bodies and the notion of *karma*: accountability for past actions.

Perfectly purified souls return to God, the creative energy of the universe, fulfilling the requirements of Divine Reconciliation – the divine plan which allows God to grow.

Looking at existence in this way we are relieved of our intellectual anxieties. It is all quite straightforward: God is electromagnetic energy, the epitome of love; each of us is likewise a tiny piece of that creative energy. Providing we love each other the overall measure of universal love must grow and as it grows, it expands. We are born, we are purified, we die, and the universe expands. We are the universe. I am you and you are me. All we have to do is love God.

This enlightenment is supported by the *Popol Vuh* in its account of God's first few attempts to make man.

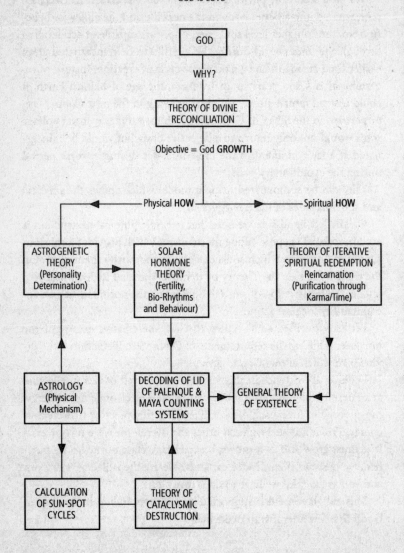

Fig 60 *A General Theory of Existence.*

The First Attempt

The first attempt at creating mankind fails and instead God makes only animals. The first forefathers after making the Earth said:

'Shall there be only silence and calm under the trees and vines? It is well that hereafter there be someone to guard them'. So they said when they meditated and talked. Promptly the deer and the birds were created. Immediately they gave homes to the deer and the birds. 'You deer shall sleep in the fields by the river bank and in the ravines. Here you will be amongst the thicket, amongst the pasture, in the woods, *you shall multiply*, you shall walk on four feet and they will support you. Thus be it done!' So it was they spoke.

Then they also assigned homes to the birds big and small. 'You shall live in the trees and the vines. There you shall make your nests; there you shall *multiply*; there you shall *increase* in the branches of the trees and the vines.' Thus the deer and the birds were told; they did their duty at once, and all sought their homes and their nests.

And the creation of all the four-footed animals and the birds being finished, they were told by the creator and the maker and the forefathers: 'Speak, cry, warble, call, speak, each one according to your variety, each, according to your kind.' So it was said to the deer, the birds, pumas, jaguars and serpents. '*Speak then our names, praise us your mother, your father…adore us*' they were told. [UOP pp.84,85]

But they could not make them speak like men. They only hissed and cackled.

When the creator saw that it was impossible for them to say their names they said, 'This is not well' and said 'because it is impossible for you to talk you will be changed. We have changed our minds: your food, your pasture, your homes, and your nests you shall have, they shall be the ravines and woods because it has not been possible for you *to adore us*…we shall make other beings.' In this way the animals were condemned to be killed and eaten.[p.85]

What we see here is that the founding fathers required the animals to do two things: (1) multiply and (2) praise them (love them). If either of these were missing then the requirements for Divine Reconciliation cannot be met. There must be a constant supply of bodies and purification of the spirit through love, otherwise the point of creation is lost.

The Second Attempt, Mud

For this reason another attempt had to be made to create and make men: 'Let us try again...*Let us make him who shall nourish and sustain us!* what shall we do to be invoked *to be remembered on Earth*? we have already tried with our first creations, our first creatures; but *we could not make them praise us* or venerate us. So then let us try to make obedient, respectful beings *who will nourish and sustain us...*

Then was the creation and the formation. Of mud they made [man's] flesh. But they saw that it was not good. It melted away, it was soft, did not move, had no strength, it fell down, it was limp, it could not move its head, its face fell to one side, its sight was blurred, it could not look behind. At first it spoke, but had no mind. Quickly it soaked in the water and could not stand.

And the creator and maker said 'Let us try again because our creatures *will not be able to walk or multiply*...What shall we do to perfect it, in order that our worshippers, our invokers, will be successful?' Then they spoke to the soothsayers saying 'You must work together and find the means so that man, whom we shall make, man, whom we are going to make, *will nourish and sustain us, invoke us and remember us!*'.[p.87]

Third Attempt, Wood

They try again and:

Instantly [the] figures were made out of wood. They looked like men, they talked like men, and populated the surface of the Earth. They existed and multiplied. They had daughters, they had sons, these wooden figures; *but they did not have souls, nor minds, they did not remember their creator, their maker*, they walked on all fours, aimlessly. *They no longer remembered the heart of heaven* and there-fore they fell out of favour. It was merely a trial, an attempt at man.

Fourth Attempt, Men

These are the names of the first four men that were created:

Sweet Laughing Jaguar
Night Jaguar
The 'Unbrushed' (Peaceful)
Moon Jaguar

They had no mother, they had no father. They were only 'called' men. They were not born of woman, nor were they begotten by the creator, nor by the maker, nor by the forefathers…*Only by a mira-cle*…were they made by the creator.[p.167]

And as they had the 'appearance' of men, they were men; they talked, conversed, saw and heard, walked, grasped things; they were good and handsome men, and their figure was the figure of a man.

They were endowed with intelligence; they saw and instantly they could see far, they succeeded in seeing, they succeeded in knowing all that there is in the world. When they looked instantly they saw all around them, and they contemplated in turn the arch of the heavens and the round face of the Earth.

The things hidden in the distance they saw all, without first having to move; at once they saw the world, and so, too, from where they were, they saw it.

Great was their wisdom, their sight reached to the forests, the rocks, the lakes, the seas, the mountains, and the valleys. In truth, they were admirable men [the first four]...

Immediately they began to see all that there is in the world. *Then they gave thanks to the creator and the maker, 'we really give you thanks two and three times! We have been created, we have been given a mouth and a face, we speak, we hear, we think and walk; we feel perfectly and we know what is far and what is near; we also see the large and the small in the sky and on the Earth. We give you thanks, then, for having created us, Oh creator and maker! For having given us being, Oh our grandmother, Oh our grandfather!' they said giving thanks for their creation and formation...they were able to know all, and they examined the four corners, the four points of the arch of the sky and the round face of the Earth...* [p.168]

At last the creator succeeds in making a creature that, on the face of it is capable of multiplying and who at the same time worships the creator, but it is not that simple:

But the creator and maker did not hear this with pleasure 'It is not well what our creatures, our works say; they know *all* the large and the small' they said. And so the forefathers held council again: 'What shall we do with them now? *Let their sight reach only to that which is near, let them see only a little of the face of the Earth!* It is not well what they see. Perchance are they not simple creatures of our making? *Must they also be gods? And if they do not reproduce and multiply when it will dawn, when the sun rises? And what if they do not multiply?* [p.169]

This is a very interesting turn-about by the creators. First of all they want intelligent beings that will multiply and praise them, but now they have created super-intelligent gods who *will not multiply.* Because they *'know all'* we must assume that these creatures understand how the universe works, about the general theory of creation (existence). And they *know* that any 'children' they produce will not be *their* children, but only reincarnated souls. Knowing this there will be no incentive to reproduce because in begetting children they are in fact not reproducing themselves at all, but simply reproducing others.

So the creators once again hold counsel:

'Let us check a little their desires, because it is not well what we see. Must they perchance be equals to ourselves, their makers, who can see afar, who know all?'...thus they spoke and immediately they changed the nature of the works, of the creatures.

Then the creator blew mist into their eyes, which clouded their sight as when a mirror is breathed upon. Their eyes were covered and they could see only what was close, only that was clear to them.

In this way the wisdom and all the knowledge of the original four men, the origin and beginning of the Quiche race was destroyed. In this way were created and formed our grandfathers, our fathers by the creator...[p.169]

It seems that what happened here was that the creator, God, blew mist (the solar wind) into the men's faces (their genes). This radiation clouded their eyes (caused genetic mutations – 12 types of personality), reducing their vision (intelligence) to a level which on the one hand accommodated reproduction as we know it today and yet on the other allowed for 'worship of the creator through individual choice'. The 12 types of personality <u>see</u> the world differently – some see far (intelligent) and some see only close (unintelligent).

And so today we reproduce and some choose to praise the maker and the universe expands, as it should.

Earlier, when discussing the *Popol Vuh* and the migration of the tribes, the passing-away of the first few fathers was mentioned briefly in regard to the encoding, 'wrapping up', of information into Maya Transformers. This farewell account, reproduced in more detail below also acknowledges the sacrifice of the first four in begetting children, in praising the creator:

And now we shall tell of the death of the first four (men): Sweet Laughing Jaguar, Night Jaguar, Peaceful, and Moon Jaguar, as they were called.

And as they had had a presentiment of this death they counselled their children. They were not ill, they had neither pain nor agony when they gave their advice to their children.[p.204]

They all had sons (except Moon Jaguar) *they were really the sacrificers*. So they bade their sons farewell. The four were together and they began to sing, feeling sad in their hearts; and their hearts wept and they sang Camucu, as the song is called which they sang when they bade farewell to their sons. 'Oh our sons! we are going away; our advice and wise counsel we leave you. And you also, who came from our distant country, oh our wives!' they said to their women, and bade farewell to each one. 'We are going back to our town, there already in his place is Our Lord of the Stags [Xipe Totec, god of Sacrifice] to be seen there in the sky. We are going to begin our return, we have completed our mission here, our days are ended. Think then of us, do not erase us from your memory, nor forget us. You shall see your homes and your mountains again, settle there and so let it be. Go on your way and you shall see again the place from which we came.'[pp.204.205]

These words they said, then Sweet Laughing Jaguar left the symbol of his being, 'This is a remembrance which I leave for you. This shall be your power. I take my leave filled with sorrow' he added. Then he left the symbol of his being, the *Pizon-Gagal* [*bundle of majesty*], as it was called, whose form was invisible *because it was wrapped up and could not be unwrapped; the seam did not show because it was* not *seen when they wrapped it up.*[p.205]

They were not buried by their wives nor by their children, because they were not seen when they disappeared. Only their leaving was seen clearly, and *therefore the bundle was very dear to them*. It was a reminder of their fathers and at once they burned incense before this reminder of their fathers.

…In this way the four died, our first grandfathers and fathers; in this way they disappeared, leaving their children on the mountain Hecavitz, there where they remained.

...They remembered their fathers; *great was the glory of the bundle to them. Never did they unwrap it. But it was always wrapped and with them.* Bundle of greatness they called it...which their fathers had left in their care as a symbol of their being...[p.206]

The *Popol Vuh* was hidden from the searcher and the thinker for 1,250 years.

The Message of the Maya

The decoded stories of the Maya Transformers tell us that Lord Pacal was a Supergod, with superhuman intellectual ability. He was the mind behind the legacy of the Maya. As Quetzalcoatl he taught his people the mathematics of astronomy spanning millions of years into the past and future. He explained the 'perfectness' of creation and in so doing explained the purpose of life.

Harnessing the skills of an indigenous Indian people he left, in the jungles of Central America, the messages of purification of the soul and of the reality of an everlasting life.

He taught the Maya mythology and created a pantheon of gods whose purpose was to come to life 1,250 years later, released after years of imprisonment in stone carvings, paintings, jewellery and architecture. In this, their final encore, they would provide 20th- century man with a mind-blowing performance, telling us that what they were revealing was of the utmost importance to us all.

This message was not aimed at the grave robber, or the ignorant, but at those who would in time understand the importance and influence of the sun in our lives – both this one and the next. Only by such a complex and dramatic encoding system could they hope to be taken seriously as they foresaw the intellectual and spiritual decline of man.

This is the way it had to be. The time has arrived when the knowledge had to be released as we approach the end of the present Iron Age of creation, 5,000 years since the same knowledge was given to Arjuna on the battlefield at Kurukshetra. Like the Maya, the *Vedas* tell of cycles of creation spanning millions of years into the past and future, of civilizations that arose and flourished, decayed and fell.

But it would be premature to congratulate ourselves, having decoded the secret knowledge of Lord Pacal. As we decoded the Maya Transformers we began to understand the 'rules' of the game of decoding. Progression from one level of decoding to a high level could only be resumed once all of the clues to each particular story were fully understood, reconciled and accounted for. Progress could not be made until the 'defects' encountered at each stage had been firstly identified, repaired and overcome.

The Transformers are telling us in the same way to examine ourselves. The way to success, to purification is therefore through self-examination of our own defects and weaknesses and failings. When these are successfully recognized, addressed and overcome then, as in the Buddha's parable of the hens, deliverance is bound to follow.

Now we are ready for the next step. First we decoded the amazing Lid of Palenque, understanding as we progressed that the Maya knew that five ages of creation exist within every cosmic cycle and that destruction of epochs is caused by geological catastrophe, as the Earth tilts on its axis in response to the sun's changing magnetic field, carrying quick-frozen mammoths to the poles.

The Maya worshipped the sun in the knowledge that it caused Venus to tilt on its axis in 3,113 BC, which they named the birth of Venus and began their own calendar.

They knew the sun brought infertility, leading to the rise and fall of civilizations on Earth. At the same time it was responsible for mini ice ages and drought to those, like themselves, in equatorial regions, as well as global glaciation.

They named their children after a recurring 'astrological cycle' based upon their sacred year, which we now know corresponds to a mutual cycle of magnetic activity on the sun.

Then Lord Pacal, using the Maya gods as actors in scenes on the Lid of Palenque, described the purpose of life on Earth; how he was able to purify his own soul to become Quetzalcoatl; and how the soul of man can return to the creator purified, or diminish and return to Earth for another try at purification through suffering. And he took us into the underworld and showed us what to expect, of Lord and Lady Death, of the goddess of Hearts who awaits us in purgatory. And he told us that it was the gravitational and magnetic pull of the planet Mercury upon the sun that caused the sun's magnetic idiosyncrasies.

Once the same decoding rules were applied to the Mosaic Mask we began to realize that not only was Lord Pacal very clever, but that he was very different. He gave life and took life away. He ruled the four corners of the sky, the heavens and as Quetzalcoatl the feathered snake he ruled the spirit and the flesh, like Krishna, Buddha and Christ before him. And as though they were comrades in arms, Pacal's appearance in the mask resembles a stained glass depiction of Christ, or of a peaceful Buddha. He bows to the audience, whom we can imagine applauding like the two stags in the story of Camaxtle, the god of Sacrifice in the Mural of Bonampak.

Look again at Lord Pacal bowing in the composite scene from the Mosaic Mask (*plate 35*). Now we are ready to begin another journey. When I slide my two Mosaic Mask acetates apart (*see Appendix nine*), two doors appear. This scene contains the instructions for opening the doors to a secret chamber which remains sealed to this day. We can only speculate as to what marvels await us behind the door.

Could this be the 'hall of mirrors' spoken of by mystics throughout the ages?

Given the Mayan obsession with time, could this secret chamber contain a 'time machine'? Could this machine take us on to the next step of understanding, enabling travel to another dimension?

Will the chamber contain the secrets of nature, of gravity and anti-gravity and in so doing explain how the ancients built their massive monuments with stones weighing hundreds of tons, without the use of the wheel?

The Supergods came on a mission to save mankind. We have revealed the messages they left for us and know now that we cannot afford to ignore them. But a wealth of super-knowledge still awaits us. This is only the beginning...

APPENDICES

The Solar System

I. The Sun

In my first book *Astrogenetics* I showed how the sun had two distinct magnetic fields. One extended between North Pole and South Pole, similar to that of the Earth (shown darker on Fig 62) and the other consists of four bubbles of magnetism equally spaced around the equatorial region.

The sun spins on its axis, like the Earth, but the sun takes 26 days to complete one rotation around the equatorial region. The polar regions move more slowly taking 37 days to complete one revolution. This is possible because the sun consists of super heated plasma, a kind of sticky gaseous substance. This anomalous relationship of movement between the sun's regions is known as the 'differential rotations of the sun's magnetic fields'.

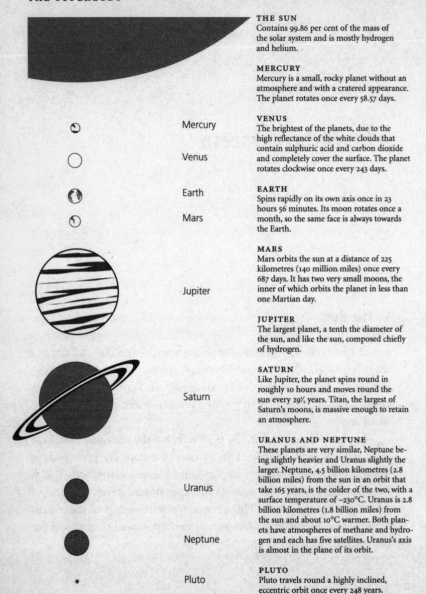

THE SUN
Contains 99.86 per cent of the mass of the solar system and is mostly hydrogen and helium.

MERCURY
Mercury is a small, rocky planet without an atmosphere and with a cratered appearance. The planet rotates once every 58.57 days.

VENUS
The brightest of the planets, due to the high reflectance of the white clouds that contain sulphuric acid and carbon dioxide and completely cover the surface. The planet rotates clockwise once every 243 days.

EARTH
Spins rapidly on its own axis once in 23 hours 56 minutes. Its moon rotates once a month, so the same face is always towards the Earth.

MARS
Mars orbits the sun at a distance of 225 kilometres (140 million miles) once every 687 days. It has two very small moons, the inner of which orbits the planet in less than one Martian day.

JUPITER
The largest planet, a tenth the diameter of the sun, and like the sun, composed chiefly of hydrogen.

SATURN
Like Jupiter, the planet spins round in roughly 10 hours and moves round the sun every 29½ years. Titan, the largest of Saturn's moons, is massive enough to retain an atmosphere.

URANUS AND NEPTUNE
These planets are very similar, Neptune being slightly heavier and Uranus slightly the larger. Neptune, 4.5 billion kilometres (2.8 billion miles) from the sun in an orbit that take 165 years, is the colder of the two, with a surface temperature of −230°C. Uranus is 2.8 billion kilometres (1.8 billion miles) from the sun and about 10°C warmer. Both planets have atmospheres of methane and hydrogen and each has five satellites. Uranus's axis is almost in the plane of its orbit.

PLUTO
Pluto travels round a highly inclined, eccentric orbit once every 248 years.

Fig 61 The motions of the planets, except Venus, are counter-clockwise.

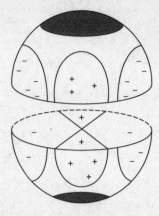

Fig 62 *Cross-sectional view of the equatorial region of the sun showing the idealised magnetic field distribution.*

The magnetic activity inside the sun results in the emission of charged particles from the sun's surface. These are negative from negative regions and positive from positive regions and are scattered like droplets from a water sprinkler throughout space. These scattering particles are known as the solar wind.

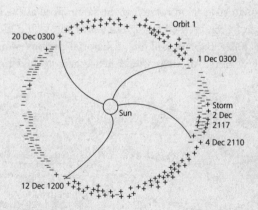

Fig 63 *The sectored structure of the solar wind as determined by interplanetary spacecraft (IMP 1 – Interplanetary Spacecraft No.1, 1963).*

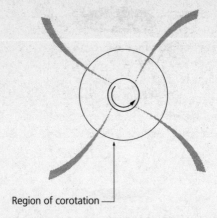

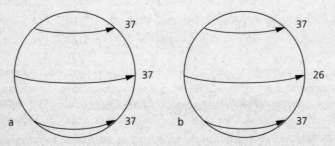

Region of corotation —

Fig 64 Solar wind. As the sun rotates, the particles of which the solar wind is composed fan out rather like droplets of water from a garden sprinkler: close to the sun, however (within the circumscribed region in the diagram), the sun's magnetic field is sufficiently strong to cause the particles to rotate with the sun as though they were rigidly attached.

Cause of the Differential Rotation of the Sun's Regions

If the equatorial region rotated at the same speed as the polar regions this could be represented by Fig 65a below and would mean that each day the polar regions and the equatorial regions would move by 9.729729 degrees. All areas would hence take 37 days to rotate once.

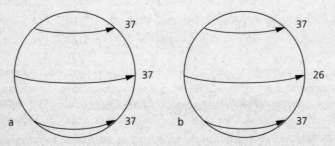

Fig 65

In reality the equatorial regions actually rotate every 26 days, amounting to 13.846 degrees per day – Fig 65b. The difference between the two true rotation periods amount to 4.116 degrees per day.

A Causal Agent

The equator of the sun lies at an angle of 7 degrees to the ecliptic, Fig 66a. The orbital inclination of Mercury also lies at 7 degrees, Fig 66b. The trajectory of Mercury is hence coincident with the solar equator, Fig 66c.

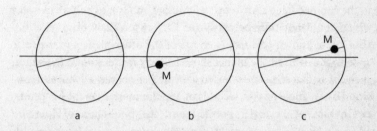

Fig 66

Mercury orbits the solar equator every 87.969 days. The daily movement of Mercury is hence 4.0923 degrees per day (4.1). This suggests that the gravitational and magnetic pull of Mercury travelling at 4.1 degrees a day drags the equatorial region of the sun by 4.1 degrees per day, such that the equatorial rotation amounts to 13.846 degrees per day instead of 9.729 degrees per day resulting in a 26-day rotational period for the equatorial regions *(see Note)*.

NOTE

A minor discrepancy exists here. The actual difference between 13.84615385 and 9.729729 degrees amounts to 4.116424846 degrees and not the 4.092350714 degrees movement of Mercury.

This means that the equatorial region excess of   4.116424846
is moving faster than the speed of Mercury at   <u>4.092350714</u>
The sun is hence moving   0.024074132
degrees per day <u>faster</u> than Mercury which seems to suggest that Mercury cannot be responsible for the increased speed of the equatorial region. But this minute error may be reconciled in the following paragraphs.

A similar problem to this (accountability of apparently excess velocity of motion) was examined by Albert Einstein concerning the fact that the perihelion (the closest approach of the planet Mercury) to the sun had been shown by U. Leverrier, in 1859, to behave in a way which could not fully be explained by Newton's law of gravitation. Due to the known perturbing effects of the other planets in the solar system, the orbit of the planet should slowly move around the sun in such a way that the closest approach (the perihelion) advances in position by an angle of 5557 seconds of angular measurement per century. In fact, as Leverrier pointed out, the perihelion of Mercury advances by an amount <u>greater</u> than the expected value by 43 seconds per century. Leverrier suggested that this discrepancy might be due to the presence of a hitherto unknown planet closer to the sun than Mercury. The puzzle was not resolved until Einstein published his *General Theory of Relativity* in 1915 (I.Nicolson, *Gravity, Black Holes and the Universe,* pp 80, 81).

Einstein showed that the excess rotation of Mercury's orbit was due to the variation in the mass of the electron as predicted in the special theory. Since Mercury travels in an elliptical orbit, its orbital velocity varies and hence its mass would vary, with its orbit being caused to rotate as a result. Einstein showed that this would account for the excess 43 seconds of movement per century.

Similarly, here I suggest that the <u>orbital</u> movement of Mercury increases the rotational speed of the sun's equatorial region. But Mercury <u>also spins</u> on its own axis. This axial rotation adds to the orbital influence to account for the missing 0.02407 degrees of movement per day.

II Effect of the Differentially Rotating Magnetic Fields

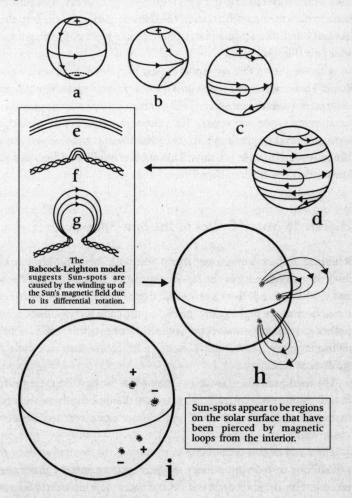

The **Babcock-Leighton model** suggests Sun-spots are caused by the winding up of the Sun's magnetic field due to its differential rotation.

Sun-spots appear to be regions on the solar surface that have been pierced by magnetic loops from the interior.

Fig 67 Babcock-Leighton model
According to this model the basic mechanism responsible for sun-spot activity is the winding up of the solar magnetic field by the sun's differential rotation.

The equatorial region rotates more quickly than the polar (Dipole) region. The polar field slowly becomes wound up to form torroidal field which varies in strength with latitude (Figs 67 a, b, c, d), below the sun's surface the magnetic lines of force get tangled up by the turbulent gas and burst through the photosphere (Figs 67 e, f, g) forming a sunspot pair (Figs 67 h, i).

It can be shown that sun-spots appear in cycles of 11.49 years on average. These cycles are carried on top of a 187-year cycle. The 187-year cycle causes the sun's magnetic field to reverse either after 3,553 years or 3,740 years (1,366,040 days). The Maya monitored this period of 1,366,040 days (3,740 years) using the planet Venus. 2,340 revolutions of Venus amount to 1,366,560 days. This magical number of the Maya was known the 'The Birth of Venus'.

III The 96 Micro Cycles of the Sun-Spot Cycle

Referring to the hypothesized 11.4929 year wave form (broken line below): at the beginning of the 187-year sun-spot cycle P (the sun's pole) and E (the sun's equator) and W (the Earth) and the hypothesized cycle all commence together. By the end of the cycle we note that the hypothesized fundamental cycle completes one whole cycle 8 time divisions before P and E and W again recommence their new cycle after division 781.

The final fundamental cycle contained in the first 187 cycle finishes 8 divisions earlier (division 773), than the new fundamental cycle that commences when P and E and W once again synchronize at division 781.

The effect of this is the same as imagining the neutral warp of the sun shifting by 8 divisions every 187-year cycle against the fundamental cycle. Fundamental cycle and neutral sheet cycle intersections hence also shift by 8 divisions as the neutral sheet scans through the 97 micro-cycle sequence, this results in an 18,139-year cycle.

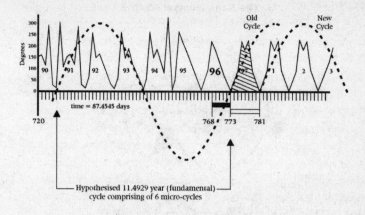

Fig 68 Hypothesized 11.4929-year cycle comprising of 6 micro-cycles.
The black horizontal bar shows the end of the 187-year cycle (96 micro-cycles) shunted forward by 5 divisions from 768 to 773. 8 more divisions separate the old fundamental, (white space bar) from the new fundamental.

IV The Sun's Neutral Warp

Normally the sun's poles are of equal and opposite polarity and the area around the equator would be expected to be neutral magnetic force. However, the differential magnetic fields distort this area such that a tilted and warped 'neutral sheet' is established (Fig 69a).

The Sun's Neutral Warp
and the five Temple Doorways

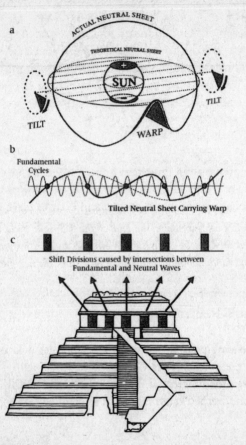

Fig 69a) Neutral warp

Neutral sheet.

Fig 69b) Fundamental cycles: 11.49-year cycles are 'carried' upon the tilted neutral sheet.

Fig 69c) Intersections between neutral sheet and fundamental cycles results in shift divisions.

Fig 69d) Temple of Inscriptions showing correspondence between neutral sheet and fundamental cycle intersections and Temple doorways.

V The Meaning of the Steps of the Pyramid

The five levels of stairs amounted to 9 steps from the ground level, 19 from the first level, 19 from the second level, 13 from the third level and lastly 9 steps leading to the temple at the highest level.

The 9s were reconciled as factors of the matrix. The total number of steps, 69, was reconciled as an anagram of the 96 micro-cycles of the sun-spot cycle.

But what about the 19,19 and 13 arrays? Why not 20, 18 and 13, or some other number which adds up to 69?

As we approach and climb the steps to the temple, we are unaware of the secrets of the pyramid. At this stage all we know is that the Maya used cycles of 144,000, 7,200, 360, 20 and 1 day to mark time, counted forward from 3,113 BC (the birth of Venus) and that such cycles were used to record dates carved into monuments. We also know they used a 'yearly' calendar which contained 260 days and that this had astrological significance. We also know that they 'worshipped' the number 9.

Setting down the cycles:

| 144,000 | 7,200 | 360 | 20 | 1 |

and the
stair levels

| 9 | 19 | 19 | 13 | 9 |

$9 \times 144{,}000 + 19 \times 7{,}200 + 19 \times 360 + 13 \times 20 + 9 \times 1 = 1{,}439{,}909$ days

Fig 70

The 5 arrays of stairs hence represent a date which adds to 1,439,909 days. This is 3,999.747222 cycles of 360.

Examining first the decimal:

$.747222 \times 360 = 268.9999$

The recurring 9999 is an invitation to 'round up' this number to 269, i.e. 260 and 9. The message here is to break the code of the numbering system, insert 260 into the cycle sequence and construct a matrix of 9 levels. This is of course what we have done and this throws up the birth of Venus number.

Next, returning to 3,9999.747222: we were invited to 'round up' the decimal part of the number and this leaves 3,999. Again we are invited to round up this number = 4,000. This confirms that the Maya understood decimals but preferred not to use them. Similarly, 4,000, i.e. the rounded-up figure × 360 actually equals 1,440,000, ten times the 144,000-day cycle period. This provides more evidence to suggest an understanding of a 10-based decimal system.

Conclusion: the number of steps on the outside of the pyramid represents a date which when rationalized tells us how to break the numbering system by insertion of 260 into the cycle sequence and by constructing a 9-level matrix. The matrix throws up the super-number of 1,366,560 days, the sun-spot cycle duration. To assist in matrix construction, the 9 levels of the matrix, 11111, 22222, etc are contained in arrays of clues in the pyramid inscriptions.

The Maya also used a base numbering system of 360 because they were concerned with angular movements of the planets and magnetic fields of the sun. The stairways date of 9,19,19,13,9 confirms their understanding of decimals and degrees, supporting similar conclusions reached in *The Mayan Prophecies* where it was also shown that the numbering system breaks down after 144,000 has been reached. This further places emphasis on the number 144,000, another clue to help us understand the life of Lord Pacal.

How the Sun's Reversing Magnetic Field Causes Catastrophes

I. Pole-Shifting and Polar Wander

The sun's field can be shown to reverse five times every 18,139 years. As the field swings from one direction to the other it tends to twist the Earth's crust around its axis. The event is recorded in the reversed magnetic field contained in surface rocks. Destructive influences hence act upon the Earth five times every 18,139-year cycle. In a worst case scenario the whole planet may shift, resulting in cataclysmic destruction, but this would not be magnetically recorded in the surface rocks.

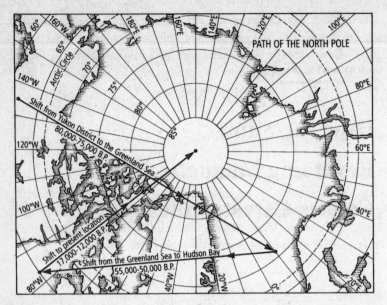

Fig 71 *The path of the north pole according to Charles Hapgood. BP means 'before present'.*

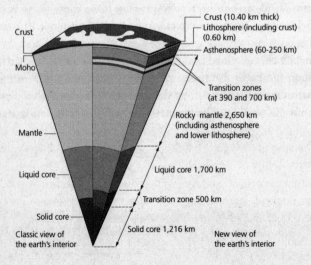

Crust (10.40 km thick)
Lithosphere (including crust) (0.60 km)
Asthenosphere (60-250 km)

Crust

Moho

Transition zones (at 390 and 700 km)

Rocky mantle 2,650 km (including asthenosphere and lower lithosphere)

Mantle

Liquid core 1,700 km

Liquid core

Transition zone 500 km

Solid core

Solid core 1,216 km

Classic view of the earth's interior

New view of the earth's interior

Fig 72

Charles Hapgood's theory suggests that the Earth's crust is free to wander and that this has resulted in shifting of the Earth's crust and polar wander at many times in the past. Such movements are enabled by a special 'wave guide layer' of 'lubricating' rock, within the asthenosphere that facilitates movement.

II Increased Infant Mutation

When the sun's magnetic field changes the Earth's magnetic field changes. At such time the magnetosphere (the Earth's protective cover) diminishes and more harmful ionising radiations are able to enter the Earth's atmosphere. These cause genetic mutations in newly born infants which leads to a higher infant mortality rate.

III Mini Ice-Ages and Drought

Sun-spot minimums bring cooler temperatures to Earth which result in mini ice ages. This results in less evaporation of water from the oceans and leads to drought. Areas of marginal rainfall, for example the home of the Maya, suffer disproportionately, leading to crop failures.

See the following graph which shows records of Solar Activity: The top curve represents the relative abundance of carbon 14 to carbon 12 in the growth rings of the Bristlecone pines. Increases in the proportion of carbon 14 are plotted as downward shifts in the curve and represent supposed decreases in solar activity. The curve here has been smoothed out to produce a long-term 'envelope' of a possible sun-spot cycle – the limits of successive maxima and minima. The remaining curves are estimates of past climate based on the mean winter temperature in England, a winter severity index for the Paris–London area, and the retreat and advance of Alpine glaciers.

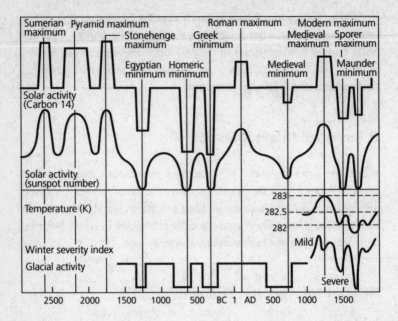

Fig 73

How the Sun Affects Personality

The particles of which the solar wind comprises travel to Earth and result in magnetic modulations of the atmosphere. These magnetic modulations result in genetic mutation at the time of conception. Personality is hence determined by astronomical influences; more commonly referred to as sun-sign astrology. These modulations can be seen to correlate to a 260-day solar cycle.

Solar radiations affect behaviour, through bio-rhythm regulation, from the moment of birth onwards. The Maya sacred year length was 260 days long. Each day in this recurring cycle of time had a ritual or astrological significance. Each day was either lucky or unlucky. Children were named in relation to the day they were born.

Planetary configurations can introduce variations to personality at conception and variations in behaviour after birth. The Maya followed the movements of the planets to compile astrological forecasts.

Determination of personality

The astrogenetic theory

This suggests that personality is a function of genetic mutations caused by modulated magnetic fields acting upon the foetus (egg/zygote) at conception. These modulations are in turn caused by solar particle interaction with the earth.

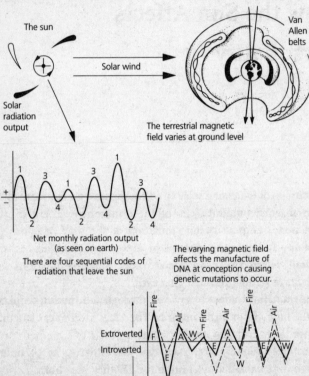

Charged solar wind particles enter the Van Allen belts, spiral from North Pole to South Pole

The sun

Solar wind

Van Allen belts

Solar radiation output

The terrestrial magnetic field varies at ground level

Net monthly radiation output (as seen on earth)

There are four sequential codes of radiation that leave the sun

The varying magnetic field affects the manufacture of DNA at conception causing genetic mutations to occur.

Extroverted

Introverted

Sun-signs and extroversion/introversion tendencies: Genetic mutations lead to variations in personality. The above graphs are the result of two studies undertaken by Jeff Mayo and the Institute of Psychiatry, under the aegis of Prof. Hans Eysenk. On the basis of 2 studies of 1795 subjects (solid line) and 2324 subjects (broken line) it can be seen that the positive signs are predominantly extroverted and the altering negative signs are predominantly introverted.

Fig 74

How the Sun Affects
Fertility

The rotating sun showers the Earth with particles every 28 days. These have been shown to affect the follicle stimulating hormone FSH which in turn regulates menstruation and fertility on Earth. Magnetic perturbations can be seen to follow the sun-spot cycle and hence the rise and fall of civilizations can be seen to reflect sun-spot activity.

The Maya worshipped the sun as the god of Fertility. They understood the cause of fertility cycles. They knew that their own civilization would decline through a disruption in fertility hormones caused by a disruption in solar radiations.

The solar hormone theory

This suggests that the human organism is bio-regulated by solar particle induced magnetic modulations after conception. Changes in melatonin affect bio-rhythms. Changes in oestrogen and progesterone affect fertility.

Charged solar wind particles enter the Van Allen belts, spiral from North Pole to South Pole

The sun

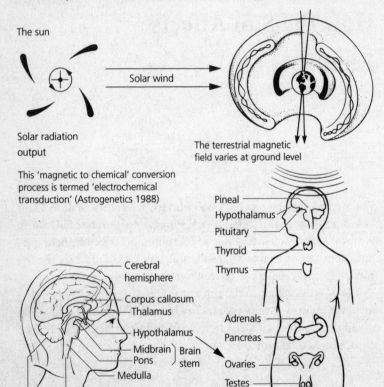

Solar wind

Solar radiation output

The terrestrial magnetic field varies at ground level

This 'magnetic to chemical' conversion process is termed 'electrochemical transduction' (Astrogenetics 1988)

Pineal

Hypothalamus

Pituitary

Thyroid

Thymus

Cerebral hemisphere

Corpus callosum

Thalamus

Hypothalamus

Midbrain ⎫ Brain
Pons ⎬ stem

Medulla

Spinal cord

Cerebellum

Adrenals

Pancreas

Ovaries

Testes

The pineal gland converts magnetic fields into the bio-rhythm hormone melatonin.
The pituitary and hypothalamus affect the manufacture and release of fertility hormones oestrogen and progesterone.

Fig 75

Some Common Questions on Fertility and the Sun

Q. If the sun's magnetic fields shower the same radiation upon all women at the same time, why don't all women menstruate at the same time?

A. The top circle on the diagram below represents the 28-day cycle of the sun and this is shown analogously, as the roof of a fairground carousel.

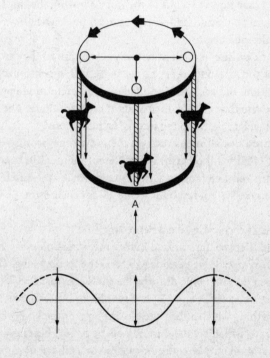

Fig 76 Here a fairground carousel is used to illustrate the principle of 'asynchronous synchronicity'.

Imagine that for every revolution of the carousel the horses and riders rise to the top and then descend to the floor once. Each passenger queues to alight the carousel at point 'A'. One passenger mounts the horse and the carousel moves forward slightly. The first passenger begins to rise off the floor of the carousel. The second passenger can now alight the carousel as the second horse has now descended to the floor. Once mounted the carousel moves forward again. The first two passengers rise higher up their respective poles. The third horse now descends to the floor allowing the third passenger to mount the horse, and so on, until all passengers have mounted. Then the ride begins.

All the riders rise and fall once every revolution of the carousel (in the case of the sun, once every 28 days). Each is 'synchronized' to the sun's radiation. But each rises and falls at a different moment in time. This is because they all took their seats at different times. The rise and fall of each rider relative to the next is 'asynchronous'.

Women do not all menstruate at the same time because each was conceived (alighted the Earth) at a different moment in time. Hence bio-rhythms (and endocrine activity) commence at a different time. Each endocrine system responds to the 28-day solar cycle.

Q. Why isn't each cycle 28 days exactly?
A. **a.** The effect of the sun is to induce menstruation every 28 days on *average*. Some periods will hence be 28 days long. Others, when the sun's pole disturbs the sun's equatorial region, will vary between 24 and 32 (28 days plus or minus 4 days).
   b. Anything which affects the bio-rhythm, or the body's metabolic rate, will affect the duration of the cycle. These agents could be stimulants like coffee or tobacco or artificial hormones oestrogen, progesterone, or anything which interferes with the bio-rhythmic signal from the sun, like overhead power cables or other electro-magnetic interference (described later).

   A news report of just such a case follows. The experiment involved placing a female deep underground to observe the effects on her behaviour. Once shielded from the sun's radiation her bio-rhythms became disturbed and her menstrual cycle stopped.

Stefania Follini, an Italian interior designer, emerged from isolation last week after four months in a cave in New Mexico. Italian scientists watched how she responded to the isolation because of its implications for space travel. Her waking days lasted 35 hours and were punctuated by sleeping periods of up to 10 hours. She lost 17 pounds and her menstrual cycle stopped. Follini believed she had spent two months underground, not four. (New Scientist, June 1989).

This has far reaching implications. If the human reproductive system is rendered ineffective, underground, then perhaps the same applies to that of other species and to infections and viruses. This is not conjecture. A link has already been shown between the flu virus and sun-spots illustrated below:

VIRUS:

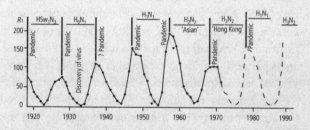

Yearly means of daily sun-spot relative numbers compared with dates of influenza pandemics. The record up to 1971 is from Hope-Simpson; the dashed curve shows the situation for the period 1971-89.

Fig 77 A remarkable coincidence exists between peaks in the 11.5 year sun-spot curve, when solar activity is at a maximum, and the occurrence of influenza pandemics associated with antigenic shifts of the virus. (Nature Magazine, 275.86, 1978, R. E. Hope Simpson).

Sun-spot maximum	Date of pandemic
1761	1761–62
1767	1767
1778	1775–76
	1781–82
1787	1788–89
1804	1800–02
1830	1830–33
1837	1836–37
1848	1847–48
	1850–51
1860	1857–58
1870	1873–75
1893	1889–90

Fig 8

And it does not end there: another report published on 3 July 1991 (*Daily Telegraph*) reported a direct link between schizophrenia and influenza. Professor Robin Murray of the London Institute of Psychiatry said his research 'showed that there was an 88 per cent increase in the number of babies, who later developed schizophrenia, born in England in the spring of 1958 following the massive sun-spot maximum which occurred in the summer of 1957. The correlation is conclusive over the period studied, from 1939 onwards ...'

Clearly, it is not the influenza which is causing schizophrenia, it is sun-spot activity. This is a little understood hormonal disease of the brain which results in mental disturbance. The sun's magnetic bursts adversely affect the hormones controlling the brain and this results in hormonal imbalance.

Seven years ago, I undertook some research with a friend, a community psychiatric nurse, to establish whether or not a link could be found between the sun-spot cycle and the administration of drugs that control the illness. This friend is now a director of the National Schizophrenic Fellowship, in the North of England. Patients who were depressed were prescribed anti-depressants. Hyper-active patients were prescribed tranquillizers. By comparing the administration of 'uppers' and 'downers' to peaks and troughs in the sun-spot cycle we hoped to prove a link between the two. Unfortunately the research became increasingly involved and impossible to complete. It was difficult, on a self-funding basis, to acquire consistent patient data and control conditions. Some were male, some female. Some menstruating females, some menopausal females, some patients went on holiday, some died, others left half way through. Regrettably the research was never finished due to lack of time and funding.

But the evidence from Hope Simpson and Robin Murray suggests that schizophrenia is indeed caused by solar activity. Removal of the radiation may therefore provide comfort to sufferers.

This also brings sense to the biblical phrase in respect to Armageddon, 'the first shall be last and the last shall be first', which seems to suggest that when catastrophic destruction frequents the Earth not only will the poles shift, and fertility decline but as the magnetic field swings, the sane will become mad as the mad become sane.

c. Females radiate hormones as a natural bodily emission. These radiated emissions, if stronger than the sun's radiation will cause females in close proximity to synchronize periods for as long as the interference continues.

I. How the Sun affects Bio-Rhythms

We have seen how the sun's codes of radiation result in the four types of astrological personalities. Once born, these infants will grow and respond positively to radiation patterns instrumental in their creation, and adversely to other radiation patterns. On good radiation days they will be more alert and responsive and on bad radiation days sluggish and more accident prone as the sun's radiation affects the operating performance of the brain.

In 1967 biologist Janet Harker undertook experiments on cockroaches to ascertain which part of the brain was responsible for awakening the cockroaches at midnight and sending them to sleep at 6am. Using an electron microscope she was able to locate the areas of the cockroaches' brain responsible for time referral. When she removed this part of the brain the cockroaches lost all sense of time and stayed awake continuously until they died. To make sure that this part of the brain was indeed the 'clock' she swapped the same parts of the brain between an Australian cockroach and a British cockroach. The two adopted the previous rhythms of the other: the British cockroach went to sleep at midnight and woke again at 6am proving that the clock was 'ticking away' after the transplant.

In a scientific paper published in 1987 entitled 'Cell membranes, Electromagnetic fields and Intercellular Communication', Dr Ross Aidey of Loma Linda Hospital, California, confirmed that modulating magnetic fields significantly affect the manufacture of Melatonin, the timing hormone produced by the pineal gland in rats, guinea pigs and pigeons, and hence bio-rhythms:

> About 20 per cent of pineal cells in pigeons, guinea pigs and rats, respond to changes in both intensity and direction of the Earth's magnetic field (Semm, 1983). Experimental inversion of the horizontal component of the Earth's magnetic field significantly decreases the synthesis and secretion of the peptide hormone melatonin, which powerfully influences circadian rhythms and also reduces activity in its synthesizing enzymes (Walker et al 1983).

By 'modulating magnetic fields' he was referring to two separate fields where one was constant, as is the case with the Earth's fields, plus another which was alternating, like the sun's fields. This of course means that neural activity, melatonin and bio-rhythms are affected by not only the sun's radiation but also the Earth's magnetic field, the longitudal and latitudal position of the subject on the Earth's surface. When removed from our place of birth the endocrine system detects magnetic changes resulting in a release of hormones.

The organism will always feel more comfortable at the place it was conceived and less comfortable when removed from this place over the Earth's surface. Thus, 'home sickness' is a real biochemical response to shifting magnetic patterns. Similarly 'jet lag' is a biochemical response to a magnetic shift acting upon the pineal gland. This is how racing pigeons 'find their way home' – once released they simply circle twice overhead, to find which position feels most comfortable; they then fly off in that direction, zig-zagging, sensing the magnetic field as they go, following the most comfortable route home, to where they were conceived. (The pigeon appears to have an 'erasable programmable memory', that is, if kept in a particular geographical location for long enough the new magnetic field wipes out the old one. The pigeon from that time on will return to the new home. This process is termed as 'homing', hence the expression 'homing pigeon'.)

II How the Sun Causes Cancer

Janet Harker continued with her experiments on cockroaches. She implanted one cockroach with two clocks, an Australian clock in addition to the British clock. The cockroach developed cancer every time the experiment was carried out, and died. This suggests that cancer is connected to desynchronization of the body with its clock. The clock is located in the sun and the sun regulates through magnetic modulations release of hormones which in turn affect the metabolic rate of the organism. We can examine this process using the diagram below:

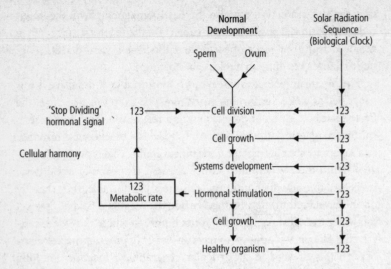

Fig 79

There are four codes of radiation from the sun: 234, 134, 124, 123. Consider an organism regulated by a 123 code. The 123 radiation generates a 123 magnetic modulation which flows across the pineal gland. The pineal and other glands release hormones into the body triggering cell division in the healthy organism. Cells divide and grow. Systems develop and the body grows. The metabolic rate adopts the periodicity of the clock, 123. The healthy system sends a 'stop' signal back to the body cells. The cells stop dividing. The organism is healthy.

Fig 80 shows an unhealthy situation. Here again the sun's signal is received by the brain and converted into hormones. Cells divide and systems develop. The metabolic rate adjusts, attempting to send a stop signal, once enough cells have been produced. But the metabolic rate is disturbed by an outside 'carcinogen', for example coffee, or tobacco (or the hormonal system is disturbed by artificial hormones, oestrogen or progesterone). The two comparator clocks can now never agree. One is counting 123, from the sun, the other, artificially stimulated, is counting, say, 134. The two will never agree and the stop signal will never be sent to stop cells dividing. Cells divide over and over

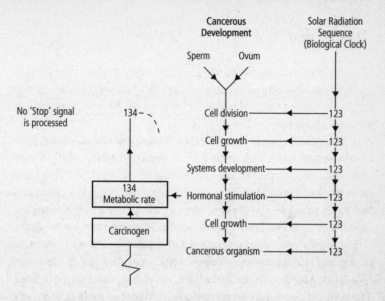

Fig 80

and over. This is cancer. Put two clocks in one body and, like Harker's cockroaches, the result is chaos.

In other cases it could be, of course, that no carcinogens are involved in the desynchronizing process. If the sun's magnetic signal, or that of the Earth is 'blocked' then again the two clocks can never achieve parity and the stop signal cannot be sent to cease cell division. It is in this way that power lines cause cancer, by blocking out the essential bio-rhythm signal from the sun.

It comes as no surprise to discover that one modern treatment of cancer, chemotherapy, is only 25 per cent effective, 1 in 4. If the treatment were scheduled to coincide with bio-rhythms then the success rate would rise to perhaps 100 per cent by matching the treatment to the correct code, 123, 124, 134 or 234.

III Body and Soul

Many believe that the Earth was created from a molten mass of dust and solar genes some 4 billion years ago. Slowly, over a period of several thousands of years, the planet cooled as the heavier elements like iron and nickel sank to the core.

A thin crust began to form over the surface and clouds of methane, ammonia and water vapour formed in the atmosphere which cooled and condensed, further increasing the rate of cooling. Ultra violet rays from the sun bombarded these gases causing them to break down into hydrogen, nitrogen and carbon. Most of the lighter gas, hydrogen, escaped, leaving behind nitrogen and carbon dioxide, the food of plants.

Life began with simple single-celled algae followed by plants that took in carbon dioxide and released oxygen, enabling the development of jellyfish, sponges, crinoids, sea lilies, bi-valve molluscs and trilobites. These were followed by armoured fish around 440 million years ago.

As volcanic activity and earthquakes forced mountains from the sea floor, marine life crawled on to land to join the already established giant dragon flies. Reptiles developed from amphibians and the dinosaur flourished from around 250 until 80 million years ago.

Biologist Charles Darwin was one of the first to describe the evolutionary process as one of natural selection, whereby the most capable flourish at the expense of the weak. Later it was determined that genetic mutations, engendered by selective breeding, was the facilitating prime mover in the selection process, although genetic mutations are also known to be caused through the action of ionizing radiations, x-rays and gamma rays which are either man-made or come from the sun.

When rays pass through matter, atoms in their path become excited in sympathy with the radiation frequency. Electrons within atoms may be so disturbed as to eject from a normally stable orbit leaving behind an ionized atom. Such atoms are known to be extremely chemically reactive causing increased enzyme activity capable of slicing sections of DNA, the building blocks of life, and hence causing genetic mutations to occur.

Similarly, magnetic fields are known to cause mutations in human cells caused fibroblasts, by affecting the manufacture of developing DNA in tissue.

Ionizing radiations and magnetic radiations from solar flares on the sun's surface and other sources have acted upon developing genera causing mutational 'leaps' in species.

Darwin would have us believe that giraffes with long necks developed from the horse and that giraffes with the longest necks had a better chance of survival that ones with shorter necks. The longer-necked giraffe had access to more leaves at the tops of trees, whereas the shorter-necked version competed more fiercely for lower leaves. As a result, giraffes with longer necks survived to interbreed, producing a new generation of long-necked giraffes.

But this does not answer the question why, if as Darwin suggests the giraffe evolved from the horse, no giraffe bones from evolving giraffes with medium-sized necks have ever been found. This seems to suggest that quantum mutation from ionizing radiations was the mutational agent. This reasoning may likewise answer the gaps in our own understanding about the ascent of man from the ape family and further explain why so many species of man exist: caucasian, negro, oriental etc., each having been mutated by different sources and levels of ionizing radiations. Moreover, it explains why apes still exist, because those apes were not ionized, a point which Darwin conveniently overlooked.

The placing of man at the highest point of creature evolution is not because man is the largest creature on Earth – he is not. Nor is it because he is more numerous than any other. The criterion used is that of intellectual ability. The intellectual nucleus in man is centred in the brain and the brain through electrical activity sends signals around the body to control the functions of organs which support the physical systems and infrastructure.

Clearly the intellectual activity of a single-celled algae, like the amoeba, is limited to chemical activity within the single cell and is negligible. As organisms grow in complexity, so the demand for electrical activity increases; animals which are mobile require muscle control for power and neuron systems to send signals up nerve pathways to the brain, which computes positions of muscles in relation to each other and to the environment as well as the amount of force required for any particular operation. Tiny chemical batteries in neurons send signals of sense, pleasure and pain to the central computer and these signals are processed. So the processing capacity of the brain grows with the complexity of the organism.

At a certain point during the evolutionary process, the voltage of the human brain must have grown to exceed that of the intrinsic magnetic field of the Earth and that of electrical activity caused by the interaction of the solar wind with the Earth. It seems that this small but growing voltage became capable of attracting electrical energy equal to, and of opposite charge to, itself from a place beyond the Earth's atmosphere.

If God is electromagnetic energy, then the growing voltage generated within the biological brain of man developed a propensity to 'tear off' a piece of this energy sufficiently to neutralize the charge between the physical body and the extra-terrestrial electromagnetic body of energy. It is at this point in the evolutionary process that man can be described as having acquired a 'soul', a piece of Godly energy.

This may explain why some lesser developed creatures are thought not to have souls.

How the Sun's Radiation Caused the Decline of the Maya

The Maya disappeared 1,366,040 days after their calendar began. The sun's magnetic field reversed in 3,113 BC and again in 627 AD leading to an increase in radiation levels entering the Earth's atmosphere. This led to infant mutation and higher infant mortality. At the same time a sunspot minimum ensued, leading to infertility and a reduced birth rate. Simultaneously a mini ice age ensued leading to drought and crop failure over Maya land. By 750 AD the Maya had succumbed to the cycles of heaven, (*see Fig 81 overleaf*).

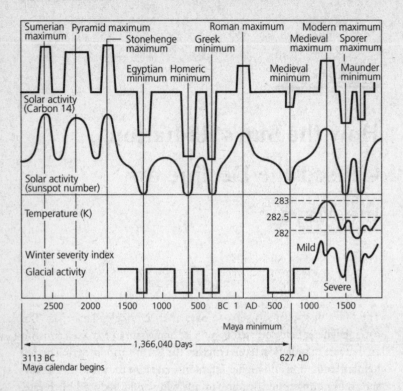

Fig 81

Why the Maya Used
Cycles of Time

The scientific understanding of the Maya is restated in their use of numbers to measure time. Numbers can be used to convey messages, once the coded system of communication is broken: the use of the 260-day astrological cycle conveys the messages that the Maya understood the dynamics of the sun's rotation and that the sun's radiation affects behaviour and fortune on Earth.

The 1,366,560-day cycle of destruction was known as the Birth of Venus (Venus was used to keep track of the accumulation of days). Venus is also the only planet which is 'upside down' – it rotates backwards suggesting that it has tilted on its axis, or that it did tilt on its axis 1,366,560 days ago (before 627 AD), and that this event was regarded as 'the birth, or rebirth, of Venus').

Elapsed Time cycles were used to measure time periods: 144,000, 7,200, 360, 20 and 1 day cycles.

Once the numbering code is broken, these periods point to the destruction period of 1,366, 560 days.

Further examination of the numbers shows that the numbering system breaks down after 1,366,560 days and that in order to continue 'counting' the system must be adapted. This adaptation reveals use of a decimal system (*The Mayan Prophecies*, M. Cotterell).

PHI, The Golden Ratio

Many experiments have been carried out to ascertain human preference of shapes and proportion. One ratio has been found to be favoured more than any other, that is the ratio of PHI. PHI is not only aesthetically pleasing, but is also compatible with human physiology, which we shall see is also related to PHI. The shape below is a rectangle. The ratio of the longer side to the shorter side is the ratio of PHI and equal (equilibrates) to 1.6180339.

Fig 82

This number has many fascinating qualities, first noticed in the west by Euclid, around 300 BC. Mathematicians ascribed the name Phi after the Greek letter PHI. Artists of the Renaissance called it 'divine proportion', the Greeks used the pentagon (which contains many PHI relationships), as a holy symbol. PHI is also referred to as the 'golden section', 'golden number' and 'golden ratio'. PHI also has many important mathematical implications; natural organisms, such as the human body, plants, animals and all living things are PHI related. In preferring PHI based proportions we are, therefore, conforming to laws of nature and responding to what appears to be a unique coding that relates to our very structure.

Artists have always sought PHI ratios in paintings: horizons for example are seldom positioned on canvas to divide the picture by say 50 per cent, but generally seek to follow PHI proportions of 1.62:1.

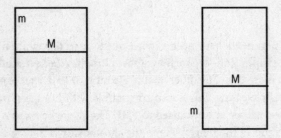

Fig 83

In the PHI rectangles above the ratio between the two sides is 1.618:1. These rectangles have a number of peculiarities. If you construct a square on the longer side, as shown here, the square taken together with the rectangle will form a new, larger PHI rectangle. The ratio between the long side **M** and the short side **m** is the same as the ratio between the long and the short sides of the larger rectangle. This is a mathematical proportion. There are also arithmetical relationships in Φ. If you divide 1 by Φ you will get 0.618. If you multiply Φ by itself the result will be 2.618. Compare these two figures with Φ and you will notice something strange about their relationship.

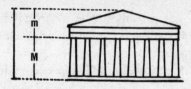

Fig 84 The Golden Section was also much in evidence in Greek architecture.

In the thirteenth century the mathematician Fibonacci discovered an interesting and puzzling series of figures, all PHI related, which proliferate in nature: 1 1 2 3 5 8 13 21 34 55 89 144 233 377 610 987 1597 2584 4181. After the series has commenced with 1, 1, the other numbers are obtained by adding the preceding two in the series together, to obtain the succeeding number. However, if any pair are then compared the result is PHI:

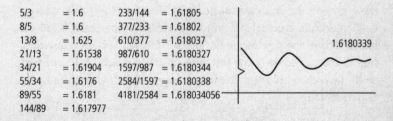

5/3	= 1.6	233/144	= 1.61805
8/5	= 1.6	377/233	= 1.61802
13/8	= 1.625	610/377	= 1.618037
21/13	= 1.61538	987/610	= 1.6180327
34/21	= 1.61904	1597/987	= 1.6180344
55/34	= 1.6176	2584/1597	= 1.6180338
89/55	= 1.6181	4181/2584	= 1.618034056
144/89	= 1.617977		

1.6180339

Fig 85

What we see is that the series alternates and reaches equilibrium at 1.6180339: the higher the number, the closer to PHI one gets. The Fibonacci series, which is a function of PHI, predominates in nature, as does F itself.

Nobody would suspect a plant like Fig 86*a* to have anything to do with mathematics; it seems to be too disorganised and irregular. But a simple investigation of its structure and manner of growing, Fig 86*b*, reveals the Fibonacci series.

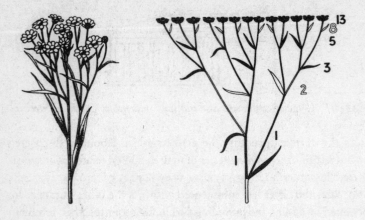

Fig 86a   Fig 86b

In Fig 87 the square **a** has been added to the small black rectangle in the centre, in the same way as in Fig 83. Together they make a larger Golden Section rectangle. If you now add another square, **b**, on the longer side of the new rectangle, another Golden Section rectangle is found. You can go on doing this with squares **c,d,e** and **f**. The corners of all the rectangles, when connected, form a spiral, such as we found in natural shapes.

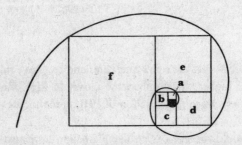

Fig 87

This shape can be seen in many other aspects of life, for example, the pine cone and the dahlia both have two sets of spirals.

Fig 88 The pine cone.

Fig 89 The dahlia.

Both the pine cone and the dahlia have two sets of spirals which relate to the Fibonacci series.

Spirals in natural shapes, Fig 88, are normally arranged in Fibonnacci numbers, which are also important to the proportions of the human body, Fig 90. Nature is full of such relationships. In most cases they can only be sensed, but here we see some of them expressed in numbers and mathematical terms.

217

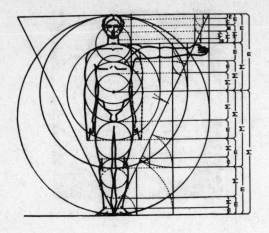

Fig 90 The Φ proportion also appears in the human body and many living things. Here, each pair of dimensions marked Mm forms a Golden Proportion.

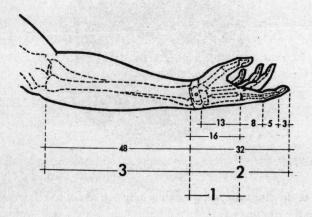

Fig 91

Phi permeates all living things.

Jade

The name jade was originally derived from the Spanish phrase '*piedra de hijada*' meaning stone of the flank, or loins, because it resembled, for the Spanish conquistadores, the flat polished pebble shaped like kidneys. They used it to describe the polished green stones stolen from the Mexican Indians in great profusion.

The term 'jade' refers to two types of similar stones either of which may be found in situ, or alluvial (boulders and pebbles):

	NEPHRITE	JADEITE
Consistency	Interlocking mass of fibrous crystals of monoclinic symmetry. Felting of crystals gives toughness.	Interlocking monoclinic crystals. Granular (not felted).
Chemical Properties	Silicate of magnesium and calcium with iron CA_2 $(Mg. Fe)_5 (OH)_2 (Si_4 Oii)_2$ Of the tremolite and (darker) actinolite family.	Pyroxine group allied to spodumene, diopside and enstatite. Sodium aluminium silicate. $NaA1 (SiO_2)_2$ with a varying percentage of the diopside molecule $CaMg(SiO_3)_2$.

Colour	From green to white 'Mutton Fat' jade. Red scale/skin of iron oxide forms on surface.	White, pink, brown, red, orange, yellow, mauve, blue, violet, black, greens. (Mauve due to manganese, duller greens to iron).
Hardness	6.5 on Mohs scale (very hard).	7 on Mohs scale (same as quartz).
Density	2.9–3.20	3.3–3.6
Refractive Index	1.6–1.627 and 1.614–1.641, reading 1.62 (PHI) on refractometer.	1.654–1.667 reading 1.66 on refractometer.
Light Absorption	4600A, 4980A, 5090A, 6890A	4330A, 4500A, 4375A (strong line) 4950A, 4375A (diagnostic).
Origin	Khotan, Turkestan in situ, 20–30 ft layer alluvial in rivers Keriya, Yurungkash and Karakash. Siberia Sayan Mountains and rivers. New Zealand (Greenstone). Swiss Lakes. Poland. Italy. Germany. Alaska. USA. (Alluvial; Wyoming, California (closest find to Mexico). Washington. British Columbia (good quantities, alluvial). Australia. Zimbabwe. Brazil.	Burma (nickname Chinese jade). California. Japan.
Qualities	Extra hard – used for tools	
Used by (in addition to where found)	Chinese, Aztec, Maya, Olmec	Chinese (18th Century), Aztec, Maya, Olmec

Only tiny quantities of alluvial nephrite have been found in Mexico itself and the large quantities worked there are not thought to be of Mexican origin. The Aztec and Maya also used jadeite, also not found in Mexico. The closest supply of both nephrite and jadeite, to Central America, is California. The materials are very hard and fashioned only by materials harder then themselves, for example diamond or carborundum tipped grinding tools. The ancient Maori, of New Zealand, and Chinese were known to cut their stones with a thin laminate of sandstone or a thin slate charged with sand and water and tools of the same materials. The Chinese drilled using water cooled hollow bamboo tubes charged with sand.

Information on Maya Transformer Books

So far I have published three books which employ the Maya Trans-for-mer decoding technique. Each is hand made and contains many 'plastic' pages which enable the decoded stories to be seen. A copy of each has been deposited in the British Library and at five other libraries in the UK. Information on how these may be seen by the public is given below.

Book Information

British Library (Museum)

The Amazing Lid of Palenque Vol 1 Shelf Mark CUP.410.C.126
    ISBN 0 9513195 1 5
The Amazing Lid of Palenque Vol 2 Shelf Mark CUP.410.C.126
    ISBN 0 9513195 6 6
The Mosaic Mask of Palenque Shelf Mark YC.1995.B.2906
    ISBN 0 9513195 7 4
The Mural of Bonampak Shelf Mark YC.1995.B.6750
    ISBN 0 9513195 3 1

1) *The British Library, Reading Room, 96 Euston Road, London NW1 Tel. 0171 412 7676 (quick enquiry line)*
   To view a copy of the book readers need a Readers Ticket available from the Readers Admission Office tel. 0171 412 7677. In addition a 'reason' to view is required; for example 'for research for a PhD' or 'because the publication is a limited handmade edition and not available elsewhere in London'.
2) *Bodleian Library, Broad Street, Oxford, OX1 3BG Tel. 01865 277 000*
3) *Cambridge University Library, West Road, Cambridge CB3 9DR Tel. 01223 333 000*
4) *National Library of Scotland, George the Fourth Bridge, Edinburgh EH1 1EW Tel. 0131 226 4531*
5) *Library of Trinity College Dublin, College Street, Dublin 2 Tel. 00 353 1677 2941*
6) *National Library of Wales, Aberystwyth, Dyfed, SY23 3BU Tel. 01970 623 816*

The above books may be ordered direct by mail from
Brooks Hill Perry & Co,
Coombe Farm,
Coombe
Nr Saltash,
Cornwall PL12 4ET

Tel. 01752 843394
Fax 01752 840945.

PRICE INFORMATION:

Amazing Lid of Palenque Vol 1	£400
Amazing Lid of Palenque Vol 2	£225
Mosaic Mask of Palenque	£ 45
Mural of Bonampak	£165

Mosaic Mask Acetates

Acetates which reveal the door to the secret chamber referred to in the Epilogue, page 170, are available from the author, price £3.50 each plus p&p, (£5 twin pack inc. p+p) c/o HarperCollins*Publishers*. Make £5 cheques payable to M. Cotterell.

Glossary

Aditi	Goddess Brahman, wife of Brahma
Agni	Aryan Fire god, son of Dyaus & Prithivi, god of South-East quadrant
Ahuilteotl (*A-will-tee-owe-tul*)	Consort of Tlazolteotl
Ahuinime (*A-wee-an-ime*)	Mistress of Ahuilteotl, prostitute
Ananta	Brahman, Serpent of Infinity
Arjuna	Soldier, main character in *Bhagava-Geeta*, Hindu
Astrogenetics	Astronomical and biological mechanisms which determine personality, bio-rhythms and fertility on Earth
Astrology	Astronomical influences, and effects on life
Aztec	Nahuatal race of Central American Indians c 1300–1520 AD

Bhagava-Geeta	Hindu epic poem of *Mahabarata*
Brahma, Vishnu, Siva	Indian trinity of gods
Buddha	'The enlightened one'. Founder of Buddhism. Name given after deliverance beneath Bo-tree (Tree of Knowledge)
Camaxtle *(Cam-axt-lee)*	(Maya) god of Hunting associated with a double-headed stag which gave him strength
Coatlicue *(Co-at-lick-wee)*	Earth goddess. Mother of gods
Chalchiuitlicue *(Chal-chee-whit-lick-we)*	Goddess of Water (Maya)
Christ	'The Anointed one'. Name of Jesus after baptism by John the Baptist
Cincalco(Maya) *(Sin- kal-co)*	The home of Maize, one of the 5 paradises
Cocijo *(Co-see-jo)*	Rain god (Zapotec)
Confucius	Chinese, Founder of Confucianism (Philosophy) 551–479 BC
Coyoloxiuhqui *(Coy-ul-sh-how-key)*	Moon goddess (Maya) Jingle Bells, goddess of Fertility
Dyaus & Prithivi	Indian Divine Couple
Ehecatl *(Air-cattle)*	God of Wind (Maya)
Four Ages	Hindi concept of time: Golden Age, Silver Age, Copper Age and Iron Age. Confluence age of destruction. 5,000 year cycle
Garuda Bird	Brahman representation of spirit
Gautama	Buddha's adult name (prior to deliverance)
General Theory of Existence	Explains the meaning of life and why we live, die and why this has to be

Huitzilopochtli (*Wheat-zillo-pocht-lee*)	God of South and Sacrifice, god of Sun (Aztec war god)
Indra	Son of Dyaus and Prithivi, Brahman, god of Weather and Eastern Skyr
Itzpapalotltotec (*Its-papa-lot-ul-toe-tec*)	God of Butterflies, Sacrifice and Purification
Itzpapalotltotechuatl (*Its-papa-lot-ul-toe-tee-quar-tul*)	Goddess of Butterflies and Scrifice
Jainism	India, Buddhism variant
Jesus	Preacher messiah of Christian faith
Kapilavasta	Birthplace of Buddha, India
Karma	Spiritual law of action and reaction. Strives to balance good actions against bad ones
Krishna	Lord, Brahman/Hindi incarnation of Vishnu
Lao-Tzu	Chinese, Philosopher, founder of Taoism c 600 BC
Lemur	Small monkey
Mahabarata	Hindu book containing *Bhagava-Geeta*
Maya (*My-ah*)	Race of Central American Indians 250–950 AD declined greatly around 750 AD. Guatemala, Mexico, Belize (Yucatan) Sanskrit word meaning 'Illusion' Name of mother of Buddha
Mictlan (*Mitlan*)	Place of the Dead. The Underworld
Mictlantechutli (*Mit-lan-tee-coot-lee*)	God of Death
Mictlantechutliuatl (*Mit-lan-tee-coo-ti-water1*)	Goddess of Death
Mitra & Varuna	Gods of Night and Day, Brahman, offspring of Aditi

Mixtec	Central American Indians 750–1500 AD Monte Alban, Mitla
Oaxaca (*Wah-hacka*)	Colonial Mexican Town close to archaeological site of Monte Alban
Olmec	Central American Indian Tribe c 1500–500 BC, La Venta, San Lorenzo, Tres Zapotes
Ometeotl (*Oh-me-tee-owe-tul*)	Original divine couple (Aztec)
Omeyocan (*Oh-me-owe-can*)	Home of Ometeotl. One of five paradises
Palenque (*Pal-en-key*)	Maya town in Chiapas Mexico
Pacal	Lord/king of Maya at Palenque 703–743 AD, incarnation of Quetzalcoatl
Pali	Sacred language of Buddhism derived from Sanskrit
Pangaea (*Pan-gay-ah*)	Single large pre-historic land mass
Parseeism	Offshoot of Judaism
Popol-Vuh	Holy book of the Maya
Puranas	Body of Brahman books
Quetzalcoatl (*Cat-sell-coe-at-el*)	God (Aztec), feathered serpent, Good god, god of West. One of four Tezcatlipocas
Quilatzli (*Kill-atz-lee*)	The Green Heron, the Sorceress (Aztec Goddess)
Satarupa	Daughter of Indian god Brahma
Sankaya	Name of Buddha during childhood
Sanskrit	Ancient language of India
Savitri	Sun god Indian
Shintoism	Japanese religious belief. Hybrid of Buddhism & Taoism
Siddattha	Given name of Buddha at birth
Siza	Japanese, variant of Buddhism

Solar hormone theory	Shows how the sun's radiation affects fertility in humans
Soma	God of Sleep, Brahman, hallucinogenic drug
Sun-spot cycles	Cycles of magnetic activity on the sun. The 11.5 yearly cycle manifests as spots on the sun's surface
Surya	Sun god (Indian)
Teotihuacan	Central American city, plains of Mexico; zenith 500–800 AD
Tezcatlipocas (*Tez-cat-lee-poke-as*)	Deities of the four cardinal points, thought to be emanations of Quetzalcoatl (West). Also Yaotl (North), Huitzilopochtli (South) and Xiuhtechutli (East)
Theory of Cataclysmic Destruction	Theory that shows how solar magnetic reversals cause pole tilting to planets, infertility cycles, increased infant mutation cycles and mini ice ages
Theory of Divine Reconciliation	Reconciles the will of the divine creator and in so doing explains the meaning of life
Theory of Iterative Spiritual Redemption	Mechanism that reconciles the purpose of physical destruction and spiritual transmigration of souls through *Karma*, time and catastrophe cycles
Three Worlds	Hindi concept, Soul World, God World and Physical World
Tlachueyal (*Clac-way-al*)	A guise of Tezcatlipoca Yaotl. Giant who lived in the underworld
Tlahuizpantechutli (*Klar-weez-pant-e-coot-lee*)	God of Ice, Venus in the Morning (Aztec)
Tlaloc (*Klal-oc*)	Wind god (Aztec)
Tlalocan	Home of Tlaloc. One of five paradises

Tlazolteotl (*Klaz-ol-tee-owe-tul*)	Goddess of Filth. Goddess of Hearts
Tomoanchan (*Tom-owe-wan-chan*)	Home of our ancestors. One of five paradises
Tonatiuh	Sun god (Maya/Aztec)
Tonatiuhcan	Home of Tonatiuh. One of five paradises, destinations of the dead
Upanishads	Body of Brahman books
Ushas	Goddess of Dawn, Brahman
Vishnu	Brahman, one of trinity of gods. Reincarnated ten times as: Matsya, Kurma, Varaha, Narashima, Vamana, Parashurama, Rama, Krishna, Buddha, Kalki
Vedas	Early Brahman books 1700–700 BC of Aryans
Vedantra Sutra	Summary of Aryan *Vedas* (Books)
Velikovsky	20th century scientist
Xipe Totec (*Shy-pee-Toe-tek*)	Fire god (Aztec), god of East and Sacrifice
Xiuhtechutli (*Shy-te-coot-lee*)	Fire god (Maya) god of East and Sacrifice, one of four Tezcatlipocas, identified with Xipe Totec god of Fire and the East
Xolotol (*Shol-o-tol*)	Venus in the Evening. Blind Dog
Zapotec	Tribe of Central American Indians 600 BC – 750 AD, Monte Alban
Zoroastrianism	Offshoot of Judaism

Bibliography

Adamson, D. *The Ruins of Time*, G.Allen & Unwin, 1975

Baudez, C. & Picasso, S. *Lost Cities of the Maya*, Thames & Hudson, 1992

Benson-Gyles, A. & Sayer, C. *Of Gods and Men*, BBC Books, 1980

Bernal, Dr I. Official Guide Oaxaca Valley, INAH, 1985

Bettany, G.T. *The World's Religions*, Ward Lock & Co, 1890

Burland, C.A. *Peoples of the Sun*, London, Weidenfeld & Nicholson, 1976

Calleja, R. & Signoret, H.S. *Ahumada A.T, Official Guide Palenque* INAH, 1990

Cavendish, R. *An Illustrated Encyclopaedia of Mythology*, W H Smith, 1984

Cotterell, M.M. *Astrogenetics*, Brooks Hill Robinson & Co, 1988

Cotterell, M.M. *The Amazing Lid of Palenque Vol 1*, Brooks Hill Perry & Co, 1994

Cotterell, M.M. *The Amazing Lid of Palenque Vol 2*, Brooks Hill Perry & Co, 1994

Cotterell, M.M. *The Mayan Prophecies*, Element,1995 (Co-authored)

Cotterell, M.M. *The Mosaic Mask of Palenque*, Brooks Hill Perry & Co, 1995

Cotterell, M.M. *The Mural of Bonampak*, Brooks Hill Perry & Co, 1995

Fernandez, A. *Pre-hispanic Gods of Mexico*, Panorama, 1987

Fullard, H. (Ed), *Universal Atlas*, Philips, 1976

Gendrop, P.A. *Guide to Architecture in Ancient Mexico*, Editorial Minutaie Mexicana, 1991

Goetz, D. & Morley, S.G. *Popol Vuh (After Recinos)*, William Hodge & Co, 1947

Hadingham, E. *Early Man and the Cosmos*, William Heinemann, 1983

Hapgood, C. *Earth's Shifting Crust*, Philadelphia/Chilton, 1958

Hitching, F. *The World Atlas of Mysteries*, William Collins & Son, 1978

Holy Bible, H.M. *Special Command*, Eyre & Spottiswode, 1899

Horizon, *Summer 1964*, American Heritage Publishing, 1964

Ivanof, P. *Monuments of Civilisation*, Cassell, 1978

Jordan, M. *Encyclopaedia of Gods*, Kyle Cathie Ltd, 1992

Milton, J., Orsi, R.A. & Harrison, N. *The Feathered Serpent and the Cross*, Cassell, London 1980

Moore, Hunt, Nicolson & Cattermole, *The Atlas of the Solar System*, Mitchell Beazley, 1985

Nicolson, I. *Black Holes and the Universe*, David & Charles, 1980

Peterson, R. *Everyone is Right*, De Vorss & Co, 1986

Readers Digest, *The World's Last Mysteries*, 1977

Roland, K. *The Shapes we Need*, Ginn & Co, 1965

Sten, M. *Codices of Mexico*, Panorama, 1987

Tomkins, P. *Mysteries of the Mexican Pyramids*, Harper & Row, 1976

Velikovsky, I. *Earth in Upheaval*, Doubleday & Co, 1955

Velikovsky, I. *Ages in Chaos*, Sidgwick & Jackson, 1953

Velikovsky, I. *Worlds in Collision*, Book Club Associates, 1973

Westwood, J. (Ed), *The Atlas of Mysterious Places*, BCA, 1987

White, J. *Pole Shift*, ARE Press, 1993

Wilson, C. (Ed), *The Book of Time*, Westbridge Books, 1980

Index